An
Invitation
to the
Cottage
by the
Loch

BOOKS BY KENNEDY KERR

Loch Cameron

The Cottage by the Loch
A Secret at the Cottage by the Loch
The Diary from the Cottage by the Loch
A Gift from the Cottage by the Loch

Magpie Cove

The House at Magpie Cove
Secrets of Magpie Cove
Daughters of Magpie Cove
Dreams of Magpie Cove

A Spell of Murder

Kennedy Kerr

An
Invitation
to the
Cottage
by the
Loch

bookouture

Published by Bookouture in 2024

An imprint of Storyfire Ltd.
Carmelite House
50 Victoria Embankment
London EC4Y 0DZ

www.bookouture.com

ISBN: 978-1-83525-179-9
eBook ISBN: 978-1-83525-178-2

For all the romantic heroes, including the Canadian loggers and the tarmac crew, and for everyone they are sweet to.

PROLOGUE

8 SEPTEMBER 1934

I have a secret place no one knows about, not even Tom. I go there when Mother and Father drink and argue because they are so loud. It is a secret cave in the rock that looks onto the water and sometimes, if I am very quiet, I can pretend I have disappeared. The birds sing to me there and I wonder what they are saying.

Sometimes I think about running away to my secret place even though it is windy, but there is a flat rock for a bed and I could make a fire to cook and make tea. I wish I could run away from them all. It would be a better future than being like Mother, or she says I could go away and work in a factory and send back money when I am older, like Molly, the daughter of the Taggart family along the way. But I have seen Molly and she looks like death warmed up and much older than eighteen, she already stoops and her face is lined. I do not think working in a factory is much fun.

Mother says, be grateful you have a roof over your head. But I prefer my cave. No one can find me here and that way no one can hurt me.

ONE

'Can you just slow down a little, Dan?' Deborah Sutherland winced as her boyfriend took a sharp turn too fast. Every time she breathed, it felt as though she was being stabbed by a bag of knives that some kindly doctor had left in her abdomen.

'I've got to get back for the football,' Dan muttered, as if that was any kind of answer. *Nice to know what the priority is here,* she thought. Dan had already made it clear that picking her up from the hospital was a huge imposition. He hadn't said it, but his manner and body language had done that for him, without words.

So sorry that I couldn't walk home, the day after a hysterectomy, she thought, bracing herself as Dan made a sudden stop at traffic lights. Pain ripped through her and she gasped involuntarily. *So sorry that I didn't catch the bus.*

Dan glanced at her.

'You all right?' he asked.

'Not too bad,' she found herself replying, and almost laughed. *Not too bad.* The most British of responses.

Actually, Dan, I'm not all right. I've just had my uterus

removed by laser and pulled out through my vagina, was what she wanted to say. *Bit sore, if I'm honest.*

All Deb wanted was to get home, right now. She was trying not to think about how she was going to get up the stairs to bed, but she'd have to do it, somehow. And then, hopefully, she could take more of the painkillers that the hospital had sent her home with, and pass out for a few hours.

It was hard to think about recovery when she was in this much pain. But, at the same time, Deb was glad that she'd had the operation. She was excited to start *living* again: her life for the past few years had been lacklustre because of her symptoms. *Goodbye, constant bleeding*, she thought, as Dan turned into the end of her street and she saw her house approach. *Goodbye, eternal abdominal pain. Ta-ra, dizziness from lack of blood. See ya, anaemia.* Maybe she could start planning a holiday now – somewhere she could wear a bikini, in a few months' time, or even a year. She could wear white underwear. Sleep on the bed without a towel under her. It was the small things as much as the big ones.

Endometriosis. It affected one in ten women worldwide, apparently, and the medical community still had no idea what caused it, or could offer any good cure, apart from what she'd had. Hysterectomy.

That in itself had been a struggle to get. Because she was in her thirties still, because she was unmarried – Deb failed to see how *that* was anyone's business – and because she didn't already have children, she had been refused the operation multiple times. *You might still want children, you see*, one consultant had said, looking over the top of her glasses at Deb. *We wouldn't want to do anything we'd regret, would we?*

We? Deb had thought. *No. I will make my own decisions about my own body, thank you. Because I am thirty-eight years old.*

The comment had rankled with her. Deb had joined an

online hysterectomy support group and found that many other women had been told the same kind of thing, or refused the operation on the basis that doctors thought they would regret it, because at some point they would want children.

Would men be doubted in the same way? Deb wondered. *Would they be questioned and queried, as if they were children, about whether they really meant what they said?* She doubted it. If a woman had made up her mind that she wanted a hysterectomy – an operation that would once and for all remove all the pain, bleeding and discomfort that was ruining her life – then she should be trusted in that decision. Not second-guessed, as if she was a child.

In the end, Deb had asked for a second opinion and been passed to another consultant, who couldn't have been more different. He'd listened to her sympathetically and, after examining her, had agreed that only an operation would solve the problem – not the other, medieval-style treatments she'd been offered in the past, like having the inside of her womb lasered off while awake, or hormone treatments that had made her suicidal and only slowed, not stopped the bleeding.

Neither had worked, and both had been distressing. But they were hoops that the medical community had required her to jump through – adding almost two years onto her suffering – before they would even consider her for surgery.

After waiting so long to be allowed to make the decision for herself, she'd said *yes*. Yesterday, they'd taken her malfunctioning uterus out. Today, she began her new life.

As Dan brought the car to a sudden halt outside her house, Deb let out a cry of pain. The knives in her abdomen felt as though they were cutting through her stomach and she bit her lip to try and control herself.

'Come on, then. Let's get you inside,' Dan said, looking at his watch. 'Almost kick off time.'

Charming.

Deb thought about the tale of the Little Mermaid as she opened the passenger side door and gingerly manoeuvred one leg onto the ground outside, and then the other. The mermaid had paid a high price to have her tail transformed into legs. To be able to walk on land, and to follow the man she had fallen in love with, she had agreed that every step she would take with her new legs would feel as if she was walking on broken glass.

This felt somewhat similar. Deb took Dan's hand and slowly got to her feet, trying to use her back and her legs and not her stomach muscles to stand. Yet, it was impossible to do that without the stabbing pain in her tummy. She felt faint.

Come on, now, she pep-talked herself. *Your life was completely untenable before this. You're going to get better, and your new life is going to start. No more blood, no more pain. It's worth it. Be strong.*

Deb took a deep breath and took a step, and then another, Dan guiding her into the house. At the bottom of the stairs, she found herself wishing that he would carry her up them, like a hero in a romance novel. But Dan just looked at her expectantly, and so she put her foot on the bottom step and began the long climb up the twelve stairs.

Every single step was agony. But every step was a step closer to her new life.

Like the Little Mermaid, she had made a choice for herself. And that was what gave her the power to reach the top of the stairs, and then to slowly lower herself to sit on her bed. It didn't matter what Dan did or didn't do. She had faced the operation and survived. Now, all she had to do was recover. And if she could do that, then she could do anything.

TWO

Deb had been having the same dream for months now. A girl in an old-fashioned smock dress and two long plaits tied with white ribbons was skipping with a rope, chanting a rhyme:

> *Granny's in the kitchen, doing a bit of stitchin'*
> *Down comes a bogeyman and knocks her out*
> *Ah! said Granny. That's not fair!*
> *Ah! said the bogeyman. I don't care.*

It was always the same dream, always the same girl. All Deb remembered when she woke up was the girl, and the sense that she was somewhere in the countryside.

Weird.

She blinked, and reached for her phone to turn off the alarm. Then, as was her habit, she sat up, put on her glasses and checked her messages, then her work emails, all of which were on her phone.

Dear Deborah,

I hope this email finds you very well. We haven't met, but you come highly recommended by my partner Zelda Hicks who I think you worked with on a House of Interiors event a while ago.

My name is Hal Cameron and I'm the Laird at Loch Cameron, based in the castle there. I'm not sure if you know it.

I like to hold regular celebration events for the community at Loch Cameron Castle, and our May Day party on May 1st is a fixture in the calendar. Looking at my schedule, though, this means that there are only five weeks to get it organised, and Zelda and myself have been asked to be in New York – at rather short notice – for at least three of those weeks.

This is where you come in! Zelda assures me that your event for House of Interiors was a great success and that you were – in her words – "an absolute darling" to work with. Therefore, I'm wondering whether you would be available to take the reins for our May Day party? Zelda and I will help where we can, but as we'll be away for a good portion of the time, we need someone we can trust to do the majority of the work.

I realise that this is rather late notice and that you might very likely be busy, but we thought it was worth asking. It goes without saying that I would be more than happy to double your usual rate, considering it's a rush job.

I look forward to hearing from you.

All very best regards,

Hal Cameron

Laird of Loch Cameron

Deb re-read the email on her phone, half-propped up with pillows on her bed.

She was seven weeks post-hysterectomy and felt about a thousand per cent better. The symptoms of endometriosis she'd been experiencing for about three years had gone.

It had been a gradual recovery and Deb had been trying to take it easy, but being self-employed meant that she didn't really have a nice cushion of sick leave to rely on. So, she'd gone back to work about six weeks after the operation, but it had been hard. She'd become so exhausted if she had to stand up for a couple of hours, and her tummy muscles got tired easily. She didn't want to push herself, but as an events organiser, her job involved being on site at the event, as well as visiting the venue beforehand to plan everything and look at the facilities. Deb mostly organised weddings, corporate parties and awards ceremonies, but she occasionally worked with magazines and other promotional type organisations for parties, launches and influencer events. That was how she'd met Zelda Hicks: at an influencer party she'd organised for *Homes and Interiors Magazine,* where Zelda was a stylist.

Deb and Zelda had got on well, and the party – at a chichi hotel in London – had been a great success. However, that had been before the hysterectomy.

A party at a castle sounded like a fun project. Though she was still more tired than she would usually be, a break in the countryside did also sound amazing. She was sick and tired of being inside all the time and she craved fresh air and a change of view. She googled Loch Cameron Castle, not sure what to expect, and when the grey stone castle with its tall, gothic turrets and manicured gardens came onto her screen, she gasped a little at its grandeur. Well... that wasn't the worst place in the world to work.

. . .

Deb walked into the kitchen to make a cup of tea, and was met with the vision of a mountain of unwashed dishes. She and Dan had agreed that it would be his job to stack the dishwasher, run it and unpack it, since Deb had been laid up. She pulled open the dishwasher door and saw that it was completely empty, and the complete disrespect of that gesture hit her hard, like a blow.

Because, it wasn't just this. There had been signs. Trigger warnings. But she hadn't wanted to see them.

Ever since she had got home from the hospital Dan had taken every opportunity to show her that he resented having to look after her. Deb didn't enjoy being dependent on anyone. She didn't want to be helped to the toilet, or into the shower, and she would have vastly preferred her own cooking to Dan's. She found the whole process of recovery mortifying.

But, she'd also read enough horror stories online to see what happened to women who tried to go back to work and normal life too soon after the operation. Serious complications could happen if you didn't give your body the time it needed to heal and, frankly, Deb didn't have the time or the inclination to go back into hospital because she hadn't done recovery right the first time. So, she had done exactly what the doctor had told her, and nodded when she'd been asked if there was someone at home who could look after her.

Deb remembered thinking about all the men with wives and girlfriends who were asked a similar question and knew without question that they would be taken care of. She envied them.

Apart from steadfastly refusing to help around the house since she'd got home from the hospital, Dan had – for years now – developed a habit of accusing her of things she hadn't done. He was critical of the smallest things that she did. He'd shouted at her for buying the wrong colour towels and for not lining all the mugs up in the cupboard to face the same way.

Both of those times – and at various other times when Dan

had been just as critical – Deb had rolled her eyes and ignored him, because that was the easiest solution. She'd found that if she just demurred, it was over faster. She didn't care whether Dan thought he'd "won" the point; she just wanted a quiet life.

However, it bothered her. More than anything, the fact that apparently Dan didn't appreciate the irony of him criticising the fact that she hadn't aligned all the mugs in the cupboard to face the same way, when he hadn't ever lifted a finger to wash a mug (or shop for new towels, or anything else that they needed for the house).

If you don't wash up any mugs, then you don't get to criticise where they go in the cupboard, Deb had thought at the time, angrily. It was just basic politeness.

At that moment, as Deb gripped the plate in fury, Dan walked into the kitchen, behind her. He put his used coffee cup down on the worktop, without comment, and walked out of the kitchen again.

Oh, hell, no.

Something in Deb snapped.

'I suppose that's your way of letting me know that my break from housework's over?' She followed him into the lounge. The only thing stopping her hurling the plate at his head was that she really liked that dinner service: it had belonged to her grandma. Instead, Deb put the plate down carefully on a side table.

'What?' He was standing in front of the TV, flicking through it with the remote control. That was another thing: since Deb was home all the time, she could see how little Dan apparently worked when he was "working from home". Like now, for instance: she'd come down to make a cup of tea, but he'd apparently left his desk for some recreational TV time.

'Listen, Dan. I appreciate that I'm up and about now, and I can go back to sharing the housework. But it doesn't mean that

I'm going to go back to doing everything, and you doing nothing.' She tried her best to be fair, and keep her voice level.

'What are you having a go at me for? I just came down for a break. Didn't know I was going to get nagged,' he replied, sulkily.

Dear lord. It's like talking to a six-year-old, Deb thought. Part of her actually marvelled at Dan's audacity.

'I'm not having a go at you,' she said, patiently, although she wanted to scream. 'I'm just saying that, if you see that there's a pile of dirty dishes in the kitchen, and the dishwasher is empty, it would be the adult thing to fill it up and put it on. It only takes five minutes.'

'I just don't have the time,' he said with a shrug. 'I'm working.'

'Excuse me?' Deb looked at the TV, and the remote in Dan's hand. She wanted to laugh, it was so ridiculous. 'I'm working too. And, might I remind you, I managed to do all the housework and the cooking and all the life admin for both of us while also running my own business, before the operation.'

'What d'you mean, life admin?' He looked up briefly from the TV.

'Booking appointments, shopping, buying and wrapping birthday presents for your friends and family as well as mine, organising holidays...' Deb listed the tasks on her fingers. She'd read an article about it in a newspaper which described all these types of activities as "life admin" and "emotional labour". They were new terms to her, but they made sense.

'Yeah, but you're just better at all that stuff than me.' Dan turned his attention back to the screen.

If Deb could have ripped his fingers off, one by one, in that moment, she would have done it. Briefly, she imagined gripping Dan by the wrist and exacting her righteous wrath upon him.

'Better than you at... housework and booking hair appointments?'

'Yeah. You know, women just are better at that kind of thing. Multitasking and all that.'

'You don't think that's basically just a pile of horseshit someone made up to make women feel better about the fact we're just expected to do everything? You'd be great at housework too if you'd been doing it since you were twelve. I'd probably have won the Nobel Prize by now if I'd spent as much time doing particle physics,' she commented, raising her voice.

'Jeez. No need to shout.' He rolled his eyes, and that annoyed Deb even more. 'No, I don't think that. What are you, a feminist now?'

Deb was momentarily speechless. She'd thought that her relationship with Dan was the kind of thing that would develop into them holding hands on the beach when they were old, huddled under blankets and drinking tea out of a flask. It wasn't hot and fiery, but she thought she could trust him.

Over the past weeks, though, Deb had realised that she couldn't. And that knowledge was killing her. She couldn't trust him to look after her and understand what she had been going through. She couldn't be open with him and know that he would hear her. She couldn't trust him to listen to her and understand how deeply disrespectful he was being right now.

'Of course, I'm a feminist. What woman isn't?' Deb couldn't believe he'd said that: as if *feminist* was a dirty word – and, even more concerningly, that they had been together for two years now and he apparently didn't know that she had always considered herself one. It was a part of who she was. She had been raised by a strong woman, raised to be independent and know she could do anything in life if she just worked hard. She was more than equal to a man, and, frankly, in this day and age, the whole idea that there was a basic inequality between the sexes seemed ridiculously outdated.

'I didn't know you were. Bit unnecessary, isn't it?' Dan shrugged. 'Moved past the need for it, I'd have said.'

'Then you would be wrong,' Deb argued. 'As this conversation is literally showing.'

'Oh, Christ, Deb, give it a rest,' Dan sighed wearily. 'I can't be doing with all this whinging. I've got a lot on my mind, yeah? It's been hard, having you at home all the time, looking after the house, doing everything while you've been up there on your arse, watching Netflix and eating chocolates. You've been skiving and we both know it. Just as well you run your own business, I'd say.'

There it was. If Deb had ever thought that Dan loved and respected her, then in that moment, it felt as though he put her heart on the floor of the sitting room and ground his foot into it. Those were not the words of a loving, supportive partner. Not someone who wanted to hold her hand on the beach under a blanket in many years to come; not someone she could share her dreams with, her insecurities, her pain and love and laughter.

Because Dan had been with her at a time when she was at her most vulnerable. And he had chosen to belittle her rather than lift her up.

'What did you just say?' She had heard it, but she still couldn't quite believe that the man she had thought loved her could say something like that.

'Deb, don't make this into one of your little dramas.' Dan sighed again, as if Deb was being completely unreasonable. 'All I'm saying is, it's been hard on me having you lying around like the Queen of Sheba, expecting me to wait on you, hand, foot and finger. I'm tired.'

'*You're* tired?!' Deb had been holding on to her anger, and now she let it go. It was a relief, in a way: an outpouring of all the hurts she had stored up over the past months, reacting to Dan's little micro aggressions.

But she wasn't going to tolerate them anymore, and the anger that coursed through her like a river felt like it nudged all of those stuck little pebbles of hurt free. One pebble couldn't hurt anyone much, but hundreds of pebbles, propelled by the strength of a raging river? That could maim anyone who got in its way.

'You're tired? How do you think I feel? I'm the one that HAS... HAD... SURGERY!' she shouted.

'Don't I know it,' he muttered.

'All you've done since my operation is complain. Don't make out like you've been working hard to keep the house together. Look at the kitchen!' she yelled. 'It's a bloody tip in there! I asked you to hoover LAST WEEK and you still haven't done it. But you have time to watch TV, apparently.'

'Do it yourself, then, if you're so worried about it.' Dan's tone was defensive. 'It doesn't bother me.'

'I bet it doesn't. But, in case you've forgotten, I can't do the hoovering for a while longer, so I asked you to do it. And you just didn't.'

'I did. You just didn't notice,' he argued, weakly.

'Dan. If I didn't notice, then that's because YOU DIDN'T DO IT RIGHT. And, while we're on the subject, you've cooked for me – very badly – about five times and heated up microwave meals the rest of the time. But worst of all, is that you have been an utter shit to me at a time that I needed you the most.'

'What? I've been here for you. I've done your laundry, cooked, cleaned, drove you home from the hospital.' He sounded exasperated. 'I don't know why we're even having this conversation.'

'Dan, I've done all of those things for you – and more – pretty much since we started living together. And I didn't think I deserved a medal for them.'

Dan swore under his breath.

Lovely, Deb thought. 'Do you know what? I'd actually be ashamed of myself, acting like such a child and refusing to do the simplest things for no apparent reason. How do you think this makes you look? It's not very grown up or attractive, let me tell you.'

'Thanks. Can't we just go back to how we were before? Since you had that bloody operation you've just been...' he trailed off.

'What? I've been what?' Deb stood in the kitchen doorway, defiantly, her hands on her hips. *I've stopped letting you get away with bad behaviour for a quiet life. And you don't like it one bit*, she thought. Somehow, in the process of making a positive choice for herself – it had been scary, but she'd done it to save herself from pain and bleeding and her whole life being governed by endometriosis – she had also become more empowered in her relationship with Dan.

'Whatever. Nothing. I'm going back to work.' He turned the TV off. 'Not going to get any peace down here, am I?'

'No,' Deb said, shortly. 'You're not.'

She thought about the Laird's email, her business brain kicking in for a moment. Business had been a little slow since she had come back from her operation because she hadn't been saying yes to as many events. She really needed a well-paying project to put her back on track, financially, and this sounded like it would at least cover the money she'd lost by being out of action. Also, it would do her good to get away from Dan. She felt like she needed some distance to work out how she felt about everything.

I deserve better than this, she thought. *I can't be around him anymore.*

'I'm going to have some time away,' she said, abruptly.

'What do you mean?' He had his back to her, leaving the room: he halted, but didn't turn to face her.

'I've been offered a good rate for a job. In the Highlands. They want me ASAP. I think it would be a good idea if I went,' she said.

'Do what you want,' he said, dully. 'You always do, anyway.'

Deb sighed. She could have responded, but what point was there, to such a passive-aggressive statement?

'I will, then,' she said, and watched him leave the room.

Well, that's that, she thought, as Dan went back up to the spare bedroom, which was his home office. She listened as he stamped up the stairs and pulled the door closed with a bang. Even though she had made the decision to go to Loch Cameron and put some space between her and Dan – the decision felt good as soon as she made it – the slammed door hurt.

She went back up to their bedroom, which served as her office too, and lowered herself carefully into the bed.

Deb wanted to cry, but she choked back the tears. She wasn't about to let Dan hear her, and she wanted to act on this decision now – to *strike while the iron was hot*, as the phrase went.

Dear Hal. Thanks for your email. I'd be delighted to take the job, if accommodation is included.

She continued the email, giving a breakdown of her fee, which was double her normal charge, and pressed SEND.

Apparently, she was going to Loch Cameron.

THREE

Deb thought that if she'd searched for "cute and cosy cottage" on the internet, then she couldn't have found a prettier and more typical little house than the one she walked up to a week later.

The cottage was painted white like the handful of other cottages up on Queen's Point, a promontory that overlooked Loch Cameron, the glinting, tranquil lake that the small village of Loch Cameron sat alongside.

Deb had done some research, and she'd learnt that Queen's Point was named because of an old legend that said Mary, Queen of Scots had met her lover there for secret romantic trysts. There didn't seem to be any actual historical proof for the story, but Deb rather liked the idea that she might be walking in a queen's footsteps.

Of course, the cottages hadn't been there in Queen Mary's time, but there had apparently been dwellings of some kind there. Something that made Mary and her lover, Lord Darnley – who she later married, and then had killed – seek out the romance of Loch Cameron for their meetings.

Queen Mary had the right idea, Deb thought offhandedly as

she walked up the little garden path to the front door of the cottage. The front door, which was painted blue, just like the window frames, was framed with a small porch over which grew a profusion of pink roses. Not that she wanted Dan *killed* – that would have been a stretch. More that she appreciated Mary's decisiveness in the matter.

The Laird had put Deb in touch with a lady called Gretchen Ross who had sent Deb directions to the cottage, which was where she would be staying while she was organising the Loch Cameron May Day party. Gretchen had explained on the phone that she had once lived at the cottage and now resided in a care home a few villages away. The Laird trusted her with managing the property, as he didn't have time to do things like organise the front door key and putting milk in the fridge.

Sure enough, as Deb pushed a large lilac hydrangea in a terracotta pot with her foot, a fob and a couple of attached keys revealed themselves underneath it, enclosed carefully in a plastic bag. She stooped to pick up the keys and let herself in.

Inside, the cottage was bright and clean, and Deb immediately felt at home in its cosy ambience. She left her wheelie suitcase in the hall, hung her jacket on the row of ceramic coat hooks by the door. She kicked off her trainers and left them next to a white painted shoe rail, where someone had left a handy pair of green wellies. Deb wondered if they'd fit her, in the event that there was a rainstorm – which was extremely likely in the countryside. Not that it wasn't likely in Glasgow, where she'd always lived. She was rather looking forward to the slower pace of life in a village as opposed to the city: it would be amazing to be somewhere peaceful for a change. Somewhere she could heal.

At the end of the hallway which was, like the exterior of the cottage, painted white, Deb found a sweet little sitting room on her right. As she walked in, she let out an exclamation of admiration at the décor.

Deb's eyes were drawn to the antique Victorian fireplace in the centre of the room, which featured light green tiles with a pink rose pattern. The room had been wallpapered with a pattern of wildflowers, just like the ones that Deb could see in the cottage garden through the window.

A comfy-looking upholstered chair with a hydrangea pattern sat on one side of the lounge alongside a vintage velvet pink chaise longue. A plain cream sofa sat opposite, and a couple of thriving tall ficus plants stood in the corner, housed in copper coloured pots. There was a brass standard lamp in another corner, and a small coffee table on which there was a stack of interior décor and fashion magazines. The cosy décor gave Deb a feeling of homeliness. She realised that she hadn't felt that for a long time: this cottage was, at least temporarily, *hers*. A girly, comfy space where she could just be. Not a shared place with Dan, which she had tried to keep nice against the onslaught of his dirty tea cups, his propensity for hanging towels over doors and the piles of auto magazines that seemed to multiply around the flat, despite her efforts to tidy them away.

She took in a deep breath and felt herself relax, a little. It would take a while, she knew, for her to *get there* fully – it had been a long drive, and she was stressed about Dan. But, she also gave herself a mental pat on the back for making the break, for moving away at least for a while, and for ending up somewhere as peaceful and pretty as this.

Deb walked through an arch that joined the lounge to a small but charming kitchen, her smile becoming wider as she explored the cottage. In the kitchen, a blue leather chesterfield sat by a blackened fireplace, and a wide window opened onto the cottage garden which was a riot of colour. Deb could see more roses, tall lupins, a couple of violet hydrangea bushes, foxglove and fuchsia bushes.

Deb sat down on the leather sofa and leaned back, closing her eyes for a moment. The chesterfield was very comfortable, despite the fact it was losing some of its stuffing.

It had been a long drive to Loch Cameron, first leaving the city and then following the satnav along increasingly narrow country roads. She had been cleared to drive six weeks after her operation, but even now, her middle felt tired and sore from having to sit in one position for so long.

Deb laid down, resting her head on the arm of the sofa and putting her feet up at the end. From her position lying down, she surveyed the rest of the kitchen: a Welsh dresser at the far end of the kitchen held a charming collection of mismatched china, and a long wooden kitchen table held a vase of flowers and a basket of fruit with a little hand-written sign that said *Welcome, Deb!*

She smiled, closing her eyes for another moment. That was a really nice touch.

I could really do with a cup of tea she thought and, though she could have lain on the sofa a lot longer and gradually let her middle revive, she got up with a sigh. She opened the little fridge that sat next to a small dishwasher under the worn wooden worktop. Inside the fridge was a pint of fresh milk from what looked like a local dairy, a packet of butter with the same logo, a punnet of tomatoes, a lettuce and a small organic-looking cucumber.

She took out the milk, amazed that Gretchen had organised groceries for her at all. Deb made a mental note to say a big thank you to her host for such lovely hospitality.

After some thought, Deb realised how to light the flame under the old-fashioned kettle that sat on the wide, old-fashioned stove, and set it to boil after half-filling it with water. She found mugs in one cupboard, and canisters containing tea bags, coffee and sugar in another. She dropped a tea bag into a mug and inspected the fruit basket while she waited for the kettle to sing.

In fact, as well as fruit, the basket contained biscuits, a fruit loaf cake, some bread rolls and a jar of locally made honey as well as apples, peaches, bananas and some golden yellow pears that made Deb's mouth water as soon as she saw them. This was above and beyond what she expected from a holiday let.

Picking up the note, she unfolded it and realised that there was a longer note inside.

Dear Deborah,

I do hope that you had an easy journey to the cottage and that you're settling in well. I've arranged a few groceries for you so that you don't walk straight into a "cupboards were bare" situation, but of course you will need to arrange groceries for yourself over the weeks you're here.

To that end, I've had a word with our local store in the village, and asked them to forward your bills to me to settle as part of your accommodation package. The same goes if you'd like to eat out at the Loch Cameron Inn – the landlady, Dotty, will take good care of you. Don't worry about paying for any living costs while you're in Loch Cameron, basically! I'm so grateful that you could come and help us out with the May Day party at such late notice.

Please give me a call if you need anything else, and I'll look forward to meeting you at the castle at 10am on Wednesday.

Yours sincerely,

Hal Cameron

Deb smiled to herself, made her cup of tea and took the packet of shortbread biscuits out of the gift basket. She carried them into the cute cottage bedroom, where she melted into a comfy, large mattress atop a white painted cast iron bed.

Propping herself up on some pillows, she sipped her tea and opened the biscuits, taking a bite of one. Its buttery sweetness filled her mouth, and she sighed happily.

Soon, work would begin. But, for today, she could put her feet up, safe in the knowledge that this job would solve her money worries for now. However, as she was self-employed, and now possibly single, Deb didn't have the luxury of a buffer or a fallback or someone to look after her if she didn't work. She'd covered her own time off, for the operation, but now it was important that she get back to it – even if she could have done with resting up for a little longer. That was how it was, being an independent businesswoman, but she wasn't complaining. Her mum, Janice, had brought her up not to complain, and it ran deep. Deb knew she found it hard to really open up and let anyone in. And even now, when Janice needed regular dialysis, she wouldn't accept the help Deb was offering.

Deb closed her eyes, propping the mug on her chest. She was tired, but she was also glad she'd come to Loch Cameron. It was good to be away from Dan, and away from the flat. Here, at least, she could think in peace.

However, she had a big task ahead of her, and she really needed the money to get back on track with work. Deb couldn't afford to have a lot of time off work unpaid. She couldn't pay herself sick pay. She needed this job, and she needed to impress the laird.

He had seemed nice in his letters and emails so far, but what if he was some kind of ultra-demanding, upper-class auto-crat? Would he be one of those work contacts who would fire off twenty emails a day at her from abroad, demanding constant updates, abrupt changes to the plan and ridiculously high stan-dards? She hoped not, but it was possible. And the fact that Hal

Cameron was willing to pay her twice what she would normally charge for a job was brilliant, but it also gave Deb pause.

Did Hal Cameron think that, now he'd bought her services at such a high price, that meant that he could make her work around the clock and answer every unreasonable whim he might have? She hoped this wasn't the reason for the laird's largesse, but whatever the reason, she'd said yes to the job now. She was here.

A thread of doubt unfurled in Deb's stomach. She hoped that she wouldn't regret taking on organising the May Day party. She could really do with peace and tranquillity right now, and a demanding boss was the last thing she needed.

FOUR

The old Loch Cameron Folly was built by the then-Laird, Donald Cameron, in 1935, as an amusement for his friends. The Laird, a renowned socialite, was known for his lavish parties and exuberant tastes. Tales are told of scantily-clad waitresses carrying crystal drinks trays on their heads, and mysterious entertainers who were said to be able to levitate and summon ghostly apparitions.

The folly can be found on Gyle Head, a clifftop five miles from Loch Cameron's Queen's Point. Gyle Head was sold to developers in 2015, but organisational difficulties meant that the land remained wild. The area remains open to the public.

Deb had waited patiently for the man to move, but he was standing in the middle of the road, on his phone, and showed no sign of having even seen her.

Which is stupid, she thought, as she beeped her horn, *because I am literally sitting here in a damned Land Rover. Can he really not see me?!*

She'd got up that morning and felt surprisingly rested, considering that she was sleeping in a different bed than her own. But, she'd woken to birdsong and a soft breeze blowing through her open window. The soft, clean flowered quilt tucked cosily around her body smelt softly of a light floral scent, with an undercurrent of that clean laundry smell that Deb associated with home. Not necessarily *home* with Dan, but *home* – her real, true home – with Janice when she was a child. Deb held the covers to her nose and inhaled a grateful deep breath.

Dan hadn't been best pleased when he realised she really was leaving. But she'd ignored his snide comments, like *I thought you weren't well enough to work yet* and *If I paid you, I wonder if you'd suddenly find the time to hoover.*

He'd said that before she'd left. She'd reminded him of her daily rate and said she'd be happy if he wanted to pay it, before pulling the car door closed and driving off.

She'd decided to go out for a drive to explore the surrounding area and, on looking at the map on her phone, saw that the Gyle Head Folly she'd read about before coming up to Loch Cameron was only a few miles away. A little drive, and a trip to find some groceries felt doable and not too strenuous. *Relax while you can*, she reminded herself. *You need all the recuperation you can get.*

Yet, here she was, in the middle of nowhere, and some guy was in her way.

It was typical. You can drive into the literal middle of nowhere, and there would still be a man, being an obstacle, Deb thought as she beeped the Land Rover's horn again. The road was narrow and there wasn't enough room to go around him.

He turned towards her and frowned. Deb expected him to step aside and let her through – the sat nav was pointing up this road, to the old ruin which was apparently at the end of it. Instead, the man approached her window and gestured with his finger that she should roll down the window.

'This is a private road,' he said, as soon as she'd wound the window down. 'I'm expecting a couple of trucks up here any minute, so you'll need to move.' He was about her age, tall – she estimated six foot two or three – and wearing a pair of grey jogging bottoms, a plain black sweatshirt and trainers. He had a trimmed black beard, and she noticed immediately that the way he stood suggested that he worked out. Deb had an initial impression of a kind of relaxed yet muscular masculinity in him, like a lion that was preserving his energy, but ready to hunt at any moment.

'Excuse me?' Deb frowned at him. His tone was dismissive, and it put her back up straightaway. 'There wasn't a sign to say I couldn't come up here. I'm looking for the ruin.'

'The folly. Yeah. It's private land,' he repeated, taking off his black aviator-style sunglasses and meeting her eyes. 'Sorry. You'll have to turn around.'

His eyes were surprising: an icy, light blue for such dark hair and beard, and with long, dark lashes that added a softness to his otherwise serious expression. Close up, Deb could also see that he had high cheekbones and a classic kind of look to his face. *Beautiful*, she thought: the word popped into her mind without her intending it to.

However, the man's tone and his insistence that Deb was wrong annoyed her. Random men telling her what to do in public had never exactly been her favourite thing: *smile, it might never happen, darlin'!* shouted at you from building sites, men at events who assumed she was on the wait staff, and not in fact the person in charge; random men in public places who thought they could tell her where she could and couldn't go.

I don't think so, she thought. *Beautiful or not.*

'The ruin is signposted on the map and it doesn't say anything about this road or anywhere in this area being private land,' Deb replied coolly, holding up her phone so that the man could see the map and the little red pin where the ruin was located.

'Am I speaking French? I just told you it was private land,' the man repeated. 'I need you to go up the lane, turn around and head out. I've got two trucks arriving any minute and they won't be able to get up here with you blocking the way.'

'Well, that's really not my problem,' Deb argued. He'd really irritated her now and, frankly, now she didn't care if she was in the wrong or not. She was damn well going to hold her ground.

'It will be if you can't get your Surrey tractor out of the lane, love.' The man raised an eyebrow. 'This is a dead end. The lane ends on my land.'

'You're very keen for me to know it's your land, aren't you?' she snapped. 'And I'm not your *love*.'

'That's for damn sure.' He returned her stare. 'And I'm not *keen* for anything right now apart from to get on with my day. So, if you wouldn't mind?' He made a circle motion with his index finger. 'On your way.'

Rude.

'You don't exactly look like a landowner,' Deb said, looking him up and down, pointedly. It was hard not to notice the faint outline of defined muscle under his sweatshirt. She blinked, looking away, not wanting to notice his tanned, muscled forearms as he pushed his sleeves up in impatience. There was a tattoo on one wrist: a black infinity sign, the figure eight on its side.

Whatever. He was an attractive man, then. But he was still unbelievably rude.

'I own the land at the end of the lane,' he repeated. 'I guess we don't all walk around with a poker up our arses like the Laird, but I can show you the paperwork, if you want.'

'That won't be necessary.' Deb closed her window and drove slowly up the lane to turn around. She was fuming. Her lovely morning of exploring had been ruined by this boorish moron. How *dare* he be so rude to her?

She turned the Land Rover in a small dirt turning circle at

the end of the lane, stopping briefly to see if she could sight the old folly. There were a few cars parked in front of a large stretch of grass that led out to the horizon; somewhere beyond that, there would be the cliff edge, like at Queen's Point, which overlooked the loch.

She couldn't see a folly, which was like a kind of pretend castle tower, from what she'd read. Rich lords and ladies in the past had built follies and grottoes and all manner of entertaining, eye-catching buildings and structures on their land as diverting objects of interest. *What a life that must have been,* Deb thought. *To build a mini castle because you had some friends coming for the weekend.*

Of course, in those days, guests might stay for weeks at a time and expect to be fed, watered and entertained. Deb imagined what it would have been like to plan a party for the Laird in the 1930s. It would no doubt have been lavish – but, in those days, the Laird would probably still have had a full staff of maids, cooks, housekeepers, drivers and butlers to do his bidding. Then, he wouldn't have needed a party planner at all, because presumably all he'd need to do was summon someone and demand something to be done, and that would be it.

There was an outcropping of trees visible to the left, and Deb thought that she could see a suggestion of brick through them. Perhaps that was where it was, then. Well, she wasn't going to get to see it today, or perhaps ever, now that this guy was guarding it like it was the crown jewels.

She drove slowly back down the lane and past the man, who was on the phone again. He watched her as she drove past, but she deliberately ignored him. If he wasn't nice enough to be polite in the first place, then she certainly wasn't going to give him the time of day now.

Deb was sick to the back teeth of men. And today's little performance from this one hadn't done anything to change her mind.

FIVE

'Good mornin'. Ye must be Deborah.' Hal Cameron strode into the large castle drawing room, a silky-eared brown spaniel trotting obediently at his heels.

Deb stood up slowly, steadying herself against the dark brown leather sofa she'd been sitting in since she arrived. She'd been shown into a large lounge that featured a huge stone fireplace, leather sofas and formal dark wooden furniture that definitely looked antique. She admired a writing desk which might have been mahogany, with a detail of ivy leaves climbing up its delicate legs; everywhere she looked, she saw something else that she loved.

This room was one of many that led off from a long, magenta-carpeted hallway. Anna, the housekeeper who had welcomed Deb to the castle, had done a mini-tour as they'd walked along: Deb had been shown a billiards room, containing a drinks cabinet, more leather sofas and leather-bound books, another large lounge, a palatial bathroom decorated in pink marble, a boot room and a corridor that led down into the cellar. Down a hallway, Anna had shown her double doors that led out to a large patio and extensive, manicured gardens.

The view over the loch was breath-taking. Rows of sharply
trimmed privet hedges reached down towards the loch in intri-
cate patterns. In the squares and triangles created between the
hedges, topiary trees in the shape of animals dotted the view
alongside evergreen trees. Wide stone steps led down from the
terrace outside the patio and, at the bottom of a grassy hill,
joined a long stone wall that ran around the whole edge of one
side of the castle. Deb had felt incredibly privileged to be
working at such a grand location, but she was also instantly
stressed by the task of having to plan a party which was fitting
for such a glamorous and spacious venue.

'Good morning,' she replied, shaking the Laird's hand and
hoping that her expression didn't show her surprise. Of course,
Deb knew Zelda, who was the Laird's girlfriend, and Zelda was
in her thirties, the same age as Deb, roughly. Yet, when Zelda
had mentioned that she was going out with the Laird of Loch
Cameron, Deb had still imagined a more portly, middle aged
man, perhaps with thinning hair and a waistcoat.

This Hal Cameron was young, dashingly handsome and in
strikingly good shape. He wore a simple white T shirt, blue
jeans and trainers with a dark blue cardigan over the top. Deb
had no doubt that even though he was dressed simply, the
clothes were of designer quality. Especially if Zelda had been
involved anywhere in the decision-making process. Deb remembered Zelda very well: like everyone at *Homes and Interiors
Magazine*, she was impeccably dressed and styled. However,
unlike some people at the magazine, Zelda was also genuine,
warm and had a great sense of humour.

'How are ye? Find it okay?' Hal asked. 'This is Finnegan, by
the way. Are ye okay with dogs? He's a friendly fella. But
gentle,' Hal bent down to stroke Finnegan's soft ears. The dog
gazed up at his owner with adoration, and sat down next to the
leather chair which was at a right angle to the sofa. 'Please, sit.
Dinnae stand on ceremony,' Hal added, and sat in the single

seater and gestured at the housekeeper who had let Deb in. 'Anna. Ye've met Deborah? She's gonna be workin' on the party organisation, so I expect ye'll have plenty o' conversations aboot this an' that.'

Anna, a pleasant-looking middle aged woman dressed smartly in dark wide legged trousers and a cream short-sleeved knitted top, nodded at Deb as she approached.

'Yes, we met just now. Happy to help with anything you need,' Anna said, politely. 'Would you both like some coffee? There's a nice madeira cake to go with it, also.'

'That'd be grand. Thanks, Anna.' Hal nodded.

'Yes, I'd love a coffee. And some cake,' Deb added with a smile.

'I'll bring it up shortly.' The housekeeper let herself out of the drawing room.

'So! You need a big community party set up for...' Deb checked her diary. 'Four weeks' time? Is that right?' she got out her laptop, which she'd already set up with a scheduling spread-sheet and a separate document for notes.

'That's right, aye,' Hal sighed. 'We committed tae it, an' then realised that we had tae be in New York for a few weeks fer some work stuff fer Zelda. I've got tae be with her. We'll be contactable, of course, but since we'll be distracted with that, an' back an' forth a wee bit, we thought it was best to outsource the party planning this year,' he added. 'We always have a May Day party fer the village. I started it again a couple o' years' back, and I dinnae want tae renege on ma promise. The villagers look forward tae it, an' it's always a hoot. Loch Cameron's a close knit community, an' they've always been so guid tae me an' my family. I think it's important tae give back, as the Laird.'

'So, what does being the Laird actually involve?' she asked. 'You own the castle, and the village? I mean, it's named after you?'

'Aye. The Camerons have been the local landowners fer

hundreds o' years.' Hal leaned forward a little in his chair as he explained. 'The first Laird was Sir Colin Cameron, who was knighted in 1280. In 1445 King James II raised Sir Colin's descendant Sir Duncan Cameron to the peerage to become the Laird of Loch Cameron. We've owned it ever since. The castle was rebuilt a couple o' times, o' course. The present building was built in the 1800s, and we've been repairin' it ever since.' He rolled his eyes. 'Another reason I'm happy tae hand the party over tae ye. I dinnae have enough hours in the day fer everythin' that needs doin'.'

'To the castle?' Deb asked.

'Aye, the castle. But, also, most o' the property in the village. I'm the landlord fer most o' the houses. The cottage yer stayin' in, too.'

'Oh, I see. That's a lot of property.' Deb raised her eyebrow, doing a quick mental calculation about the possible value of the Laird's estate.

'Aye. A lot o' responsibility.' He nodded. 'Still, it's also a great honour.'

'Of course.' Deb wondered how Zelda had met Hal Cameron. Even if you worked for chichi magazines, it wasn't every day that you ran into a titled landowner who owned a castle and looked like this.

'So, the party.' Hal clapped his hands together. 'May Day is historic, up here. In Edinburgh ye may have seen the big bonfires at Samhain.' He pronounced it *sow-in*. 'That's the old Celtic fire festival. New Year for the Celts, though we call it Halloween now,' he clarified.

'Ah. I have seen the bonfires,' Deb replied. 'People are quite into getting back to the old rural traditions nowadays, aren't they? In Cornwall they parade a horse's skeleton around the streets. And in Wales, too, I think. And there's Krampus, isn't there? That big, scary goat thing. Is it a goat? But that's in Germany.'

'Aye, you're right. People like tae keep that connection to the old traditions, especially now they're interested in nature more. Over the past five, ten years, we get more people up here foragin' for wild mushrooms, wantin' tae do wild swimmin', all that. When I was a kid, nobody was bothered,' he laughed. 'All those old festivals like Samhain and May Day – well, that was called Bealtaine, in the Celtic times – they're based on the farming calendar. They're just the times when the crops were harvested or when the land was fertile for plantin'.'

'I see. That would appeal to people who are getting interested in working sympathetically with nature, nowadays,' Deb mused.

Anna walked into the lounge, carrying a tartan patterned tray with a pot of coffee, two large ceramic mugs and a plate with a whole madeira cake. She set the tray on the table, the nutty, chocolatey smell of the coffee making Deb's mouth water.

'I'll let you both help yourselves. There's milk in that jug, sugar in the bowl. A knife for the cake, and some plates and napkins.' The housekeeper had a friendly and unassuming manner that Deb liked. She was relieved, because as Anna was probably going to be her main point of contact at the castle for organising everything, it made a huge difference if Anna was easy to talk to or not.

'Thanks, Anna. That cake looks gorgeous. Did you make it?' Deb asked, admiring the golden crust of the madeira loaf cake. Anna had cut the end off already, and Deb could see the yellow, light textured sponge inside.

'Oh, no. This came from the local market, I must confess!' Anna grinned. 'We have a lovely one here; I'll take you, if you'd like to come next time it's on. There's a fabulous bakery stall that I always stock up on cake and bread from. There's a great grocery stall too, and other stuff: a vegan wholefoods stall, if that's your thing. Jam and honey, locally made soaps. They're lovely, actually, all very natural and gentle. Crystals, even, sometimes.'

'That sounds gorgeous. I'd love to.' Deb poured some coffee from the pot into one mug, and then the other, for Hal.

'Well, I'll let you know. I expect we'll be seeing a lot of each other, anyway.' Anna nodded. 'Anyway, I have to get on – we've got French polishers coming in and I have to show them what needs doing. Catch up soon, though?'

'Definitely. Thanks, Anna.' Deb reached for the knife to cut a slice of the moist-looking cake. 'And, I've been Mother here and poured you one, but you can put your own milk and sugar in. I know I'm fussy about that,' she said to Hal.

'Thanks.' He took the cup. 'Anyway, in the past, the Camerons always had a big bonfire in the castle grounds and a big knees-up for the villagers. Kindae tae say thanks fer all their hard work over the year. Let them blow off steam, promote community cohesion. I was readin' in the auld journals down in the family archive that some o' the auld Lairds used tae hear grievances from the villagers in the afternoon, before the party, an' sort them out so that there'd be nae bad will goin' forward.' Hal chuckled, pouring a little milk into his coffee and giving it a cursory stir with a silver teaspoon that Deb noticed was monogrammed with the initial C and with a crest. It was the Cameron insignia, she guessed. 'I don't do that now. But we do have a ceilidh, a free bar, food, the bonfire. I like tae be able tae give back.'

'I'd like to see the records of the previous parties. Might be useful.' Deb made some notes on her laptop.

'Yer welcome tae. Get Anna tae take ye down tae the archive room sometime,' Hal said. 'Lots o' good stuff down there, though there's also a lot o' auld records o' cattle yields, land allocations, maps, that kindae thing.'

'That sounds amazing, thanks.'

'Aye. Couple of years I didnae hold the party, after my wife was ill and she passed.' Hal looked reflective for a moment. 'Then I met Zelda and she made me realise that Maggie wouldnae have wanted me tae stop doin' the party. So she helped me reinstate it.'

'I'm so sorry for your loss.' Deb felt the familiar ache in her middle and leaned back in the sofa to stretch out her muscles a little. 'Sorry. Do you mind if I just change position? I had a hysterectomy a couple of months ago and I'm fine, but I get a bit sore if I sit in one position for too long.'

'Oh, of course, do whatever ye need.' Hal looked concerned. 'Can we get ye a hot water bottle or somethin'?'

'That's kind, but I'll be fine. I might just get up and walk around for a minute, though,' Deb said, touched at the offer. Hal was a total stranger and had made a thoughtful suggestion: Dan had been her partner, and called her the Queen of Sheba for taking too long recovering. She took out a couple of over-the-counter painkillers from her handbag and swallowed them with a sip of coffee.

'Okay.' Hal took a slice of cake. 'Well, let me know if ye need anythin'.'

'I will. Now. How many people are we expecting at May Day? From what time, until when? And you said there's a free bar and catering, and a ceilidh. Any other main features we need to add in? And do attendees have full run of the castle, or just restricted areas? What about serving staff, do you have a place you usually get them from? Just off the top of my head, to start with.' Deb paced around the lounge, feeling the pain in her middle start to abate.

'Wow. That's a lot of questions. Okay, let me think. One by one?' Hal grinned.

'How many people are we expecting at May Day?' Deb smiled, holding up one finger.

'About three hundred or so.'

'All right.' She'd organised events for more people in her time, though three hundred was quite a lot.

'From what time, until when?'

'I'd say five p.m. tae late. Often, it's the early hours. Three, four a.m.? I dinnae put an end time on it. At a certain point, I just go tae bed and leave 'em tae it.'

'Free bar and catering?'

'Aye, of course. All on me.'

'Ceilidh?'

'There'd be an outcry if there wasnae.'

'Okay... let's see. Serving staff?'

'I'll give ye the name of the firm I usually use. An' the contacts fer the band, an' Dotty an' Eric in the village – at the Loch Cameron Inn? They'll run the bar.' The laird fed some cake to Finnegan the dog, who had been waiting patiently at his heels.

'That would be great, thanks. Yes to all helpful contacts, especially if they've done the event before.'

'Aye, o' course. I recite a poem too, do a bit o' performance. I did it once years back, an' people seem tae expect it now. So...' He shrugged.

'That must be quite a sight,' Deb chuckled.

'Ha. Ah do my best.' Hal stroked Finnegan's ears. 'So Zelda tells me yer quite the pro at this kindae thing. I was thinkin', we have our traditions, but by all means feel free tae suggest different activities. I'm open tae suggestions.'

'Hm. Well, I did think about maybe a signature cocktail for the event. Seeing as you've got a local distillery here, I think? That might be nice?' Deb suggested. 'And I don't know if you usually do goody bags, or small gifts, but that might be good? If you have the budget?'

'Aye, the budget can stretch.' Hal nodded. 'The Loch Cameron Whisky Distillery, aye. Ben Douglas is the owner, an' his partner Liz. They're great, an' I'm sure Liz would be up for helpin' out. You should give her a call.'

'I will. That's great. Whisky cocktails, of course. With a yummy non-alcoholic alternative.'

'Goes without sayin',' the laird chuckled.

'And if there are other local business owners you think would be interested in helping, that would be great,' Deb continued. 'I guess in this situation, though, you're the local landowner, so all permissions just go through you?'

'That's right.' Hal nodded. 'Though I've sold off some land recently to a developer. But that shouldnae affect anythin'.'

'Oh, really? Would the developer be interested in sponsoring the party, maybe? I mean, I know you have a generous budget, but there's no harm in suggesting it. Sometimes, companies like to sponsor an event to develop a good relationship with the community, or just get brand exposure.'

'Hm. In this case, I'd appreciate if ye didnae approach him,' Hal said, shortly.

'The developer?' Deb asked, noting a subtle change in Hal's voice. He seemed suddenly a little colder than his usual warm manner.

'Aye. I dinnae think there's much in the way of community spirit there.' Hal sounded dismissive. 'Zelda says hi, by the way. She's sorry she couldnae make it today but she's off in Edinburgh just now.' He was changing the subject, and Deb briefly wondered why, but she supposed Hal had his reasons.

'That's all right. Say hi back, and I'll see her soon, I hope.'

'Aye. You might do, but we're away to New York later this week,' Hal explained.

'What are you up to over there?' Deb asked, curiously. 'I mean... I assume it's important, otherwise you wouldn't be going.'

'Aye, right. Yeah.' Hal rubbed his beard with the back of his hand. 'Zelda's been asked to work on this interior design project for a celebrity client, so she'd be away a few weeks tae do that. Usually, I'd stay here, but she's also up for an award at this posh magazine do. For her interiors. An' apparently the award has a lot o' press associated wi' it, an' they asked if I could be there. So, of course, I'll go an' support her.'

'Wow. That sounds very impressive.'

'Aye. She's a powerhouse.' Hal sighed, with a smile of fond longing on his lips. 'An' she's done so much fer me an' the castle, an' the estate, it's only right that I should support her career. Anyway, I'm proud tae be on her arm.' He shrugged, smiling.

'Zelda is awesome,' Deb agreed. 'That's so exciting for her!'

'Aye. She's all fingers an' thumbs in the meantime though, aye.' Hal laughed. 'Nervous as a cat.'

'All the more reason for her to have her man by her side.' Deb felt a twinge at seeing how much Hal supported Zelda. They really were partners, in the way that you were supposed to be: Hal had Zelda's back, and vice versa. It stung when she thought about Dan, who complained about stacking the dishwasher and relied on her to do everything.

'Aye, well. That's what ye do, isn't it?' Hal replied, simply.

'You would think so,' Deb replied, a little archly, and looked down at her notepad. Work was a good distraction from her love life, which, unlike Zelda and Hal's, was significantly less than ideal.

'Now. Where were we?' She uncapped her pen, trying to ignore the feelings of loneliness that came from comparing her relationship with Dan to Hal and Zelda. But perhaps she needed that comparison: perhaps she needed to see that settling for something you perceived as easy wouldn't make you happy. It hadn't, despite the fact that she had thought it was a safe option.

If her mother, Janice, had been here, Deb knew that she would have suspected Hal of deviousness in some way: she wouldn't have believed that a man could be so pure of heart, or so devoted to the woman he loved.

It seemed to Deb that you got what you expected in life, and Janice had expected a hard life in which she could trust no one. It wasn't her fault: that was how she'd been brought up herself.

Maybe I can expect more, she thought. Half of her was intimidated by Zelda and Hal, living in an actual castle and jet-setting all over the world. It was a wildly glamorous and apparently unattainable lifestyle. Yet, the other half of her could see beyond that: the look in Hal's eyes when he talked about Zelda transcended wealth and glamour and awards ceremonies and parties at the castle. That was love, and Deb knew that was what would remain if all the other trappings were gone.

That was what she wanted, but she had never allowed herself to have.

In fact, it was love that was intimidating; not anything else. To open yourself up to another person that deeply was something she had always – if she was truly honest with herself – been afraid of. She was still afraid of it, but, Deb allowed herself to imagine for a moment what it would be like to be loved that deeply. And to love someone else as thoroughly.

The thought was terrifying, but it also drew Deb like a magnet and refused to let go. What might life be like with that kind of love?

SIX

'Morning, Mum. How are you?'

Deb had been dreading her twice weekly call to her mother, Janice. Not because she hated her mum, or anything as dramatic: they'd always got on fairly well. Rather, she felt guilty about being away for a few weeks, and not being as available.

'Can't complain, poppet.' Her mum sounded tired, but she always did, nowadays.

'How's the dialysis?' Deb asked. Her mum had been diagnosed with diabetes some years ago, which she now needed two sessions of dialysis a week for.

'The same. I wish they'd refresh the magazines in the treatment room. I've started listening to audiobooks. You can get them from the library, you know.'

'That's good. How about when you get home?'

'Well, I'm done in, obviously,' Janice said, briskly. 'Four hours of your blood being pumped out of your body, cleaned and then pumped back in will do that to you.'

'I know, Mum,' Deb replied, evenly. She was all too aware that it was unlikely that Janice would have much energy to cook dinners and do the housework after dialysis.

If Janice didn't get a kidney transplant in the next couple of years, things didn't look great. People could be on dialysis for years: the doctor had told them that. But, over time, Janice's kidneys would get weaker, and she would get more vulnerable, and more prone to complications. 'Has the taxi been okay?' Usually, Deb drove her to the clinic a couple of times a week for her treatments, with a local taxi taking her there and back on the days Deb couldn't manage. Deb already hadn't been able to drive her mum for six weeks after the hysterectomy, and she'd felt hideously guilty about it. Now, as she was away in Loch Cameron, her mum would be taking the taxi for even longer. Deb was paying for it, which she didn't mind at all, but she still felt awful.

'It's fine. Taxi drivers are a bit predictable. Always going on about the state of the roads, or politics,' Janice sighed. 'However, I had a nice conversation with one of them the other day about music. He was a Cher fan, of all things.' Janice never liked talking about her treatment. 'We had quite the discussion.'

'That sounds good. As long as they're not coughing all over you.' Deb was referring to the time that Janice had caught a bad cold from one of the taxi drivers who were on a contract with the hospital. In her immune-compromised state, what had been a normal cold to him had put Janice in bed for weeks.

'Don't worry, Deb. I sit in the back and make them put the plexiglass guard thing up,' Janice tutted. Deb could imagine her rolling her eyes. 'Don't fuss.'

'I'm not fussing.'

'How's the little village?' Janice changed the subject.

'It's nice. I'm staying in a really cute little cottage. You'd like it.'

'Ah, lovely. Nice views? You said it's on a loch, isn't it?'

'Yes. I'll send you some pictures.'

'In the post? All right. Or a postcard, if they have them.' Her mum sounded pleased. Deb laughed.

'No, Mum. On your phone. You can view pictures, remember? I showed you?' Deb had bought Janice a smartphone six months ago, but her mum had been very resistant to learning how to use it. It had taken Deb a month to persuade her to leave it on and not turn it off "when she wasn't using it" so that she could call Deb in an emergency – or Deb could get a hold of her mum when she needed to.

'Do, darling. That would be lovely. I'll try to remember how to view them.'

Deb rolled her eyes and resisted the urge to say "Just tap the screen, Mum," but even at the age of thirty-eight, she knew she couldn't get away with any sass with Janice.

'So, how are you feeling? How were the appointments this week?' Deb knew that she had to push her mother to talk about her dialysis. Janice never wanted to admit that there was anything wrong with her. Janice was the most stubborn person Deb had ever known – and she'd met some divas in her line of work, organising fancy events.

But, the thing was, Janice was vulnerable, and they both knew it. Janice needed help, not only in being driven to and from her appointments – she had never learned – but around the house, too.

But, Deb had never known how to persuade her mum to accept help. She was absolutely, pathologically incapable of accepting help, apart from in the direst of circumstances when a) she was unconscious or b) there was literally no other option.

'Oh, you know. The usual,' Janice tutted. 'Nothing out of the ordinary. Fine.'

'Right. And you had your check up with Dr Gupta. How was that?' Deb knew that Janice wouldn't volunteer any information without being harassed for it.

'It was fine. Nothing to report,' Janice said, airily. 'So, tell me about this big job! At a castle! That's exciting.'

'*Mum.* Otherwise, I'll just have to call Dr Gupta.' Deb tried her best to boss her mum around, but Janice was having none of it.

'You will not, missy. The doctor-patient relationship is confidential. I'm not batty yet.'

'I know that, Mum. I just want to know what's going on.'

'I'm fine. That's what's going on.' Janice's voice became a little steelier. 'Can we change the subject, please? I have to be at that bloody clinic for far too much of my life, as it is. I don't want to waste my time talking about it when I could be hearing what you've been up to.'

Deb sighed. 'Are you sure you're okay, though?'

'Sure, I'm sure. Now. How are things between you and Dan? And then tell me about the castle,' Janice instructed.

'Ugh. Not great when it comes to Dan, I'm afraid,' Deb sighed. 'I think we're... on a break? I left it open, I guess, but I haven't heard from him and I don't really want to.' She brought her mum up to date with her argument with Dan, which had started with dirty dishes, and ended up with her realising that Dan didn't respect or care for her at all.

'He's been such a prat.' Janice was not one to mince words. 'You know that I've never thought he was good enough for you, pumpkin.'

'I know. But he was nice, in the beginning. Kind,' Deb said with a sigh.

'They all are.' Janice snorted. 'It doesn't last.'

Deb had never known her father: according to Janice, he had been a one-night stand who hadn't even stayed the night. Two months later, she'd realised she was pregnant. *I was blessed with a beautiful daughter*, Janice would say, if she was questioned on the subject. *I got his DNA and frankly that was all I needed.*

'Well, I wanted it to,' Deb replied. 'Not now, though.'

'So, you broke up?' her mum prompted her. 'Lucky you had this job, I suppose. To give you a bit of space.'

'Not officially broken up. We're having some space. But, yes, basically.'

'Do you know what you'll do?' Janice probed. 'If it was me, I'd be out of there. You deserve better, darling. You're a catch.'

In fact, Janice had never settled down with a partner since Deb was born. She'd had a boyfriend here and there, but nothing serious. Deb had always wanted her to find someone, but she'd remained fiercely independent. Deb respected that, but, particularly as her mum had got older, she wished that Janice would let someone into her life. Not least, so that the burden of caring for her could be split with someone else. It was hard, being just the two of them. Deb felt utterly responsible for her mum.

'I'm not sure that I feel like it at the moment, but thanks,' Deb said. 'And I can't have children anymore. So, not really a catch.'

Before her hysterectomy, she actually hadn't thought much about the fact that having it would mean she wouldn't be able to have children, after. She had been so focused on ending the horrible symptoms of endometriosis that she insisted that she'd never really wanted to be a mum. It wasn't in her life plan.

Now, even though motherhood still wasn't in her plan, Deb felt more aware of her loss. The operation had been a huge gain – she had regained her health, her body, her energy. It had been a success, and she was so, so happy that she'd done it. But, now that her uterus had gone, there was no going back. It wasn't like a vasectomy, which could be reversed. This was final.

After she'd had the hysterectomy, her mum had dropped round some magazines for her to flick through. They weren't the ones she would usually read: in fact, they weren't what Janice would usually read, either, but her mum had explained that she'd "borrowed" them from the hospital waiting room.

So, Deb had flicked through them, looking disinterestedly at articles on autumn fashions from two years ago, at recipes and real-life stories.

One article had drawn her attention. It had been a collection of inspirational real-life accounts from women with fertility problems who had all had babies with the help of IVF, herbal medicine, having faith against the odds, surrogacy, adoption, and a variety of other methods.

Reading the article, Deb couldn't help wondering where the woman was who either didn't want children at all, or for whom none of these things had worked. The header to the piece read:

WHAT WOULD YOU DO FOR A BABY?
Six women told us how they achieved a woman's greatest goal –
becoming a mum.

What about the ones that don't? Deb had thought. She was absolutely supportive of any woman who wanted to have a child, and she knew what barriers could stand in the way. She admired all the women that she read about in the article, and was happy for them, that they got what they wanted.

But, having a baby was not every woman's goal. It had never been hers, particularly.

Did it make her less of a woman, though, now that she couldn't have one anymore? She knew, intellectually, that it didn't. A woman was more than the sum of her physical parts. But Deb also worried that, maybe, other people would see her differently when they knew she couldn't have children. They would think less of her, somehow. The memory of the article nagged at her. *A woman's greatest goal.*

If that wasn't her goal, was that wrong in some way?

'That is ridiculous, Deborah,' her mum interrupted her. '*You* are a catch. And, so what if you aren't able to have a baby the normal way anymore? You could still adopt, or use a surrogate, if it came to it. But, take it from me, and I mean this in the nicest possible way, because you know I love you very much. But, having a baby isn't the main aim of life, and frankly it's not all it's cracked up to be. Other things are just as important. I wouldn't worry about it, if I were you.'

'Wow. Thanks.' Deb shook her head, knowing that her mum meant well, but that she could also be hurtfully blunt sometimes.

'Deb. You know I wouldn't change a thing, having you,' Janice sighed. 'But all I'm saying is, you are not worthless or less of a woman, just because you can't now grow a baby in your uterus. And I somewhat feel that if you'd been so desperate to do it, you would have at least tried before the age of thirty-eight.'

'But... I didn't meet the right person,' Deb protested. 'It's not as easy as that.'

'Life is as easy or difficult as you make it.' Janice tutted, and Deb knew that she'd never get her mum to change her mind now: she had launched into her personal philosophy of zero-tolerance-for-excuses-and-pure-unfettered-independence. Deb knew that Janice had learned this from her own mother, Grandma Elsie.

Deb's grandma had tried to insist that people call her Elise, because it was classier, but everyone ignored that, and called her Elsie. Even after she'd changed her name by deed poll in her fifties. This was something that Deb had only found out when Grandma Elsie had died, and she and her mum were going through her papers. In retrospect, Deb thought how cross she would have been if she had wanted to be known by another name and everyone had ignored her wishes. Still, it was too late now: Elsie was long gone, though her legacy remained strong.

Grandma Elsie had died when Deb was in her teens, but it was obvious where Janice had got her fierce independence from: it seemed that it ran in the family. As if every woman in the Sutherland family had inherited a ramrod of steel for a spine, and an imperious raised eyebrow to be directed at any and all perceived wrongdoing.

'Life is not a birthday party. It's tough. You've got to be tough to get through it,' Janice lectured.

'I know, Mum,' Deb sighed. The thing was, Deb didn't always want to be tough, or think of life as a battle to be fought every day. She wanted some lightness in her life too: some joy, some love, some ease. Was that really so much to ask?

'I wonder if you do know. God knows I tried to teach you, like Grandma taught me. Be thankful *she* wasn't your mother,' Janice exhaled, half-crossly.

'I loved Grandma,' Deb replied, truthfully. She had. Grandma Elsie had had that same complete stubbornness as Janice, but Deb had always thought that she also had a flair of whimsy that was absent in her daughter, shown by that more poetic, dreamy name.

Despite all of her family, and most of her friends, continuing to call her Elsie, Grandma had known who she was, and she wasn't afraid to change it, so that, at least legally, she was who she wanted to be. Deb had always respected Grandma Elsie's oddly tenacious grip on her dreams. Even though the world around her hadn't agreed, she had made her dreams a reality.

'I know you did. And I'm glad. But, remember that how she was as Grandma, with you, was different to how she was as Mum, for me.' Janice sounded distant. 'All I'm saying is, you don't know everything about her.'

'You've got to respect the way that she lived her life, though,' Deb insisted. 'She was independent, and with the name thing, she changed it legally, despite the fact that everyone refused to call her Elise. In her mind, she was Elise, and that was all that mattered.'

'Poppycock.' Janice sniffed. There had always been bad blood between Janice and Grandma Elsie, and Deb had never

known why. Both of them had refused to talk about it, but there
was always an atmosphere when they were both around. Deb
had preferred it when it had just been her and Grandma. 'I
couldn't respect that woman. Such vanity.'

'She was your mum,' Deb said, appalled at Janice.

'She was damaged,' Janice replied, crisply. 'She had no business bringing up a child.'

They'd talked about Grandma Elise – which was how she
had wanted to be known, and Deb thought it was respectful of
her to call her Elise rather than Elsie, even though she was dead
now – many times over the years, and Janice had told Deb that
Grandma Elise was an unhappy person. She had been made to
leave her home when she was young, and she'd never got over it.
Janice had intimated that other things had happened to
Grandma Elise afterwards, but she'd never said what. When
Deb had asked, Janice had said, *too much water under the bridge*
or *there are some things that should be forgotten.*

Once, Deb remembered vividly, she had been ten, and
they'd been on their way home on the bus from Grandma
Elise's flat. Janice had been at work – she worked at the supermarket then, stacking shelves. It had been the summer holidays
and Deb had been spending every day with her grandmother.

They'd spent most of their time on the allotment, which
Deb loved. She remembered Grandma Elise saying she was
brown as a tree trunk from being in the sun all day – Janice had
made her wear a hat and sunscreen, but her skin still darkened
every day – and she came home every day with a little prize for
her good work: a bag of ripe, cherry-red tomatoes, a tub of small,
sweet strawberries and, once, a whole carrier bag of runner
beans. Janice had raised an eyebrow at the bag and said, *what
the hell am I supposed to do with these? You don't like green
beans.*

But, because Grandma Elise had grown them with such
patience, and because Deb had helped to water them and train

them up the wooden frames her grandmother had made, Deb had said *yes I do*. Even as a child, she'd sensed that there was tension between her mother and her grandmother. If someone had asked her then whose side she would have chosen, it would have been Grandma Elise's.

That day, in the kitchen with the carrier bag of runner beans in her hand, Janice had said *You're just like your grandmother. Changeable. One moment you hate green beans, the next moment you love them.* She'd dumped the bag on the table with a sigh. *She's always been like that. She'd say black was white and up was down, then switch as soon as you agreed.*

I'll eat them, Deb had insisted. *Grandma isn't like that. Neither am I.*

Don't forget, I know more about Grandma than you do. Janice had raised an eyebrow. *You're more alike than you know.* Janice had hesitated, perhaps gauging for a moment whether Deb was old enough to understand what she was going to say. *There are things she'll never tell you. Things that you couldn't understand, sweetheart*, she'd said, in a more gentle tone. *Reasons for why Grandma is the way she is.*

Grandma Elsie – *Elise*, Deb thought, she should really use the name that her grandmother had preferred – had, in Deb's opinion, suffered from depression. Possibly, it was post-natal, or perhaps just depression overall. Not that there was simply a "just" when it came to something like that. Deb knew that depression could destroy a person. She was grateful that she'd never suffered with it, but she knew people that had.

She was damaged. The words rang in Deb's ears.

'That's a horrible thing to say.' Deb knew she was on thin ice, being so direct with Janice, but she had loved Grandma Elise, and she felt that she couldn't let it go without defending her memory.

There was a pause on the line; Deb wondered if she'd gone too far.

'Oh, God. I know.' Janice sighed, after a moment. 'And I loved her. But she was difficult. And all the fuss about the name...' there was another pause... 'Eh. Water under the bridge.' There was a shrug in Janice's voice, but Deb knew that it was a pretence. If things between her mum and Grandma Elise really were "water under the bridge" then she would have no problem being open about it.

'Poor Grandma,' Deb said.

'Hmph. You don't know half of the stuff that happened in my childhood.'

'I would if you'd tell me,' Deb protested. 'Was it that bad? At least Grandma was there for you. She looked after you.'

'Hmm.' Deb could tell from her mum's voice that she was frowning. 'Let's just say that I was fed and had clothes and went to school, darling. But all the bedtime stories and gardening and baking and hugs... she saved that for you. Don't get me wrong. I'm glad she did. But, as I've said, that wasn't the woman I knew. She... lost a lot, as a child, and I don't think she ever really recovered.'

'That's vague. I know she had to move house when she was young, but that's not that bad, is it?'

'Well, it was more than moving house, sweetheart. But I don't think we should get into it now,' Janice said.

'You never want to talk about Grandma.'

'No. It's best left in the past,' Janice said.

'Fine,' Deb sighed.

'Well, this ended up being a deep conversation,' Janice chuckled. 'Are you all right, darling? Missing Grandma?'

'A bit. And you. It's just been a bit of an upheaval, coming over here to work, and what happened with Dan.'

'I imagine. But you're strong. You'll manage.'

'Hmm...' Deb thought for a moment about the strange appeal of *not* managing. How nice it would be, not to be so capable. To be one of those people who just let other people do things for them.

But, it just wasn't who she was. Hewn of the same granite as Elise and Janice, with the same ramrod spine.

Was this why she was single again? She'd snapped, eventually, at Dan's terrible behaviour. Maybe, another woman would have taken it for longer.

Maybe another woman would have had children, and been married, and settled down like you were supposed to.

There was something in the back of Deb's mind that she wasn't quite ready to verbalise – not yet. A shadowy sentiment that said something like, *maybe the women in our family are too hard, too stubborn and intransigent to be truly loved.*

Or, let ourselves be loved.

Maybe we aren't natural mothers. Not the maternal type.

'All right, Mum. I've got to go.' Deb felt a lump in her throat as that horrible thought emerged. She didn't want to explore where that sentiment led: what did it say about her? 'I love you.'

'I love you, too, darling.' Janice sounded tired. 'Don't let the world get you down. Remember that you're a winner. I didn't raise a reedy little girl that would break in the slightest breeze. I raised an oak, Deborah. An oak.'

'I know, Mum,' Deb replied, trying to control the wobble in her voice. She certainly didn't feel like an oak, most of the time. 'I know.'

'Good,' Janice said.

Deb put her phone on the table as the call ended. She admired Janice and Elise very deeply, and loved them both.

But, did she want to be like them?

Not entirely.

Not when it came to having a stone heart, toughened in the flames of loss and hardship.

What do you want, then? Love and roses? she asked herself.

Yes, came the answer. Would that be so terrible? A life of love, and ease? Of never having to struggle and fight, ever again?

No, it wouldn't be terrible at all.

Was it likely? Also no. But, perhaps, Deb could at least allow herself that dream.

It seemed that Grandma Elise had believed in her dreams. But Deb wondered what Janice was hiding about her. What was it that she refused to talk about? Was there something terrible at the root of her mother and her grandmother's relationship? Something that threatened to shake the foundations of her own sense of self? And if so, what was it?

SEVEN

'DOWN WI' NEW BUILDS! PRESERVE OUR LAND!' the group of women shouted as Deb approached the end of the road where she had had her first run-in with the man with the piercing blue eyes.

It was a lovely day and she'd thought she'd walk up to Gyle Head and see if she could find a footpath around the building site and get a glimpse of the old folly. Even though there was, of course, Loch Cameron Castle – which she had now visited, and had tea with the Laird – she was intrigued to see something that was more of a ruin.

Plus, she needed some distraction.

Deb had always loved old castles, and though Loch Cameron Castle was breathtaking, the romantic in her had been slightly disappointed that it was fully operational. A castle with tiled bathrooms, washing machines and a digital security system was practical, but not necessarily the stuff of epic novels. Part of her had wanted to see broken, moss-covered walls and spiral turrets that had crumbled away to reveal their stairs within. Gothic, arched doorways with heavy, creaking doors that opened onto ruined ballrooms; slitted windows that over-looked a twisted, ancient forest.

The folly on Gyle Head looked like a real beauty spot, according to the pictures she'd found online. It did have a forest to one side, though Deb had no idea if it was ancient or not. The ruins weren't anywhere near as big as a castle's would have been, as the folly had only been built as a party feature for the then-laird's amusement. In fact, looking at the pictures of the original structure which some keen local historian had posted online, it looked fairly small, but remarkably picturesque. She was keen to try again and see if there was another way she could get to it.

Built in grey stone, there had been two main towers which were edged in white – whether they had been painted originally or whether it had been a white stone of some kind, Deb couldn't tell – and grand double doors with black cast iron hinges. Unlike a real ancient castle, the windows had been glazed and were much bigger than the customary arrow slits an older structure would have needed. Deb had found a few pictures of the original inside décor, which had been done in a faux medieval style with a large round table at the centre of the main room – there didn't seem to be an upstairs – which the laird of the time had apparently used to host King Arthur and the Knights of the Round Table dinner parties.

Cute, she'd thought. She'd worked on some impressive parties in her day, but it looked like the Scottish gentry had been kicking up their heels in pretty fine style in the 1930s, too.

Yet, today, there were about ten women at the end of the little road, all ages, carrying hand-lettered signs and marching in a circle. One of them – an elderly black woman with short grey hair and a kind yet stern expression, approached Deb. She wore shiny purple wellies, black harem pants and an elegant, draped top under an equally elegant shawl in a black and white geometric pattern.

'Hello, dear. Sign our petition? This awful property developer, Kyle Abernethy, wants to build houses on protected land. There's rare local wildlife up there – red squirrels and capercaillie. Building work is going to drive them out.'

'Oh. Right. Yes, of course.' Deb took the pen from the woman and signed the paper. 'Not many signatures so far,' she said, handing it back. Despite the fact that she had had a run-in with this Kyle the other day, she couldn't forget his muscled forearms, and the figure eight tattoo on his wrist. About the knightly set of his face, his beautiful, startling blue eyes. Thinking about Kyle, too, was a distraction from worrying about Janice, and a welcome one, at that.

'Aye, well. We've just started. But don't worry. When the group gets the bit between their teeth, we're unstoppable.' The woman smiled broadly. 'I haven't seen you round here before. June Hyland.' She held out her hand, and Deb shook it.

'Deb Sutherland. Hi, June.' She shaded her eyes from the spring sun that slanted through the trees lining the road. 'You're a group? Of what kind?'

'Our weekly club at the community centre. We crochet, chat, and provide a low-cost lunch for anyone who wants to drop in. We fundraise a bit too. For the local families usually, if people need a bit of extra help or what have you. Toddler group, the elderly, meals on wheels, that kind of thing. We call ourselves the crochet coven.'

'Sounds like that keeps you pretty busy.' Deb was touched that something like the crochet coven existed at all. It was lovely that a small community like Loch Cameron looked out for its more vulnerable members. She wished something like that existed where her mum lived. Granted, the small block of flats where Janice lived was quite a friendly community, as many people had lived there a long time. But there was nothing as organised as the crochet coven. Deb thought that Janice would probably quite enjoy having a group like this to hang out with.

In the days when Janice's health had been better, Deb could imagine that she could have got quite into demonstrating against things and putting her natural obstinacy and outspokenness to practical use.

'Aye. I guess you could say that's what we have in common. Women that like to be busy. Some might say busybodies, but I couldn't comment,' she laughed. 'Of course, when you look at Scotland's history, you do wonder how many busybodies were falsely accused of being witches. It wasn't always good to be a woman with an opinion.' She raised an eyebrow, archly.

'Nothing wrong with being busy. Or having an opinion. If you want something done, ask a busy person, so they say.' Deb nodded. 'I always think, more, if you want something done, ask a middle-aged woman. Goodness knows men are useless at concentrating on more than one thing at a time.'

'Heartily agree, dear. I was a nurse all my working life. Rarely found anyone as unflappable with sixteen things going on at once as a middle-aged woman.'

'I'm an event organiser. Much the same, but not saving lives, of course,' Deb chuckled. 'That's why I'm here, actually. I'm organising the May Day party for the Laird.'

'Ah. I see. Well, if you want any help with catering or organising, do let us know. We've supplied baked goods to the party in previous years, and Mina runs a food company with her husband.' June pointed out a black-haired woman marching in a circle who was wearing smart black wellies, a pea green wax jacket and jeans, and carrying a sign that said SAVE THE SQUIRRELS.

'That's good to know.'

'Aye. Pop in and see us at the community centre one day and we can talk about how we can help,' June pointed to a green car that was parked up on the verge of the road adjoining the one they stood on. 'We've got tea and cake over there. Go and help yourself.'

'That's really kind. Thanks!' Deb looked up as a shiny black truck approached. The windows were tinted, but as the driver's side window rolled down, she saw Kyle behind the wheel.

'Hey. I told you,' he addressed June, abruptly. 'Move. This is private property.'

'I think you'll find it isn't, actually,' June replied, crisply. 'We've done our research and Abernethy Construction has bought a large area of land on Gyle Head, but you don't own the road leading up to it. The road is for public access, and we're just expressing our views, as is our right. On a public right of way.'

'Fine. But you're blocking access to my land, and I need access to run the business. Restricting access to a commercial site is an offence,' he replied, smoothly. 'Move.'

Deb looked over, drawn to his voice, and Kyle met her eyes as soon as she did so. He nodded imperceptibly at her. Deb looked away, her cheeks flushing. Yet, before she looked away, there was an unexpected spark of connection between them that she felt in her groin, heart and stomach, simultaneously.

Dear lord.

She looked away, feeling that everyone nearby must have also felt that zing of sexual power passing between her and Kyle, like a bolt of electricity burning a trail along the ground. Yet, no one seemed to have noticed.

'You're spoiling an area of natural beauty. And an important wildlife habitat!' June raised her voice as Kyle began moving forward slowly in his truck. It was a huge thing with bull bars on the front and massive wheels: it looked like some kind of monster truck, completely out of place in a little Scottish village.

'I won't tell you again,' he said to June, as he rolled up his window. 'Move, or I'll come back with the police.'

The women stood to one side, booing as Kyle drove through. Deb watched him through the windscreen: he was frowning, and she could feel the stress radiating from him. Her heart went out to him. It wasn't easy, dealing with this kind of opposition, and she wondered whether he was the villain that the women were making him out to be.

As Kyle drove past her, he met her eyes again – and, as he did, his expression changed. His brows were heavy, and his jaw clenched, but as he looked at Deb, something shifted just for a moment in his face. He smiled and, just for that moment, it was a secret between them. She smiled back, unable to stop herself, and then he was gone.

EIGHT

She had the dream again.

It was the same girl in the same old-fashioned smock dress and two long plaits tied with white ribbons.

> *Granny's in the kitchen, doing a bit of stitchin'*
> *Down comes a bogeyman and knocks her out...*

Deb had no idea why she was having the dream. She couldn't recall having a recurring dream before, either. In fact, she'd never been one to remember her dreams at all.

That morning, she had woken up from the dream with the desire to go for a walk, and decided to try her luck on Gyle Head again. She'd driven over and parked a little way away from the main site. Then, she'd walked up through the forest around the building site, heading away from the noise.

It was beautiful. Deb took in a long, deep breath and let it out slowly as the trees enveloped her in their gentle, leafy canopy. Clusters of oaks led her into the forest: grandfatherly trees with their thick trunks and dark green leaves. Sycamores and Ash trees grew harmoniously alongside the oaks, and, in a small clearing to the right of the pathway, a lone yew tree spread out its ancient, curved branches as if in invitation to stop and take a moment under its wise aura.

Birdsong filled the air: she was no expert when it came to bird life, but she enjoyed their trills and melodies spiralling around her in layers of bright joy. She could smell the moist, dark earth and a floral scent in the air.

It felt good to walk. She was supposed to do daily exercise, and some days she didn't get around to it because she was sitting at her laptop all day or on the phone. Her doctor had said that walking was ideal exercise, and there were so many beautiful spots around Loch Cameron. Yet, there was something special about this place, though Deb couldn't say exactly what it was.

It was a feeling that drew her here more than any particular feature. She walked through the forest at the edge of Gyle Head, and found an opening into a small meadow. It seemed to be totally enclosed, and even though there was an active building site nearby, there was no noise at all, except for birdsong.

Deb climbed over the wooden stile at the edge of the trees and hopped down onto the long, soft grass on the other side. She walked slowly along the edge of an ancient-looking hedge, where thrushes and blue tits flew in and out of their nests. She could believe that the hedge was old, as it contained so many intergrowing plants: holly, hawthorn, even some bramble leaves. It was a shame that it wasn't autumn, at which time the hedge would be full of berries.

When she'd come to Gyle Head originally, Deb had been interested to see the remains of the old Folly. However, that wasn't why she'd returned: there was something else drawing her here, and she didn't know what it was. The land here just felt right under her feet and in her soul. She took in a deep breath of the pine-scented air.

Home. That was how it felt.

She walked along the hedgerow, noting the flattened parts of the grass where rabbits had run across it at dusk. *Home* was a strange feeling. She thought of Janice's small terraced house in Glasgow as home, because that was where she'd grown up. Yet, Glasgow had never felt as comforting as this place did. And she'd had her own home for many years, more recently, shared with Dan. Had it ever truly felt as rooted and right as this land did to her? No.

It was, on one hand, understandable to feel an affinity for the Scottish countryside: after all, Deb had lived in Scotland most of her life, apart from a few stints in London for work. Yet, she'd never been to Gyle Head before. And the feeling was specific to here: she loved the village of Loch Cameron, but she hadn't felt this – not this exact feeling of rootedness and belonging – there.

Slowly, she turned around, stretching her arms out around her and spun around slowly, just for the sheer pleasure of it. She watched the landscape flash and merge with itself as she sped up, laughing like a child at her increasing giddiness. The green of the meadow merged with the blue of the sky, and the trees seemed to spread and waver at the edge of her vision.

Deb was so happy, just in that moment, feeling completely alone and caressed and supported by the land-scape. She felt like a child: carefree and full of excitement and adventure, but also safe and protected. She belonged here, and she knew it at a cellular level of herself, though she couldn't say why.

'Wow. You really can't keep away, can you?' A deep voice broke her reverie, and Deb stopped spinning as soon as she realised that someone was standing in front of her.

'What? How are you here?' she gasped as she stopped whirling, trying to regain some sense of balance. She reached for the hedge to steady her, but her hand clasped around holly. 'Ouch,' she withdrew her hand and shook it.

'You all right? Not going to fall over?' Kyle Abernethy took her arm to steady her.

'I'm perfectly fine, thank you,' she pulled her arm away, and they stood there, looking awkwardly at each other. 'I was just enjoying a walk. No law against that.'

'No, no, indeed. Same here. I like to walk over this way for a break sometimes. It's beautiful. I'm Kyle, by the way.' He removed his hand from her arm.

'Deb Sutherland.'

'Good to meet you.'

'And you,' she said more as a reflex than anything. 'Yes, it is beautiful,' she said, guardedly. 'And, I know your name. The women at the protest filled me in. This isn't your land too, is it? I'm not trespassing again?' She knew that there was an edge in her tone, but she couldn't help it. *Just try and tell me to get off your land one more time*, she thought. 'There weren't any signs if it is.'

'No, I don't own this part. It is part of Gyle Head, but the development's just at the top. I couldn't do anything with this, anyway. Forest and protected land. I couldn't if I wanted to.'

'How come it's not all protected?' she asked. 'The habitats, and all that?'

'The habitats *are* protected. That's this bit.' Kyle waved a hand at the forest behind them. 'This hedgerow's hundreds of years old, as are the trees here. I know all about the bloody protected habitats and ecosystems up here. I had to sign more agreements to protect badgers and voles and pygmy nuthatches than you'd believe before Hal Cameron would sell that piece of land to me.'

'Pygmy nuthatches? Are they indigenous to the area?' Deb asked, raising a playful eyebrow.

'All right, I was making that bit up. But, you get the idea.' A grin lurked around the edge of his mouth.

'The ladies from the community centre don't think a lot of

you. I'd go so far as to say that they wouldn't believe you're protecting anything.' Deb raised an eyebrow.

'They can believe what they want,' Kyle replied, noncommittally. 'None of my business, is it?'

'No, I suppose not,' Deb frowned, trying to work him out and failing. She had a sense that Kyle was holding something back, but, she reasoned, they'd only met briefly, so whatever he was thinking or not thinking was also really no business of hers.

'If you walk that way, and over the stile at the end, there's an amazing view of the loch.' Changing the subject, Kyle pointed ahead of them at the end of the meadow which led into trees again. 'Through the edge of that part of the forest, just follow it along and you'll come to a little pathway. Follow that to the right and you'll find it. It's a lovely spot.'

'Oh. Thank you,' Deb was taken aback. 'That's... very kind.'

'Welcome.' He shrugged. 'I was actually going that way myself.'

'Oh. Well, let's go, then. You can show me.'

'Right,' he strode off, and she had to scurry after him a little to keep up.

'So how long have you been working on this development?' she asked as she caught up.

'Over a year, but the site hasn't been up long.'

'Listen, I wasn't part of the protest group, the other day. They were just there when I was, and we got talking. Actually, some of them will be useful contacts for the party.' Deb knew she didn't have to explain, but she felt she wanted to anyway.

'Party?' He glanced at her. Deb couldn't help admire his face in profile. The black beard highlighted his high cheekbones and noble face. His nose was straight and his brow was strong but not overwhelming like some men who had that caveman brow look.

'Hmm. The May Day Party at the castle. I'm helping Hal out.' She looked away, not wanting to be caught staring. Kyle nodded as he vaulted the stile and held out a hand for her to climb over it. Deb shook her head and climbed over herself.

'You're, what? A party planner?' He strode into the trees, hardly waiting for her to keep up.

'Yes. Events Manager. I do a lot of freelance work.'

'Cool. You must be very organised.' Kyle held back a leafy branch for her as she walked under a tree.

'On a good day. I like lists.' She took the branch from him and let it go when she'd passed by.

'Same. You can't go wrong with a list. I can't bear people who complain they're disorganised yet do nothing about it. Just make a list, power through it.' He shrugged. 'Simple.'

'Well, I guess not everyone finds it that easy. Hence why I have a job. I'm grateful for the disorganised.'

'Fair enough. You're one of those compassionate people, I suppose.' He rolled his eyes, and then laughed, which was unexpected. 'Always seeing the good in others. Not me, I'm afraid.'

'I don't know about that, but I suppose I always try to understand people.' Deb thought about it for a moment. 'Mostly because I value being understood myself.'

'Yeah, it makes sense. I'm just a hothead.' He gave her a wry smile. 'Tend to jump into things. Act first, think later. Not always a great thing.'

'Well, at least you get things done,' Deb said, politely. 'Oh! Wow, what a view!'

They had come out of the trees and were standing on an open viewpoint above the loch, but at a point that Deb had never been at before. Before them, the widest part of the watery expanse stretched out and into the distance, surrounded by the heather-covered hills and mountains. As clouds scudded across the sky, the sun and shade changed the colour of them from bright mauve to a dark greenish grey. From where she stood, the mountains looked as if they were covered in velvet pile which changed colour depending on which way it was stroked. To the right, Deb could see Loch Cameron Castle in the distance, with the village opposite it – from here, everything looked tiny.

'Where does it go?' Deb pointed to the loch on their left, as it stretched out and thinned into the distance.

'Eventually it runs into the sea,' Kyle explained. 'Most lochs aren't sea lochs, but this one is, technically, though it's very shallow and small at that end.'

'I didn't know that,' Deb confessed, taking in the view, and watching a bird of prey as it circled above them on the thermals. 'What's that?' She pointed at it.

'Red Kite, looks like. They went almost extinct here for years and were reintroduced. Seem to be thriving now, I see them fairly frequently up here.' He followed her gaze. 'Beautiful, isn't it?'

'Yes. I don't think I've seen one before.'

'You might look around for some discarded feathers here and there. I've found them sometimes. They can be quite large.' Kyle's eyes never left the kite and it swooped and hovered in front of them.

'I will, thanks.'

He looked back at Deb, and smiled surprisingly warmly. 'Those type of birds, in other countries, they'd have a legend or a tale attached to them. Like, a power animal meaning, or something. Birds like eagles and hawks, they're really important to other cultures. I always think it's sad that we don't have those kinds of legends about animals, here.'

'I can see that. They are majestic creatures.' Deb was bemused. Far from the rude, dismissive man she thought Kyle was, here he was waxing lyrical about the local wildlife, and the spiritual significance of birds of prey.

'Mmm. Well, I should get going. Break's over.' Kyle sighed. 'Believe me, there's nothing I'd like more than to stay here looking at this wonderful view with you.'

With me? Deb thought. Despite herself, a glow of warmth bloomed in her chest.

'Sure. Thanks for bringing me here.'

'Welcome. Nice to share it. You remember the way back?'

'I think so. I'll stay a while longer.'

'All right, then.' Kyle nodded, and turned back, heading into the trees. 'Good to see you, Deb.'

'And you, Kyle.'

Deb watched him go, feeling confused. Kyle had been friendly to her for no reason. They'd met in a random field, completely unexpectedly, and shared a moment of beauty. It was... odd. But, it wasn't at all unpleasant.

She turned her gaze back to the circling kite, and wondered what meaning it might have. A totem, or an omen of some kind? And, if it was an omen, an omen of what?

NINE

'And that's a canasta.' Gretchen Ross tapped her wrinkled index finger on the row of six Kings and two Jokers that were laid out in front of Deb. 'Impure, of course, because you used a couple of wild cards. So, it scores a bit less, but now that you've got it, you can go out when you want to.'

They sat at a wooden dining table in the sitting room of Gretchen Ross' flat. Hal had given Deb Gretchen's details, saying that Gretchen could help answer any questions about the cottage. In an email, he'd written:

> Gretchen is a mine of local information, history and – dare I say it – gossip. She's a great lady, as Zelda would say, and she loves company, so do pop up and give her a visit at the care home if you've a mind to. She does still get the odd bit of post delivered to the cottage, so you might take it up to her.

There had in fact been a stack of mail in the hallway of the cottage, addressed to Gretchen, so Deb had decided to take it up to her. The drive to Gretchen's care home looked like it took in some lovely scenery, so she'd taken advantage of a beautiful blue sky and the clear air of a spring morning and hopped in the car after breakfast, having called Gretchen to check whether she was up for a visitor.

Deb was glad that she had, because the drive over the moors and fields, on a twisty tree-lined road was absolutely beautiful. Along the way she had passed fields with sheep grazing, others with shaggy, brown cows with long horns and cute stone cottages dotted along the landscape, sometimes arranged in a tiny village that she had driven through before she knew it was one. The odd signpost pointed to something intriguing as she drove past: castle ruins, burial mounds and a sign to a stone circle that she thought she should definitely go back and discover.

Deb wound her window down and breathed in the fragrant, herb and heather-infused air of the highlands and sighed happily. There was something so healthy and free about the air up here. As if breathing it really could give you a new life. Remake you from the inside.

I could do with being remade, she thought as she drove along. *I've had one troublesome organ removed, so maybe it's just my heart and brain that need replacing, or at least, cleansing.* What was it that people did now? Waving sage smoke over themselves to cleanse their auras? Deb hadn't tried it, but she thought that a good walk in the Scottish countryside would probably have the same effect.

Gretchen's apartment at the care home was delightfully cosy, with a modern white kitchenette to one side and Gretchen's bedroom and bathroom to the other. A log burner glowed in one corner of the sitting room, and as well as the wooden table and chairs, Gretchen had bookshelves lining one wall of the sitting room, and a brown leather sofa facing them, as well as an ergonomic recliner type chair, also in brown leather. A large window looked out onto a large garden, with oak trees along one side, and a wide lawn that had been mowed in neat stripes.

Framed book posters lined the walls: Deb recognised various bestsellers of the 80s and 90s. She'd even read a few of them.

Deb had seen a quite lovely common room, stacked with books and comfy chairs, and the gardens on the way up to Gretchen's flat. All in all, it looked like a pretty nice place.

When she'd got there, she'd asked about the playing cards on the table – Gretchen had been playing patience, but she'd suggested that she teach Deb canasta.

'Okay.' Deb frowned at her hand of playing cards. 'And the aim is to go out first?'

'Usually, but timing is everything. Ideally, you want to wait until I've got a handful of cards and nothing much on the table, and then go out. Because everything still in my hand will count against me. But if I've got a lot of points on the table, and a few canastas, then it's worth thinking about who's going to come out with more points, because you only get a hundred points for going out first. A bit like life, really.'

'Ha. Which part?' Deb laid a four of hearts on the giveaway pile of cards next to the stack of playing cards on the table between them.

'Holding your cards close to your chest doesn't always pay off, and dying early's a gyp,' Gretchen explained, grinning. 'Far better to lay all your cards on the table, get as many points as you can, take risks but also be a bit canny, and live your life for as long as you can. I could add some more card-playing metaphors here, but you get the idea.'

'Playing the game. Luck changing on the turn of a card. Being dealt a bad hand. That type of thing,' Deb chuckled, and took a sip of the tea that Gretchen had brewed in a lovely blue and white bone china teapot. The design featured a country scene, with a castle in the background and a figure depicted against trees in the foreground.

'Exactly. I rather feel that no one gets dealt an entirely bad or good hand, most of the time. It's very much what you make of it. Of course, some people have terrible luck. I've been quite fortunate, all in all. Still, I worked hard for it. And there have been ups and downs, I won't deny that.'

'I could say the same.' Deb thought about the hysterectomy. On the one hand, it had been bloody painful. But, on the other, it had given her freedom. She thought again of the Little Mermaid, and the price she had paid for her legs. It wasn't as bad, of course, because, unlike the character in that fairy tale, Deb's operation wouldn't make it feel like she was walking on glass for the rest of her life. That part had only lasted a month or two. And, now, she had the rest of her life to look forward to, which would be pain and discomfort free. Whenever she thought about that, she felt a little bubble of excitement in her stomach.

'So, the laird gave you my details?' Gretchen asked, as she studied her hand of cards.

'Yes. He said to ask you if I needed any local info, and he's arranged for me to be able to get groceries in town, on his tab, and dinners and lunches at the Inn, if I want. He's been incredibly generous,' Deb explained.

'Ah, Hal's a good egg.' Gretchen nodded. 'I don't want that four, dear. Throw away something I want next time.' She winked at Deb, and picked up a card from the pile. 'Oh. That changes things somewhat.' She whistled under her breath and laid down four eights.

'Haha. That's not the aim of the game,' Deb replied. 'And it looks like you did better on the pickup.'

'I did. You're right. So, what do you think of Loch Cameron so far?' Gretchen had a shrewd gaze, and she fixed Deb with her bright eyes.

'I like it. It's very quaint, and the castle is beautiful.'

'It is stunning. Lovely view on Queen's Point. I do miss it,' Gretchen sighed. 'My family were tenants for years. I grew up there.'

'It's a gorgeous little place,' Deb replied.

'It certainly is.' Gretchen looked wistful. 'I moved back there for some years when my daughter was young. She loved it there too. That whole area has a real magic to it. I miss it.'

'I bet. But this place is nice,' Deb added. 'Your apartment is really nice, and I saw a cinema and a beauty salon on the way up here.'

'Oh, it's not bad. I know I'm lucky to be here. But hanging out with old codgers all the time does rather grate, after a while.' Gretchen rolled her eyes. 'That's partly why I like to be the point of contact for tenants at the cottage and help Hal out. It means I get to chat to people under eighty who have different things going on in their lives. I like to stay connected to what's going on in the outside world. Hip rather than hip replacement.' Gretchen made the peace sign with one hand, and Deb laughed.

'I get that. You're hip, Gretchen.'

'Down with the kids, as they say.' Gretchen shot Deb a playful smile and looked at her over the top of her glasses. 'I read a lot too, and I always think that's a good way of staying up to date with society. I love all these new young authors. Writing about sex and identity and gender and feminism and all sorts. Very eye-opening.'

'I noticed your book posters. And all the books, of course.'

'Ah, yes.' Gretchen turned to look fondly at the books lining her wall. There were also piles of them on the floor in front of the shelves, and all of the shelves held two rows of books.

'Yes. Books and my daughter were my world.' Gretchen sighed. 'I worked in publishing all of my career. It was wonderful, for the most part.'

'Do you get to see much of your daughter now?' Deb asked.

'No. She died a few years ago.' Gretchen looked back at Deb. 'Accident. Luckily I have my grandson, and he visits. Not all that often, but enough. I wouldn't want him to be here all the time, anyway. He's a young man. He's got a life to lead.'

'I'm so sorry to hear that, Gretchen. About your daughter.' Deb instinctively reached for the older woman's hand. What Gretchen had said about her grandson had reminded her of Janice – it was exactly what she would have said.

'Thank you, dear. It's a difficult thing. You never think you'll outlive your child,' Gretchen sighed. 'Still, I had her in my life for a good amount of time. I was blessed to have her at all.'

'I'm still sorry. I can only imagine how awful that must be to live with.'

'Ah, bless you.' Gretchen patted her hand, and withdrew hers. 'So, tell me about you. What brings you to Loch Cameron?'

'Oh, goodness. Where to start?' Deb laughed and picked up her cards again.

'Wherever you like, dear. I'm not going anywhere.' Gretchen sipped her tea. 'Tell me everything.'

TEN

'So, that's my story,' Deb finished. They were still playing cards, and Gretchen had laid down another canasta. Deb had never played before, so they were treating it as a practice game. She thought that was just as well, because she was definitely losing.

'If you don't mind me saying, I don't think you're missing much if you're not with this Dan.' Gretchen picked up a card from the centre stack, frowned and returned it to the throwaway pile. 'Tell me if it's none of my business, of course. But I always found that being alone was better than being with someone you didn't truly love.'

'I know that, intellectually. I understand that. But I guess in the past I was too scared to be alone.' Deb played an eight, and then realised she shouldn't have as Gretchen picked it up immediately and added it to a row of eights she already had on the table. 'Did you... did you ever find love? Real love?'

Deb knew it was a very personal question, but she felt like she could ask Gretchen. There was something about the woman which gave Deb a sense of being in a safe place.

'I did. More than once.'

'Did you ever get married? I know you said you had a daughter...'

'No. Marriage wasn't for me. I adopted my daughter and raised her on my own. That was how I wanted to do it.' Gretchen played a three of clubs. 'You can't pick up the pack with that one, by the way. But if you have a red three you put it to one side on the table. A hundred points each, five hundred if you get all four.'

'Right.' Deb frowned, trying to remember all the rules of the game. 'But you had relationships.'

'Of course. I wasn't a nun.' Gretchen laughed. 'Nor should you be, dear. Life is for living.'

'I don't feel like I've been very lucky in love so far,' Deb confessed. 'And with the hysterectomy I just feel like I'm less of a good prospect now. I can't have children, and I don't feel very confident. In bed.' She blushed. Why was she telling Gretchen this? Yet she felt that she trusted the woman.

'So? Dear, we aren't just baby-making machines, you know. We burned our bras for more than one reason.' Gretchen gave her a stern look. 'Now, you listen to me. There has been a huge change to your body, and you have to give yourself time to heal. Believe me, there's plenty of time for all that, and your body will let you know when it's ready for a new lover. Until then, see the world as full of possibility, not restriction.'

'You're right. I keep thinking about the Little Mermaid. How she sacrificed her tail for legs but then she was tortured by the pain forever. All for love.' Deb studied her cards. She had absolutely no idea what she was doing in the game, and Gretchen now only had two cards in her hand, which she suspected was a bad sign. 'That's how I felt after the operation. I put myself in this painful position to be able to get my freedom back. It worked, but damn, it was painful.'

What would you do for a baby? The headline of the magazine article Deb had read popped back into her head. There was such sacrifice implied in that question. Give up your independence, your health, your money, in some cases? Your time? Possibly, your career – or, at least, a chunk of time at work, and probably change your working hours for a few years after that. Not that sacrifice was wrong for something that was worth it.

'Well, if you will allow me to interject, *The Little Mermaid* is a stupid, anti-woman story.' The old woman adjusted her headscarf haughtily. 'She gives up all her sovereignty – being a mermaid, a wonderful, magical creature – for a man, and we're supposed to think that the pain is worth it. As my friend Zelda would say: what a crock.' Gretchen got up, went to her bookshelf and scanned it for a moment, and then came back, holding a book. 'Here. If you want fairy tales, this is better.'

'What is it?' Deb turned the book over in her hands.

'Angela Carter. Rewritten fairy tales that are not all about suffering for some *man*.' Gretchen raised her eyebrow. 'You'll like it.'

'Thank you.' Deb opened the paperback curiously and flicked through the pages.

'You're welcome, dear.' Gretchen sat back down, looked at her cards and smiled. 'And that, as they say, is that. I'm out,' she said, laying her final cards on the table. 'Good game, Deb. Not bad for a beginner.'

'Oh! Well done. I don't think I knew what I was doing at all,' Deb chuckled.

'You'll get there, dear. Remember, life is like cards. It just takes patience, learning the rules and then making the game work for you.' Gretchen winked. 'The great irony of life is that when you finally understand it, you're too old to enjoy it in the way you want to. I can't remember who said it, but *if I knew what I know now, and still had those legs*.' Gretchen smiled ruefully.

'It sounds like you did quite enjoy your legs, though. Unlike the Little Mermaid.'

'Ah, I did. I did,' Gretchen laughed. 'I've enjoyed my life, and I enjoyed my figure, when I had it. And I enjoyed being a mother. But, listen, dear. That can still happen for you, if you want it. I adopted my daughter, remember. And if you don't end up being a mother, then that's also completely fine. It's not the only thing there is in life for women. You're a smart girl. You know that.' She looked at Deb as if she was checking if Deb really *did* know that.

'I know,' Deb agreed. 'Thanks, Gretchen.'

'You're welcome. Remember, you're not a character in a fairy tale. Not a princess or a mermaid or a helpless little fairy. You are a grown woman, and you're strong and capable.' Gretchen pushed the plate of cake over the table towards Deb. 'Come on, now. Eat up. There's nothing on you.'

Deb felt that, although she was a strong and capable woman, it would be unwise to disagree with Gretchen Ross. She helped herself to another slice.

'Hm. Now, go and pop the kettle on for me, would you, dear? I'm parched.' Gretchen sat back in her chair, looking tired. 'And then, I might need to say adieu; I'm in need of a nap after all that high-stakes game playing.'

'Of course. It was kind of you to have me over,' Deb said, getting up and taking the tea things into the kitchenette.

'Not at all, darling. Not at all.' Gretchen yawned. 'It's good to have young friends. Keeps me youthful and sharp. I recommend it, when you're old.'

'I'll bear that in mind.' Deb smiled to herself. If she made it to Gretchen's age, and she was half as bright and charming, then she would consider that a life well lived.

And, the conversation had helped her put the thought of children into perspective: Gretchen was right. It was a great thing to be a mother, but it wasn't the *only* thing one could be. And that made her pull her thoughts and feelings about the hysterectomy together into a more settled and harmonious place.

Spending so much time with Gretchen made Deb think again of her grandma Elise. She hadn't been able to stop thinking about what Janice had said, or rather what she didn't say. Janice had said her grandmother shouldn't have had children, but clearly there was more to that story. Deb was determined to find out what Janice was keeping from her.

ELEVEN

'That's really good. I couldn't put it down.' A voice over her shoulder made Deb jump, and she looked around her in dismay.

Kyle Abernethy was standing behind her, his hands in his pockets.

'Oh. It's you,' she said, without thinking.

'Indeed. And it's you.' He gave her an amused look.

'What are you doing here?' she demanded, and then realised how stupid that was. *Looking for a book, presumably.*

'I didn't mean to startle you. I just recognised the book, and I always think a personal recommendation is worth more than a cover blurb. You know, with those – when it says "Brilliant" or whatever on the cover? I heard that the publishers have to use a quote from a person, but, say that someone's review was "this isn't brilliant", they can still cherry pick the "Brilliant" part and put it on the cover, with the newspaper that said it, or whatever. Technically, it's not wrong.' Was it her imagination, or was Kyle talking too much? He cleared his throat. 'Anyway...' he trailed off.

Was he nervous?

'I'll bear that in mind.' The book Deb had picked up was a

spooky Victorian thriller set in an asylum. 'You like this kind of thing?'

'Yeah. Big reader.' He nodded. 'Kyle Abernethy.' He held out his hand, and she shook it with the hand that wasn't holding a book.

'I know,' Deb chuckled. 'I do recognise you, you know. We've met twice before.'

'Well, I just wanted to make sure you knew who I was. Nothing worse than someone assuming and chattering on and then you go past the point of being able to ask.'

'Duly noted. Deb Sutherland.'

'The party planner.'

'Indeed.'

'Listen... I know that I was quite rude to you, the first time. I was stressed. Wasn't an excuse to take it out on you. I should have said something when we were at Gyle Head the other day, but actually it was just such a lovely day, it sort of slipped my mind.'

'Oh. Well, that's nice of you to say.' Deb was a little taken aback: more so because as she shook Kyle's hand, a jolt of powerful energy zinged between them. Her eyes widened a little as she looked up into his. *What was that?* she wondered.

'Yeah. I'm not usually that much of an idiot. Certainly not usually rude to strangers,' he murmured, meeting her gaze. Just for a moment, there was a kind of smouldering, intense look in his eyes that she hadn't seen in a man for a long time.

She was a grown woman. She knew what that look meant, and it made her feel as though her insides were made of melted butter.

Deb looked away, feeling awkward, and let go of his hand.

'So, what are you looking for? Books wise?' she asked, brightly. *As if he'd think you meant anything else,* her internal monologue chipped in. *He's unlikely to be looking for a post-hysterectomy survivor.*

'Oh. Looking for a present for my aunt.' He picked up a book from a pile on a nearby display table. 'And, if I'm honest, a break from the site. I love it, but sometimes it all... gets a bit much.' His expression clouded over for a moment.

'Hmm. I know that you said you're protecting the ecosystems up there, but I don't think anyone knows that.' Deb picked up a book about Scottish history and turned it over. 'You should talk to the people in town more. Open up.'

'I tried. Before we started the project, I did an open community consultation about the process. No one interacted with it. Now that I finally got the go ahead to begin on the project – which, by the way, is providing essential low-cost housing to the area, which is desperately needed – the local Women's Institute have decided to get their knickers in a twist over it,' he sighed.

'Crochet coven,' Deb corrected him.

'Excuse me?' he frowned. 'They're a coven? Like... witches? Should I be concerned that they're going to curse the site?'

'Ha. I said the same thing, but no. It's just what they call themselves – although, I would say, now that I've met one of them, they do seem to be a group of quite powerful women.' Deb grinned, thinking of June and her efficient, no-nonsense aura. 'Maybe they didn't know about your consultation. Perhaps if you just talked to them?'

'I can't see the benefit. The project has begun. I can't stop it now, even if I wanted to – which I don't. It took so long to get all the permissions and the finance: I've been working towards this type of large-scale development for years. I'm not about to let a group of busybodies get in my way.'

The stubborn set to his jaw reminded Deb that Kyle Abernethy was apparently not a man who enjoyed being argued with.

'Well, I guess I don't know all the details,' she said, diplomatically. 'All I'm saying is, maybe it's worth meeting with the locals and seeing if you can iron out some of the issues. Just from a PR point of view, if nothing else.' She shrugged. 'I've worked in events a long time, and I've seen what a bad PR strategy does for a project. And, the worst PR is usually the people who don't know how to communicate their project properly. If you were clear and open about what you're doing up there, instead of just shooing people away, then maybe they'd be less invested in protesting at the bottom of the road. Just a suggestion.'

'Hmm. I'll think about it.' A smile lurked around the edges of Kyle's mouth. 'You're a part of this coven, are you? Sent to influence me, undercover?'

'Ha. Well, for one thing, witches aren't spies, as far as I know. And, no. I'm not a local, remember, just a temporary guest while I work on the party. But I can see how much this project means to you, and the people in town. So, I want to help if I can.' She put the book about Scottish history down and walked over to a shelf of beautiful notebooks. Kyle followed her.

Are we browsing together now? she thought.

At that moment, the shop door opened and a woman walked in. Deb looked over and met Mina's disapproving eye.

Oh, no. Deb knew immediately what Mina was thinking as she looked from Deb to Kyle.

'Hello, Deb. I see you've found the bookshop,' Mina said archly as she made her way over to them.

'Er... yes.' Deb was both at a bit of a loss for what to say, and was also struck with the obviousness of the statement. *I mean, we are standing in it*, part of her wanted to retort.

'Mr Abernethy.' Mina inclined her head. 'We haven't met, but I'm part of the community protest group that was at the site recently. We'll be back, too,' she said, airily.

'I look forward to it,' Kyle said, evenly. All traces of his former affability disappeared, and he crossed his arms across his chest. Deb was reminded of how much he could look like a human battering ram or a brick wall.

'Well, you shouldn't.' Mina raised herself up to her full height, which wasn't much, especially compared with Kyle. However, she still managed to remind Deb of an angry duck with its feathers fluffed out to make itself look bigger. *A duck with a sharp bite*, Deb thought to herself, half amused at both of them and half alarmed that Mina would probably now have a go at her for the cardinal sin of even being seen with the most hated man in town.

'Mina... perhaps you should listen to what Kyle has to say,' Deb said, gently. 'You both really care about Gyle Head.'

'I'll listen to him when he listens to us,' Mina scoffed. 'Anyway, I don't negotiate with terrorists, and I don't have time to stand here and argue the toss. I've got shopping to do. Deb, lovely to see you.' She shook her hair, which was tied up in a glossy black ponytail, and nodded briefly to Kyle before going to the counter, paying for something and leaving, slamming the door after her.

'I seem to remember Margaret Thatcher using those same words.' Kyle raised an eyebrow.

'Don't,' Deb giggled, despite herself. 'She cares. She's just... passionate, I guess.'

'That's one word for it. Other people might say rude.'

'Well, I couldn't possibly comment.'

'You're a diplomat, see. I knew it.' Kyle flashed her that warm smile again, which was so very different from the way he looked just now with Mina.

'Is that wrong? I grew up with a tough mother. You learn to pick your battles.'

'No, it's not wrong. It's a gift. I told you, I'm not like that.'

'Well, we all have different qualities,' Deb said.

'Indeed. How's the party planning going?' he asked. 'That's a nice one.' He nodded as she picked up a notebook covered in red silk. 'Suits you.'

'The notebook suits me?'

'Red. Because of your colouring,' he added, hastily. 'You've got that same dark hair, like me. Though yours is a lot prettier, of course.' He looked immediately uncomfortable. 'Sorry. I just meant... you know...' he trailed off. 'Because it's long. And... silky.'

'You're just making it worse now, really.' Deb started to giggle at his obvious awkwardness. Kyle had gone from bolshy property developer to awkward school boy in a matter of seconds.

'I know. Please take pity on me and pretend I didn't just say that.' He put a hand over his face and laughed. 'Tell me about the party.'

'Well, it's a big project,' she replied, knowing that she could have taunted him for longer, but also that he was mostly a complete stranger. The thing was, Deb felt strangely comfortable in his presence, and comfortable in teasing him too. Even though the first time she'd met him, they'd argued. But, then, even that was unusual for her. Deb wasn't usually someone to argue with a complete stranger, but she had felt totally fine about expressing herself with Kyle.

What did that mean? Perhaps, post-hysterectomy, Deb was just less keen to take bullshit from *anyone*. It made sense: once you'd laid on the operating table, seen the anaesthetist come at you with that big needle and know, when you woke up, that your uterus would be gone – once you'd weathered that and survived, and survived the pain afterwards, then a little bit of standing up for yourself in public didn't seem like that much of a big deal.

Yes, she'd always be a diplomatic sort of person, most likely. But that didn't mean she couldn't be strong when she needed to be.

'I bet. Have you worked for the Laird before?' he asked.

'No, actually. This is the first time for me, but he seems great.' Deb opened the notebook and inspected the pages inside:

it was nicely made, with ruled pages and a ribbon bookmark. The type of smooth paper that was a delight to write on. The stationery geek in her wanted to stroke it, but she controlled herself. 'It's quite a lavish occasion, by the sounds of things. Perhaps you'll get an invite.'

'I very much doubt it.' Kyle raised an eyebrow, and looked away.

'Why?' Deb frowned, remembering that Hal had hinted that there was some kind of undercurrent of difficulty between him and Kyle. *What was the issue*, she wondered?

'Oh, you know. This and that,' he said, evasively. 'I'm guessing I'd get one if I was extra nice to you, though.' He smiled, suddenly. Was he flirting with her?

'Haha. The Laird is in charge of the guest list. So, you really would be better off being nice to him.'

'Hmm. I was thinking of asking you out to dinner. To charm my way onto it.' He gave her an unreadable glance. 'I'd rather have dinner with you than Hal Cameron. You're much prettier.'

'Errr... well, I...' Deb felt herself blushing, not knowing how to respond.

'What about if I just wanted your company?' He put the book he was holding down on the table and faced her. 'And to apologise for my rudeness on the first time we met?'

'Oh,' Deb prevaricated. 'Really? I'm not sure if that would be a good idea.' Mostly, she was thinking about how unpopular Kyle was in the village. Not that she owed the crochet coven her unwavering loyalty, but, still. She was aware of it.

'You can say no. Sorry, I just thought...' he trailed off. 'I didn't mean to make you feel uncomfortable.'

'No! I'm not,' she said, quickly. 'I'm just... not used to being asked out.' It wasn't a lie – she *wasn't* used to it. But there was also a voice in her head that was saying, *do you really want to go out with the least popular man in Loch Cameron?*

'I can't believe that,' he chuckled. 'You're gorgeous.'

'Thanks,' she mumbled. 'I just... ummm... ugh. That makes me feel really uncomfortable.' She laughed, uncomfortably. She didn't want to explain about the operation, and how she hadn't felt attractive for years because of the endometriosis.

'Well, the offer stands.' He reached into his pocket and handed her a business card. 'I know it's very 8os, but what can I say. I'm a retro kinda guy.' He flashed her that smile again and her stomach did a little somersault.

'What?' She looked at the business card, aware that her heart was beating faster than usual and she was having trouble focusing on what Kyle was saying.

What was happening? She had no idea. All she knew was that, in his presence, she felt like a hot mess. Was she ill? Perhaps she was coming down with something. Surreptitiously, she put her hand on her forehead to check for a temperature. It felt normal.

'Business cards. I know no one uses them anymore, but I like 'em.' He shifted his weight from one foot to the other, slightly awkwardly. 'Anyway. Good to meet you properly, Deb. Short for Deborah, I take it?'

'Yes. My mum's the only one who calls me Deborah.' She cleared her throat and tried to focus.

'I like Deborah. Queenly. Like something from the Old Testament.'

'Oh.' She blushed, and hated herself for it immediately. 'I don't think that was the intention. Mum isn't overly religious. Also, I feel like any queens in the Old Testament probably got their villages razed to the ground for being idolatrous harpies, or something.'

'Haha. You're probably right. I kinda like that, though.' He grinned. 'I'm enjoying the image of you as a sexy Old Testament queen. In robes. Throne room. Line of suitors. I'd fight them all off for your attention, of course.'

'I'll bear that in mind.' She looked up and met the eyes of

the young woman behind the till at the shop, who gave her a curious look. 'And... I'd like a drink, if you're serious. I don't really know anyone in the village and it would be nice to get out and see Loch Cameron while I'm here.' She lowered her voice a little, feeling self-conscious. But, then, she thought: *you're a grown woman, and free to do what you want. If you want to go for a drink with this guy, then go.*

'That would be awesome. Give me your number and we can arrange a time. I'm free tomorrow night. Or most nights this week, actually.' He reached into his pocket for his phone. 'I tend to go to the gym most nights, but I can have a night off.'

'I could do tomorrow.' Deb tried – and failed – not to think about Kyle in the gym, as she rattled off her phone number. Today, he was wearing light blue jeans that hugged his large thighs, heavy work boots and a tight blue shirt that showed off a heavily muscled chest. The sleeves of the shirt were rolled up to expose tanned, muscular forearms.

Dear lord, she thought. Did men like Kyle just walk around in the normal world all the time, and she'd just never noticed them before? Or was he some kind of aberration? A tall, built, sexy aberration that exuded testosterone and masculinity like a prowling tiger?

Maybe, since the operation, she was slowly becoming aware of men again, now that she had her body back. She was still healing, but something was starting to happen to her. She felt more connected to her body than she had in years, and she felt... different. She felt *alive*.

'Great. I know a really nice restaurant. I'd love to take you there. I can pick you up, if you want? Or meet you there if you'd prefer?'

'I can meet you there,' Deb decided. At least if she had her car then she could leave whenever she wanted to. Independence was important, and she might not have been out on a date for some years, but she wasn't an idiot.

'All right. I'll text you the details.' Kyle looked like an excited schoolboy. 'Awesome.'

'Well, I should probably get going.' Deb picked up the books she'd placed on the table.

'Okay. Me too. I've got a site meeting in half an hour. I was taking a little break. I guess it was meant to be, right? That we met? It's the fourth time. Like fate is trying to push us together.'

'I don't know about fate. I don't really believe in it. But... maybe.' She felt her cheeks colouring again and thought, *what am I DOING?* She couldn't think of a time that a man had actually ever made her blush. It was ridiculous.

He went to the counter and paid for his books – a crime thriller and a nonfiction book about ancient Peru, Deb noted. She followed, standing behind him and waiting for him to finish at the till. From behind, she could also admire his physique, and watch his back flex and move as he took the books in a bag from the shop assistant. God, he was beautiful.

'See you soon, then.' He paused, turning towards her. For a moment, Deb thought Kyle was going to kiss her, but he just smiled. 'I'm looking forward to it.'

Somehow, she'd gone into a little local bookshop for something to read, and come out with a date.

Not just that – a date with a man that made her go weak at the knees. This definitely wasn't what she'd expected when she'd taken the last-minute job in Loch Cameron.

TWELVE

The next morning, there was a knock at the cottage door as Deb was doing some gentle stretches. Slowly, her fitness was returning, though her middle still felt weak after a few hours of sitting up, or after a walk. Still, she was slowly returning to her body, like an old friend she used to know. She had missed feeling strong and flexible; and, the more she was able to exercise, the happier she felt. Yoga had always been good for her mind as well as her body.

She walked into the hallway and opened the door, expecting some book packages for Gretchen, but the postman handed her a parcel wrapped in brown paper addressed to her.

'Deborah Sutherland?' he asked. 'I know it's usually post for Miss Ross but I know you're renting here.' He was probably in his fifties, with an Irish accent, and was always chipper.

'That's me,' Deb smiled, taking the package curiously. Who was sending her packages? 'Thank you.'

'Just look at that view. If I wasn't working, it would be a perfect day for a picnic and a couple of beers,' he sighed, looking out at the wide expanse of the loch, which, today, was reflecting the clear, crystal blue sky. It reminded Deb of those pictures you saw of lakes where you didn't know where the sky ended and the water began. As they both gazed at the view, two hawks circled lazily on the thermals, high in the cloudless expanse. There was something so calming about looking at such a wide panorama: it gave Deb a feeling of freedom, as if she was one of the hawks.

'Well, at least you get to be outside,' Deb said, wriggling her toes in the spring sun. 'I think I'm going to bring a cup of tea out here for a while and enjoy it, though. You're right.'

'Indeed, indeed.' The postman tipped his baseball cap to her. 'Enjoy the sun. Vitamin D!'

As it was so sunny, Deb sat on the front step and unwrapped the parcel, frowning as she took out a small, ring-bound notebook with a plain brown cardboard cover that featured the name of a company she didn't recognise and the word NOTES. It looked old: the pages had that yellowish-brown tinge at the edges, and felt fragile. The font of the text on the cover was old-fashioned. She opened it, looking curiously at the childish handwriting within.

Strange. Who would send her a child's journal, or was it a diary?

There was a note with it, which Deb unfolded and read.

Dear Deborah,

I was sorting through some of Grandma's things and remem-bered her old diary. I know we talked about her the other day and when I saw it, I thought that you should have this. I found it hard to read, but you and Grandma were closer than she and I were. I think she would want you to have her things, not that there were many.

Love, Mum xx

So, this was Grandma Elise's book. Deb carefully flipped to the first page, forgetting that she had intended to make herself a cup of tea, and started to read.

15 March 1934

Played with Tessie and the other girls. I skinned my knee and Mother put salt water on it. Ouch! Tom ate the last biscuit. I told Mama but she said there's no more hush your whining.

20 May 1934

My birthday. I got a new blue coat and some flower seeds to plant. Tom drew me a card that said Best Sister. The seeds are sunflowers and some others that Father dried from the woodlands. I hope it will be poppies. Mother made me a cake. It has jam in it.

Deb flicked through the childlike entries, smiling at her grandma's childish observations. There was a long gap in the dates recorded, until a flurry of entries in 1935.

3 September 1935

Mother says we have to leave the cottage in two days. The Laird came round and gave us a basket of food and said we were good not to cry. Tom said there was cake in the basket and hot chocolate powder but I didn't see it because Father took it away and put it in the cupboard and said not to look.

6 September 1935

We are living in a house with my aunt Lotty but Father says she is a hussy and we cannot stay here long because she keeps house like a slut. Mother said shush when she saw me listening and sent me to bed. But there is hardly room for us here anyway.

Tom and I are sleeping in the same bed, top to toe and we share a room with Mother and Father which is Aunt Lotty's bedroom and she is sleeping on the chair in another room. Tom kicks in his sleep. I pretend to be asleep when Mother and Father come to bed but they smell of sherry like at Christmas and argue loudly. Tom says he sleeps through it but I know he is awake.

I miss our cottage even though it was never tidy and Father used to shout at Mother for being a sluttish housekeeper then too but at least it was home. I don't know why we had to leave.

28 September 1935

Father says we must leave Aunt Lotty's house because there is no room for us. I overheard Father and Aunt Lotty – who is my Mother's sister – arguing and him saying he wanted to leave me and Tom here but Aunt Lotty said no, what would she do with two bairns and this was only a temporary arrangement. Father called Aunt Lotty some bad names like he would say to Mother sometimes when he had been on the drink but unlike Mother Aunt Lotty called him some names back and said get out of my house you ungrateful drunk and so we all had to leave.

Deb's heart clenched. Poor Elise. She'd had no idea that anything like this had happened to her grandmother. It would have been heartbreaking to read a diary like this belonging to any child, but knowing that this was something that happened to someone that she loved was terrible.

14 November 1935

It has been three weeks since Mother and Father left us, and I don't think they are coming back. Tom and I got so hungry and cold begging on the streets that I thought we might die and then Tom said lets go in the Church here and sleep on the pews at least it will be out of the wind.

So we did and the vicar found us but instead of shouting he said where are your parents and when we said they have gone sir and we don't know if they are coming back he said we were poor lambs of God and gave us some soup and a couple of new cardigans from a box in a room at the back of the Church.

A family called Smith is looking after us now and they are very Godly and tell us that we are heathen children for not knowing how to pray or have good ways but that they will set us on the Straight and Narrow. Tom says at least we have a bed again and food but I miss our real home and I wish we were back there even if Mother and Father were always arguing.

Deb flicked through the pages of Elise's little diary, written in her careful childish hand. It was full of spelling mistakes and odd capitalisation – and Elise didn't appear to know how to punctuate a sentence – but Deb wondered how much schooling she had been able to have. Certainly, if she and Tom had been going to school in their village, then their education would at the very least have suffered a break when they became homeless. Deb wondered if the Smith family had sent them to school. She looked ahead in the diary. The entries were sporadic, but Grandma Elise had only been eleven. For a child undergoing such disruption, it was amazing she'd written a diary at all. She continued reading.

20 December 1935

I hate it here. Mrs Smith never stops telling us we are ungodly children and need correction. She beats us with a wooden walking stick across the back, hands and knees. Mr Smith does not help us, just tells us that we should be grateful that him and Mrs Smith took us in at all because The Lord told them to. Tom couldn't walk for a week after Mrs Smith hit him hard on the ankles with the stick for forgetting a line of The Lord's Prayer. He is hobbling around now and it is breaking my heart to see him. I hate Mrs Smith.

Deb looked up from the page, tears springing to her eyes. How could someone do something like that to a child? Now she knew why Janice had found the diary difficult to read. This was heartbreaking, and it made Deb wish that she had known this while Grandma Elise was still alive. Not that she could have done anything about it, but at least perhaps Deb could have talked to her about it.

There was a few months' gap until the next entry.

8 April 1936

I am at a new family now and I hope it will be better than Mr and Mrs Smith's house. The vicar had us moved when he found out about Tom's broken thumb and his ankle which is good but neither of them healed right and he says they ache.

However this time we did not get to stay together and even though I asked for Tom's address the vicar did not give it to me because he says what would stop me running away from my new home to see Tom and such disorderly behaviour will not be tolerated by our new families that have been so kind as to take us in being the ungodly heathen children of sinners.

So I do not know when I will see Tom again and I miss him terribly even though he could be annoying at times. The new people seem all right so far but I keep mostly to my own room when I can though Mrs Ainslie has a new baby and twins

that are two years old and I am to help with them so I don't get
much time to myself.

I don't like the baby because it screams all through the
night and Mrs Ainslie cries all the time. The bairns are nicer
sometimes though they are always hungry and cry for food. I
am also hungry most of the time. I am never having a baby.

Deb had never known that Grandma Elise had lost her
brother as well as her parents. She'd never even known that her
grandma had a brother; that meant Deb had a great-uncle,
somewhere, if he was still alive. Or, she had had a great-uncle,
and he had passed away now before Deb had ever had an
opportunity to know him. That was an awful feeling: to think
that there was a member of her family out there who she had
never known, and that she might already have lost him.

Deb felt choked up, thinking about this and imagining what
it must have been like to have been abandoned by your parents,
and then to lose the only family you had left. No wonder
Grandma Elise had been sad, and raised Janice to be as fiercely
independent as she had. What other option was there, given the
life she had?

She took her phone out of her pocket and called Janice, but
her mother didn't pick up her landline. Deb frowned for a
minute, then remembered that her mum was likely on her way
to a dialysis appointment. She would call tomorrow and see
how it went, and talk to Janice about the diary. There was no
point calling later today, as her mum would be too tired to chat.

Deb still felt bad that she wasn't there to take her mum to
her appointments like she usually would, but getting over to
Glasgow and back in a day would be a challenge if she was to do
it more than once every so often. Still, she missed Janice, and it
was hard not being around to look after her mum, despite the
fact that Janice resisted any notion of 'being looked after'.

She picked up the phone and called her mother, but the

landline rang and rang. Deb tried her mother's mobile phone, but it was – of course – switched off.

Deb sighed. She really wanted to talk to Janice, now that she'd read the diary.

She needed to see if Janice had known about Grandma Elise going into foster care, and being abused. She needed to know if Janice had known about Tom. Had she ever made an effort to find him, or had she known him and just never told Deb? That seemed unlikely – Deb hoped that wasn't the case, because it would have been a huge betrayal on Janice's part, and she didn't think her mother was capable of that. Still, Janice had alluded to things that Deb didn't know, related to her past and Grandma Elise. There were things that Janice had refused to talk about. Was this what she'd meant?

Had Grandma Elise ever reconnected with her brother, or had they always remained lost to each other? There was so much Deb wanted to know, now, and she had a million questions for her mother. Why wouldn't she pick up the phone?

THIRTEEN

'Hello, dear. Ah, now, don't tell me...' The elderly black woman with the lined face and bright, inquisitive eyes held up her finger as if waiting. 'Debbie? We met at the demonstration the other day, didn't we? June Hyland.' She held out her hand and Deb shook it.

'Deb. Yes. Hi, June.' Deb looked around her at the community centre, which seemed to be a hive of activity that day. On one trestle table there were a few open Tupperware boxes containing a variety of cakes: as they were labelled with clear, hand-lettered cardboard signs, Deb could see that there were oatmeal cookies, chocolate and beetroot cupcakes with a cream cheese frosting and lemon curd slices. Her belly rumbled: breakfast seemed a long time ago. There was also a hot water canteen, a stack of mugs and a tub of tea bags as well as a carton of milk and a sugar canister.

Her phone buzzed, and she grabbed it from her pocket, hoping that it was a reply from Janice about the diary. She was desperate to talk to her mum about Elise, but so far, she hadn't had a reply to her texts and voicemails. Instead, she was surprised to see a message from Dan.

Missing you. Can we chat?

I don't think so, she thought, deleting the message.

Deb wasn't ready to talk to Dan yet. She didn't know what to say. What could she say? That she was sorry for having an operation? That she was sorry for leaving home and coming to work in Loch Cameron? Neither of those things were true.

Deb couldn't think about that now. Instead, she looked curiously around the little community centre: it was a sweet little place, with white walls covered with children's finger paintings and crafts and colourful displays.

Most of the activity seemed to be centred around the other tables, where groups of women were painting more protest signs like the ones Deb had seen them carrying up at Gyle Head. There were more women sitting in plastic chairs in the corner, sewing. Deb couldn't see exactly what they were doing, but they all seemed to have a corner of something large that bowed in the middle of the group, like a tablecloth.

Again, Deb thought of Janice. She knew that her mother was terrible at responding to texts and calls, but it could be hard to have to reassure herself that her mum hadn't passed out or fallen over in the bathroom.

Deb wished she could bring Janice here, to have a bit of company, some cake and some gossip. She knew that her mum would enjoy it.

'Welcome! You're just in time to paint a sign. Oh, and help yourself to cake. We do ask for a small donation, but it's for charity.' June nodded towards a teacup that held some loose change.

'Of course. I'd love a lemon slice in a minute, I think.' Deb looked back at the cake table. 'I wanted to talk about catering for the May Day party, though. If you were all still interested.'

Deb had walked past the centre a few times on her way up and down the high street, but after meeting the demonstrators a few days ago she'd meant to come and check out their weekly meeting, since June had mentioned that they'd helped with the May Day party food in previous years.

She'd had a spare hour in her diary that day, between seeing the florist for decorations and a chat about themed corsages and buttonholes, and meeting with the band to make sure they were happy with the space they'd have in the Great Hall, and to talk about the ceilidh.

'Oh, yes, of course. Let me wave at Mina and Sheila. Hang on.' June gesticulated at two of the women who were in the sewing circle. 'We're doubling our efforts for the demonstration at Gyle Head, as you can see. That Kyle Abernethy's got another think coming if he continues with construction up there. Which I suppose he will.' June pulled her lips into a tight line of disapproval. Deb smiled politely, glad that she hadn't mentioned her upcoming date with Kyle – not that it was anyone's business – and trying to swallow the feeling of awkward discomfort. She felt like a liar, which was ridiculous, because she had no responsibility to tell any of these women about her love life.

You're just here for a few weeks, she reminded herself. *You're allowed to have dinner with a hot guy and for it not to be some kind of career-killing incident. If you were a man, you wouldn't be worrying about it.*

That was true. Deb thought that was something Gretchen might say, and it made her feel slightly better.

'Mina, Sheila, you remember Deb, from the protest? She's helping Hal organise the May Day party.' June introduced the two women, both of whom Deb remembered. Mina waved.

'Hi, Deb! Nice to see you. I don't think we said hello, but I did see you there. Having a few words with that evil property developer,' she *tsked*. 'Very happy to supply snacks for the party, though. My husband and I have a food business. We can do dips, chutneys, that kind of thing? It's been nice before with a cheese board?'

Deb balked at *evil*, but chose not to pick Mina up on it. Like June, she struck Deb as rather no-nonsense and direct, which was a wonderful quality – but both of them felt like women she'd rather have as friends than enemies. *I'm going out with Mr Evil*, she thought. *Save me.*

'I wouldnae say he was evil, Mina.' Sheila rolled her eyes, echoing Deb's thoughts. 'Hi, Deb. Sheila. Happy tae sort ye oot fer a few cakes.'

'Ah, that would be brilliant, thank you. I'd need enough for about three hundred guests, though. That's not too many?'

'No, it's fine. I'd likely do a few big cakes and then a lot of cupcakes, if ye dinnae mind. Happy tae suggest options, like a lemon drizzle cupcake wi' lemon icin', or chocolate's always popular. A bit like the one over there.' Sheila nodded to the trestle table with all of the refreshments on it.

'Cupcakes sound ideal. I could arrange them on those nice tiered stands. Perhaps lemon and chocolate? Half and half?' Deb suggested.

'Aye. Give me yer number an' I'll message ye some options. I dinnae mind givin' ye samples to try.' Sheila reached into her pocket and passed Deb a pen and a piece of paper.

'Great.' Deb wrote her number on the piece of paper and handed it back to Sheila. 'What was that you were doing over there? Sewing?'

'We're making a protest quilt!' Mina interjected, excitedly. 'It was my idea. We like to crochet in the group but I also like quilting and embroidery. It keeps me busy in the evenings when I'm watching TV, although of course I don't have an awful lot of free time, with the business and the children. I have three children,' she added proudly, and Deb sensed that Mina, while very friendly, was also perhaps not the shyest person in the room.

'Come and see where we are with it.' Sheila winked as she and Mina led Deb over to the sewing circle. There were three other women working on the American style quilt, and two empty chairs where Sheila and Mina had been sitting. 'Sue, can you turn over the bit you're working on? This is Deb. She's new to the crochet coven.'

Deb wanted to point out that she hadn't, to her knowledge, *joined* the crochet coven. Still, she didn't want to be rude, so she just smiled and looked curiously at the square of embroidery that Sue was holding up.

'What's the design?' Deb asked. Sue's square featured a red squirrel among leaves, which was very pretty: Deb recalled that red squirrels were one of the species that were under threat from Kyle's development project.

'It's going to say WOMEN SEWING AGAINST ECOSYSTEM COLLAPSE.' Sue, a woman with long brown hair in a plait and a dark green smock dress explained. 'There's a proud tradition of quilting and crafts in political resistance. We thought we'd try and display it permanently at the entrance to the building site.'

Oh, no. Deb felt a twist of anxiety in her stomach. This felt like a step up in activity from haranguing Kyle at the entrance to the building site.

'Wow. OK.'

Kyle probably didn't know how incensed these women were.

This put her in a difficult position, because now she felt like she had to tell him about the quilt when she saw him. She imagined that the notion of a quilt might not disturb Kyle that much – it wasn't as if Mina and Sheila were planning to fire-bomb the building site – but there was something about the concentration required to make a quilt that spoke of an intimidating sense of determination on the part of the women.

'Is that the risk? Ecosystem collapse?' she asked, looking back at Mina and Sheila. 'That seems quite an... intense outcome. Obviously, I'm on the side of the animals,' she added, quickly.

'It might be.' Mina sounded slightly peevish, as if she didn't appreciate Deb questioning the group's message. 'But anyway, he shouldn't be doing what he's doing. People are angry.'

'But isn't he just building houses that people need?' Deb asked, which she regretted instantly as Mina's expression went from frowny to thunderous.

'No! He isn't!' she snapped. 'He's going to wipe out whole populations of red squirrels and capercaillie, and he's going to land us with more commuters, clogging up the roads,' she continued, becoming more cross.

'Would it really be that many more commuters?' Deb asked, mildly.

'It's the principle,' Sheila interrupted, crossing her arms across her chest. 'The point is, we dinnae want the development. It's no' something that Loch Cameron needs.'

'Right. Well, you know best.' Deb didn't want to make enemies of the crochet coven. 'I mean, I'm just visiting. I'm not here to get involved in local disagreements.'

'Right, well,' Mina huffed. 'It's important, though. Maybe, if we've finished the quilt by the time of the party, we could reveal it then. In a kind of ceremonial way.' She looked hopefully at Deb, who thought that was definitely not a great idea, but had no idea about how to say that and not offend Mina.

'Hmm. Maybe!' Deb said, noncommittally. 'We'll have to see if we have time. The schedule is already packed, so...' she trailed off. It wasn't that she didn't want to be supportive, but the May Day party was a fun event for the community. It wasn't the place for political demonstrations. Plus, again, it put her in a difficult position with Kyle.

'Well, you're in charge,' Mina sniffed. 'Hal would have let us. Maybe I'll just give him a call. I'm sure he'd understand.'

'Hal's in New York,' Deb replied brightly. Mina wasn't the

first stubborn diva she'd had to deal with in her career, and she wouldn't be the last. 'You can call him if you like, but he *has* handed authority and responsibility for the party over to me. He is super busy, so I'm not sure if he'd really appreciate being asked... but it's up to you, of course,' she said, politely, but with an unmistakeable firmness.

'Hmm. Well, I might.' Mina flashed her a smile that said she was letting it go for now, but maybe not forever. 'I'm sure you know best, Deb.'

'Let's stick a pin in it for now, shall we?' Deb suggested, diplomatically. 'The quilt looks amazing, though.'

'Ta.' Sue smiled and returned to her embroidery.

'So, you guys really aren't keen on Kyle Abernethy,' Deb said as she went over to the cake table and got herself a chocolate and beetroot cupcake, and made herself a cup of tea. She was keen to dig a little deeper and find out if there was any reasonable basis for why he was so disliked, apart from the housing development.

She slipped a couple of pounds in the donation box as Sheila tidied up the work surfaces.

'No. He's no' endeared himself tae the community,' Sheila said. 'Rude fella, too. He couldae been polite, but he never is. Could listen, but he doesnae. Could be nice, but he cannae,' she finished with a shrug. 'Don' tell me you're friendly with him or somethin'.' She shot Deb a questioning look.

'Oh, no. I've met him a couple of times and I didn't like him at all,' Deb lied. 'Unnecessarily rude.'

Deb thought about the time she'd spent with Kyle looking out over the loch, watching the Red Kite. It had been so beautiful.

'Aye.' Sheila shook her head in disbelief. 'Some people, ye just wonder how they get through life, bein' like that. Like he doesnae care what people think o' him at all.'

'Hmm,' Deb said, noncommittally, and sipped her tea. He

did seem to have a blatant lack of ability to play nice, sometimes.

He'd said himself that he could be hotheaded, and was certainly direct in saying what he thought.

Would she, at some point, have to prove to the coven that Kyle wasn't the monster they thought he was? Or would she just have a few dates with him and leave after the party with no harm done?

The latter was the logical option. Yet, something in Deb wanted to be able to convince Mina, Sheila and the rest that they were wrong about Kyle Abernethy. It wasn't fair that they had such a bad opinion of him.

Was that her responsibility? No. Kyle was a grownup and responsible for managing his own reputation. But, still, it nagged at Deb, and made her uncomfortable. She couldn't shake the feeling that all this bad feeling being directed towards Kyle wouldn't end well, and she had no desire to find herself in the middle, with Kyle on one side, and the crochet coven on the other.

FOURTEEN

'So, tell me about you.' Deb tried to remember what people did on dates. In the absence of having any "moves" – the thought of it was ridiculous – she reverted to what she was good at: asking questions. Being an event planner meant that she spent her life asking questions and getting answers to them. If anything, Deb was aware that she was a serial over-questioner, but there were worse things in life. Probably.

It had been years since she'd even gone on a first date with someone new. Deb had surprised herself by actually enjoying getting ready for it that evening. She was feeling particularly relieved because she had at least managed to get Janice on the phone, albeit briefly, because the soaps were about to start and Janice was waiting for her neighbour Beatrice to come around so they could watch them together.

Deb had asked Janice about Grandma Elise's diary, but her mother had been quite dismissive. *I just thought you should have it, darling,* she'd said with a sigh. *Since you're so curious about Grandma. Now you know.*

But when Deb had pressed Janice, her mother had

demurred, not wanting to talk about it anymore. *Beatrice is at the door, love. I'll speak to you soon,* she'd said, and rung off.

Deb had been disappointed not to be able to talk about the diary, but she'd also been excited to get ready for her date. She'd treated herself to a long soak in a bubble bath, washed her hair and blow dried it and selected an outfit that she felt comfortable and pretty in: some white jeans, a pair of heeled sandals and a V neck yellow T shirt that was made of a soft, drapey cotton.

When she was dressed and ready, she'd looked at herself in the mirror with a slight sense of disbelief. Was this the same Deb as the one who had struggled to make it up the stairs after her hysterectomy, feeling like a bag of knives had been left inside her? The same Deb as the one who had, at one time, thought that her future lay with Dan? She had lost weight since the operation: much of the bloating that came with endometriosis had gone. Her face looked different: some of the weight had come off there too. Her cheekbones were more prominent, and her eyes had more sparkle. She was sleeping better and deeper, enjoying a bed all to herself at night without Dan rolling over and snorting like a pig in the night, so the dark shadows that used to lie under her eyes had gone. She looked younger.

Deb had sacrificed her uterus for improved health, but she had gained so much more. The stresses of her old life were melting away, bit by bit, and it was visible in her face. Her skin looked less stressed. It even had a *glow*, even though she felt strangely self-conscious thinking that.

Was Kyle someone she could have a long term relationship with? It remained to be seen, but it was nice to be going on a date again. It felt good.

'What do you want to know?' Kyle looked at her over the top of the wine menu. They were sitting at a table by the window at a small restaurant with about ten tables total, with white painted brick walls displaying modern paintings. Overall, the look was clean and sophisticated: on each table, a simple glass vase held a bunch of heather and locally sourced flowers. Deb knew that, because there was a note on the menu that said so.

In fact, she hadn't even had to drive here. The restaurant – The Fat Hen – sat at the top of a hill at the edge of town, at the far end of the high street to Queen's Point. The restaurant was a lovely old red brick building with a white front door. Large hanging baskets outside boasted a profusion of orange geraniums and red poppies. Kyle had been waiting for her at the door, which she was grateful for, because she hated walking into a bar or restaurant on her own if she was meeting someone there – never mind for a date.

She'd walked from the cottage, and it had only taken her about twenty minutes or so. On the way, she'd walked past the various shops on the high street shutting up for the day, pulling in their wooden signs and blackboards from the street. As she'd walked past the bookshop, she had nodded a shy hello to the girl pulling in a cart of discounted paperbacks, the same girl who had been standing behind the shop counter when she'd met Kyle there.

'I don't know. Tell me about your childhood.' Deb tucked her hair behind one ear, thinking that she could really do with visiting the local hairdresser for a cut.

'Oh, is that all?' Kyle chuckled. 'Well, I was born, my parents were nice enough, then I went to school, I was pretty okay at maths but I hated geography. Played some sports. Grew up.'

'That's the briefest version of a childhood I think I've ever heard.' Deb raised an eyebrow, smiling. 'What sports?'

'Rugby and rowing. Preferred rugby.' Kyle smiled at the waitress, who came to the table. 'Hi there. Can we order some wine? What would you like?' he asked Deb, handing her the wine list.

'Dry white would be good, if you don't mind? What do you recommend?' she asked the waitress, who had remarkable, two-tone hair. One side of her impeccably cut bob was raven black, and the other side bright pink. 'Can I just add, I love your hair?'

'Ah, thanks.' The waitress grinned. 'Luckily the chef doesnae mind it.'

'Haha. Loch Cameron seems like a fairly relaxed place,' Deb commented. 'Has the restaurant been here long?'

'A few years, I think. Rory, that's the chef and owner, he's run it at least five years or so, anyway. I'm Kathy, by the way.'

'Hi, Kathy. I'm Deb. I'm working at the castle for a few weeks, organising the May Day party this year,' Deb explained.

'Nice tae meet ye. Let us know if ye need any help wi' the caterin' fer the party. Rory's great and we've helped before.' Kathy pointed to a wine on the list. 'I recommend this one.'

'Looks great. Thanks, and I'll definitely bear that in mind.' Deb nodded, pleased to be making some more local contacts. The people of Loch Cameron were all so keen to help her out. She liked that. She liked their kindness, which wasn't something you found so much in big cities, where people could seem like they were more focused on themselves. 'Oh, this is Kyle Abernethy, by the way.'

'A pleasure,' Kyle said, a little guardedly.

'I recognise ye. From the housing development, aye.' Kathy shook her head. 'My friends aren't happy with ye, no' at all.' She made a *tsk* noise at Kyle.

'Sorry to hear that,' Kyle said, in a tone that implied he wasn't sorry at all. 'Perhaps you should tell your friends to come along to the next open community consultation, rather than blocking the end of my access road for no reason.'

'Listen, I'm no' getting' involved.' Kathy held her hands up in a defensive gesture. 'I hardly have time tae do ma grocery shoppin', what with workin' here an' finishin' ma PhD. Ye can all fight it out amongst yerselves,' she told him with a shrug.

'However, when I see the group, I'll tell them there's a... what did ye say? Community consultation?'

'Yes. There was actually one before the project began, but I thought I should probably hold another one, since there has been such virulent local opposition to the new houses. Which, I might add, will be affordable and sustainably built.' Kyle met Deb's eyes. 'It was good advice. Thank you.'

'You're welcome.' Deb was surprised that Kyle had taken in what she'd said. She was uncomfortable at being seen by someone from the crochet coven with Kyle, though: even though Kathy seemed all right about it, she could only imagine what June and Mina and the rest of them would say. Deb was immediately on edge. She couldn't relax, knowing that Kathy might recount everything she and Kyle did back to the group. *Ah, they looked very cosy*, Deb imagined Kathy saying. *I doubt there's many secrets between them. We cannae trust that one, aye. Sleepin' wi' the enemy.*

'All right, well, let me get yer wine. An' ...point taken.' Kathy nodded, and retreated behind the small corner bar.

'Sorry, if I was a bit terse, just then,' Kyle said with a sigh. 'I just get really annoyed with all of this negativity around the project. I've done everything by the book and people just seem to want to make up their own version of the truth.'

'That's okay. I guess I'd be frustrated if the same thing had happened to me.' Deb smiled thinly, but she couldn't stop thinking about what Kathy might tell the crochet coven.

'Hmm. You okay?' Kyle gave her a penetrating look. 'That didn't upset you, did it? It's just business. It's not personal. I don't want you to think... I dunno. It looks bad for you to be seen with me.'

Deb was surprised at Kyle's intuition of what she was thinking.

'I don't think that,' she said, not entirely truthfully. 'It's just... I do want to keep the crochet coven on side, while I'm working on the May Day party. They do seem to be quite influential.' She lowered her voice. 'I feel like they could make things difficult, if they wanted to.'

'No kidding. I can't relate to that at all.' Kyle rolled his eyes. 'But, listen. Don't worry. I'm the big bad wolf here, not you. Okay?' he reached for her hand across the table.

'Okay.' The warmth from Kyle's hand lent a glow of pleasure to hers: she didn't want him to take his hand away.

'Shall we change the subject? You were saying you played a lot of rugby at school?' This evening, Kyle was wearing a fitted dark blue jumper and black jeans. Deb had definitely noticed how good he looked in both: the jumper wasn't by any means skintight, but it skimmed his large, muscular arms and shoulders and made her look at his corded, strong neck. For some reason, just looking at his neck made Deb think about what was under that jumper.

For goodness' sake, she berated herself. *What are you, a teenage boy?*

But I want to strip that jumper off him and kiss everything underneath, her inner horny teenager whined. *It looks so gooooood.*

Deb allowed herself a small half-smile: she'd had a good look at the menu and had had somewhat the same reaction to the fillet steak. She was, in fact, thinking about Kyle more or less like a piece of meat. She'd never thought this way about a man before, but... she actually didn't hate it. Goodness knows where it was coming from – maybe she was in the midst of a perimenopausal hormone rush, but *damn* she wanted to jump on that fine looking man.

Deborah. Really. She tried to discipline her thoughts, while also trying not to giggle. Hormones definitely made sense, actually, in a way, though she'd kept her ovaries in the hysterectomy. You could have them removed, and that would cause immediate menopause: her gynaecologist had advised that she might as well keep them, as that wasn't where the problem was for her.

But maybe there was something in the fact that she suddenly wasn't in pain, or uncomfortable, or constantly bleeding anymore. Whatever it was, it was a revelation.

'Yeah. I like to stay active.' He smiled as Kathy brought over the bottle of wine and a basket of aromatic, yeasty bread. 'That looks awesome. Thanks.'

'Welcome.' Kathy nodded. She shot Deb a friendly smile, which made her feel a little better. Kathy didn't seem to have a problem with Deb. Maybe she wouldn't gossip to her friends about her and Kyle – or, if she did, maybe she would be kind. 'Can I take your orders?'

They both ordered the steak, which amused Deb. She broke off some of the warm bread and sighed happily as she put it in her mouth. It was completely delicious: soft on the inside, with a salty, buttery crust.

'Okay, then. Tell me about why you're single,' Deb said, her mouth full of bread.

'You're really interviewing me here.' Kyle frowned.

'You don't have to answer, if it's too personal.' Deb folded her napkin into a tight square, purposefully looking away from him. 'Sorry, I can be too inquisitive, I guess. Force of habit.'

'I was seeing someone until about a year ago. Right person, wrong time, maybe. I don't know.' He looked away. 'Sorry. I don't really want to talk about it. Bad breakup.'

'Sorry to hear that.' Deb swallowed her bread and reached for more. *God, it was good bread.* 'It's hard when you think you've found the right person, but things can get in the way. Life stuff.'

'Yep.' He nodded, but she could see she wasn't going to get any more from him. *Not keen to talk about your love life, then,* she thought. *Me either.*

'What about you? You're single, right?' Kyle looked at her hand. 'No wedding ring.'

'Not married, no. I was in a relationship until recently.' Deb let out a long breath. 'I knew it hadn't been working for a while if I'm really honest with myself, and then it all came to a head when I had an operation. It's okay, I'm fine now.' She anticipated what he was going to say from his expression.

'What operation? If you don't mind me asking.' He took a sip of wine.

'Hysterectomy. I had endometriosis. It's a gynaecological condition.'

'Oh, I'm sorry. I've heard of that.' He sounded sympathetic. 'But you're okay now?'

'Yes. It takes a full year to totally heal, internally. Or so I've heard,' she said. 'But I'm good enough to be back to normal, more or less. I still get a bit tired sometimes if I've been very active, but the doctor says normal activity and exercise is good for me. I've re-started yoga again but I think Boat Pose is going to take a while to achieve again.'

'I don't know yoga, though I always think it would be good for me. All I do at the gym is strength training. I could do with some flexibility.'

'Ah. Boat pose is where you sit down and lean backwards and raise your feet and legs off the ground at the same time. You sort of bring your body into a V shape.' Deb held her hands together in a V at the wrists to demonstrate. 'Hard on your core. Does give you a great tummy if you do it enough, but my core has taken a bit of a battering recently. I'll get there again one day.'

'Ah, well, there's no rush for these things.' Kyle smiled. 'You look great, anyway.'

'Thank you. Back atcha.' Deb felt a little colour rise in her cheeks.

'Sorry – if you don't want to talk about it, I do understand.

But I'm confused, why did the operation break you up?' Kyle frowned, and then looked up as Kathy arrived holding two plates, each holding a delicious looking steak fillet. 'Ah, wow. Thanks, this looks amazing.'

'I had the op, and he was basically an idiot afterwards,' Deb said after Kathy had gone. 'It was a time when I needed his support, and he was great for about a week. Then, he started making remarks about me being lazy, getting back to work. We were living together and he didn't like it that I wasn't there to cook and clean for him.'

'It's like a six-week recovery for a hysterectomy, right?' He spooned some buttery dauphinoise potatoes onto his plate from a dish that Kathy had brought to the table for them to share. There was also a dish of fresh seasonal greens. 'My Executive Assistant was out for about eight weeks with hers, a couple of years back.'

'Yes. Exactly. And that's just to get back to reasonably human. It's much longer, really. Months until you feel normal again,' Deb helped herself to some greens. 'And you can't even sit up that well after a week. Never mind do the hoovering.'

'I know, I remember Stella. I popped round every week to help out and see if she was OK. She was in a right state, bless her. Fortunately, her husband took good care of her. Doesn't sound like you were as lucky.'

'No. I wasn't,' Deb said, shortly. The whole thing with Dan was still hurtful.

'Sorry, for men. They can be real shits sometimes.' Kyle rolled his eyes. 'I know I'm not directly responsible for them, or anything. But I still feel the need to say it.'

'Thanks. And it's not your responsibility by any means, but I appreciate the thought.' Deb smiled. Kyle was proving to be something of a surprise.

'Ah, well. What is it we say nowadays? Now you've binned the wrong guy, the universe can give the right one to you, right?

You've set boundaries. Made space and all that.' He shrugged, a half-smile playing on his lips. 'Personally, I'm not happy that this guy was such a shit to you, but I'm very happy that you broke up with him.'

'Haha. Thank you.' Deb blushed. 'I don't really know what to say now. Apart from, can I just say that I have a little bugbear about when we say the universe is *giving us* things? Like the universe gives a stuff about what you or I want.' She rolled her eyes. 'I catch myself saying it and sometimes I think, *what?*'

'Ha. No apology necessary. I'm a fan of facts over vague beliefs that the universe will or won't do things for me.'

'Yeah. I guess I was raised to believe that we're responsible for ourselves. My mum was tough. Is tough,' Deb corrected herself, thinking about Janice. She hoped her mum was OK – she'd texted before she'd left the cottage to walk to the restaurant, and got a brief reply. 'She would say that the universe doesn't give two hoots about you. That life is hard, and then you die.'

'Well, I can't necessarily disagree with that, though it's kind of bleak,' Kyle chuckled. 'Sometimes, life is nice.' He shot her a sudden smile that made his icy blue eyes light up. Deb felt her stomach melt.

Yowza.

'Here's to life being nice sometimes.' Deb poured wine into both of their glasses. 'And, a sometimes kind universe.'

'The universe.' Kyle clinked his glass with hers. There was a comfortable silence. 'So, how's the cottage? And, this steak is awesome, incidentally. Wow.' He pointed at his mouth with his fork.

'I know. Mine is too.' Deb grinned. 'Ah, it's lovely, actually. The Laird organised it for me and it's such a cosy little place. And the views over the loch are amazing. There's something about the wide open spaces here... the panoramic view. Wide skies. It's so calming,' she sighed. 'And I feel like the slower pace of life is... I don't know. It sounds silly.' She halted, feeling his intent gaze upon her.

'What?' he prompted her.

'Oh, you know. Healing?' She looked away, not wanting to sound like a flaky person. But, that was how she felt about it here.

'I get that. Part of the reason I wanted to build up here is the quiet. I know that sounds counterintuitive.' He smiled, a little uncharacteristically shyly, and Deb's heart skipped a little. 'But when I came to Loch Cameron for the first time and visited Gyle Head, I just thought... what a great place to live, you know? I could imagine kids playing up here. Fresh air. Views.'

'That's really nice,' Deb said, meaning it.

'Not quite the monster some people would have you believe, I guess.' Kyle held her eyes with his. Deb felt heat roll in her belly and expand up her body. *Dear lord.*

'I will say, though, that there's a dripping tap in the bathroom and it's driving me mad at night time.' She changed the subject and looked away, breaking the intensity of the moment. 'But, other than that. Gorgeous.'

'He'll fix that for you, I'm guessing? The Laird?'

'I guess he would usually, but he's off in New York right now.'

'Ah, right. Well, I could look at it for you. If you wanted.' Kyle looked a little shy. 'I'm pretty good at DIY.'

'Oh, that's not necessary. I'm sure I can find a handyman around the village,' Deb protested.

'I'm happy to do it. I have a toolbox in the car.' He shrugged. 'Really, it's no bother.'

'You have a toolbox in the car? Who has that?' she chuckled.

'Me?' He shrugged. 'I'm a property developer. Yeah, it's mostly meetings and looking at plans, overseeing the building and what have you. But I started off as a builder. Old habits die hard, I guess.'

'Well, let's see, shall we? I don't want to put you to any trouble.' Deb was touched, though. It was a nice offer. Or was Kyle just looking for an excuse to get into her cottage?

'It's no trouble,' he repeated. 'Anyway, it would be a pleasure. A way to make up for being so rude to you before. I'm sorry about that – again. I was just... sometimes work can be stressful. And I guess I can be a bear with a sore head from time to time. My breakup... wasn't the easiest, and I, I'm still getting over it. Not that there's ever an excuse for bad behaviour. I know that.' He put his hand on his heart.

'I accept your apology.' Deb almost reached out to squeeze his hand. She wondered what kind of awful breakup Kyle was still suffering from. She felt a wave of compassion for him: you never knew what people were hiding under their personas. Especially people with a gruff exterior, like him. 'And I'm sorry. If you want to talk about it sometime, then I'm here.'

'Thanks.' He held her gaze with his for a moment, a smile playing around his mouth. 'That's good to know.'

There was a subtext to his words, and Deb could feel that same attraction zinging back and forth between them again. She really had never felt anything like it before.

Here she was, having dinner with the most hated man in Loch Cameron. And she was enjoying every minute.

FIFTEEN

'So.' Kyle had walked her to the door of the cottage and was standing close to her, under the porch. A light rain had just begun, but the drizzle added to the gloomy feel of the evening: there was something intrinsically *Scottish* about the smell of the wetness in the air and the distant heather scent from the moors surrounding the village. Deb closed her eyes for a moment and took a deep breath, enjoying the moment.

'So.' She opened her eyes, and gazed up at him. 'This was lovely.'

'It was.' He smiled, and brushed her hair away from her face softly. His fingers traced the line of her cheek, and then the softness of her neck. Deb shivered; she realised that she had been craving his touch the whole evening. 'That restaurant is gorgeous. Thanks for coming with me: I've been wanting to go for a while now.'

'You're welcome,' she replied, a little shyly.

'Did you want me to have a look at that tap for you?' He gestured at the car. 'I brought my toolbox.'

'Don't be silly. I don't expect you to fix a tap at 10pm, after you've just taken me out for a lovely dinner,' she protested.

'I offered, and I meant it. I'm not one of those guys who's all hot air.' Kyle shrugged. 'I don't mind. It's my way of showing you I like you.'

'DIY is your love language?' Deb chuckled. 'I don't think I've heard of that one. Taps.'

'Acts of service.' Kyle grinned. 'It's a thing.'

'Fair enough. Come on, then.' She turned and unlocked the front door to the cottage.

Kyle ran to his car and returned with a tool box, which he set down in the hallway.

'Thanks. Wouldn't mind a cup of tea,' he added. 'Is that rude? That dinner was quite rich, I feel like I need something to even it out.'

'No worries.' She went into the kitchen, filled up the kettle with water and set it to boil on the hob. She felt a little nervous, inviting Kyle into her cottage. It wasn't that she didn't think she was safe. It was more that she wasn't sure what was happening between them, and what she wanted to happen. There was a crazy hot energy between them: she could practically feel it zinging off the walls. 'Bathroom's through there.'

'Right you are.'

Deb smiled at the sound of Kyle whistling in the bathroom; there were some hmms and ahas, and various clanking noises for a while. He reappeared in the kitchen soon after, laying his dark blue jumper on the side of the aged leather sofa.

'Don't want to get that dirty,' he explained. Deb nodded, handing him a mug of tea she'd just brewed. Under the jumper he'd been wearing, Kyle wore a plain white T-shirt. Deb could tell it was good quality, but it was also fine enough material for her to detect the shadow of some tattoos underneath it. Not only that, the shirt was fitted enough so that his biceps strained against the sleeves. She looked away, not wanting to gawp, but it was hard not to.

'Hmm? No, of course.' She nodded, and picked up a tea

towel purposefully, as if she had some important business with it. 'I'll just, errr... carry on here.'

'Won't be long. Thanks for the tea.'

Deb took her mug of tea and sat at the kitchen table, facing the garden window. Though it was night time, she'd left the window open, and she closed her eyes again for a moment, listening to the soft sound of the rain on the grass. It was a tranquil moment, but there was something playing on her mind – and it wasn't Kyle's bulging biceps.

Well, it wasn't *not* his biceps, she corrected herself. Whenever she saw Kyle, Deb couldn't help but think about sex. And, for Deb, sex felt problematic.

Thinking about sex, in itself, had become unusual for Deb. Even before the endometriosis had destroyed her sex life, she'd never met anyone who prompted such graphic thoughts or feelings as Kyle did. But she'd gone such a long time, suffering with pain and bleeding, that she could hardly remember what it was like to have these kind of lusty thoughts and feelings about someone.

Now, though, since her body was apparently waking up after the operation, she had found herself having dreams where she woke up, desperately aroused, and not knowing why. The details of the dreams were hazy: it was a feeling more than any details in particular, but the feelings were... definitely *something*. If she was honest, she was faintly mortified about it. She felt like a horny teenager, especially around Kyle, and she just wasn't used to it.

She'd never had the experience of lusting after a man – in real life – like she did with Kyle. Sure, she'd had crushes on movie stars just like anyone else. But this was new, and faintly unsettling.

The thing that was playing on her mind as he clanked around in the bathroom was that they'd had a lovely time. But, she wasn't sure that she wanted things to get physical.

It wasn't like anyone was taking notes, but Deb felt like Kyle was expecting something. And she didn't know if she was ready to go there. Not yet.

Deb hadn't had sex since the hysterectomy. The doctor had said that she would be safe to have sex around six to eight weeks, but that she should do it when she felt comfortable, and take it nice and slow when she did. *Don't go mad. Be careful, and remember that the end of your vagina is now only held together with stitches.*

Before, where her cervix had sat at the end of the vagina, at the entrance to her womb, there was nothing. Deb had looked it up online, and technically, if you broke your stitches, then all that was behind your vagina was now your other internal organs, and if that occurred, then a prolapse was possible. A prolapse, Deb had learned, was when your intestines slipped into your vagina and could even come out of your vulva.

Even though her body seemed to have its own sexy agenda nowadays, Deb was having trouble coming to terms with her new reality. What if something terrible happened during sex? What if her body malfunctioned in some way? What if it hurt, or bled, or the dreaded prolapse happened?

Kyle reappeared in the kitchen, making Deb jump. She had been lost in her thoughts for quite a while.

'All done.' He handed her the towel he'd been using to wipe his hands. 'Sorry. I'll take that back in a minute. Just needed a new washer. I had one, so it's all done now.'

'Oh, thanks so much.' Deb was nervous. Despite the fact that she had got to know Kyle a little now, and felt comfortable in his presence, he still made her flustered. It was an odd combination of feelings.

'Of course. All part of the service.' Without warning, Kyle took her in his arms and kissed her deeply. 'Mmmm,' he breathed as he kissed her. It was a deep, intense kiss, and she could feel herself responding to it instantly.

Deb felt herself dissolving into Kyle, but the worry about the operation lurked at the back of her mind, and it made her freeze up in his arms a little.

Prolapse was not exactly a sexy thought, and not what she wanted to be thinking about when Kyle was kissing her. Yet, it was now the only thing she could think about.

She knew it was ridiculous. But the thought that a kiss might lead to touching, and that might lead to more caused a wave of panic to engulf Deb's body. And, there was something else. The way that Dan had pressured her for sex, afterwards. It had spooked her, being so vulnerable, and him not seeming to care.

'Stop. Please.' She pulled away suddenly as Kyle's embraces grew stronger. 'I... I just need a minute.'

'What is it?' Kyle asked, slightly out of breath. 'I'm sorry if I kind of jumped on you there a bit... I just... well, you must know what you do to me.' He stroked her cheek again, and leaned in to kiss her again. Deb stepped backwards, and hit her thigh on the edge of the kitchen table. She winced.

'No. Please, Kyle.' Her voice tightened; stress had taken over, and whatever pleasant energy had been between them vanished. 'Stop.'

'What is it?' he repeated. 'Have I done something wrong?'

'No... I just... it doesn't feel right.' Deb didn't know what to say. She had told Kyle about her operation and he'd been sympathetic, but Deb was still paranoid that it might make him think that she was less of a woman. Or, old and lacking in some way. Unsexy, or, worse – in some way *unable* to do it, now. She hadn't tried yet, and she was anxious about it. Logically, she knew that she wasn't old or lacking or unsexy, but the fear of them danced in her brain and taunted her.

The sudden fear that Kyle might not want her, once he stopped to think about it, filled her with an irrational terror.

'Okay.' He stepped backwards and nodded. 'I... okay. I'm not sure what just happened.'

'I just... I'm sorry.' Deb didn't know what to say. She couldn't help but feel that there had been an unspoken pressure on her since he'd walked in the door tonight: was there an expectation they were going to sleep together? She'd felt it, but she didn't know if that was an echo of something in her brain rather than the reality of the situation.

Come on, you're being dramatic. That was what Dan had said. He had implied that she had purposefully withheld sex from him, after the hysterectomy. That she had used the operation as an excuse. And she hadn't, not at all. But the thought of sex, when she was still hurting so much, had been unbearable.

On top of her worries about her body and whether it would work, this was an extra layer of anxiety now: the possibility of Kyle pressuring her for sex.

'I'm just not ready. For... anything more.' Deb felt mortified. Now it sounded like she'd assumed that she and Kyle were going to sleep together. But the more she thought about it, the worse she felt.

'That's okay. I didn't assume anything.' His tone was kindly.

'I asked you in, but that didn't automatically mean we were going to sleep together,' Deb added, defensively.

'I know,' he replied, slowly. 'Did I say that I assumed that?'

'No, but... you were acting as though you thought you did.' Deb was hyped up, now, eager to defend herself, and the words were coming quickly. She said what was on her mind, and, really, she knew she was talking to Dan. But Dan wasn't here. 'And it made me uncomfortable. You don't have the right to assume anything. You don't have the right to my body if I say no.'

'I know that,' Kyle repeated, frowning. 'I just kissed you. And I stopped when you asked me to. I respect your choice, and I hear what you're saying. I don't know what's going on here –

maybe some crossed wires. It seems like a good idea if I leave.'
He picked up his jacket and slung it over his shoulder. 'Good
night, Deb. I had a great night.'

'Good night,' she said, her voice flat. She watched him leave,
her heart plunging to the depths of her. She felt awful, but it
would also have felt awful having him stay, and expect things to
happen when she couldn't. She just *couldn't* be physical with
Kyle: she was too tense, and too afraid of what might happen.

It was better if she never put herself in that position again.
She couldn't see him again, not after this: she'd embarrassed
herself too much to go back.

Her heart ached, but she knew she'd done the right thing.
Deb just wasn't ready for a man yet after all: perhaps she'd
never be ready. The thought filled her with desolation, but there
was a dreadful acceptance in there too. *Perhaps it was never for
me,* she thought, as the front door clicked closed. *That kind of
intense feeling. It's just too much.*

She'd never understood what the fuss was about before, but
now that she had met someone who gave her those feelings, Deb
was starting to realise that whatever it was – lust, love, attraction
– wasn't plain sailing. It wasn't just a question of walking off
into the sunset with someone, because life got in the way of
sunsets. Your brain could get in the way of sunsets and sailing
off into the horizon very effectively.

Was that what had just happened? Or had she been right to
say no to Kyle? Deb put her head in her hands and let out a long
sigh.

If this was love, then you could keep it.

SIXTEEN

'Morning, Deb.' Anna, the castle housekeeper, opened the door to the rather grand castle library where Deb was working at a leather-topped desk and enjoying the view onto the manicured castle gardens. 'How's it going?'

Deb had been largely working from the cottage, as most of what she did could be done with her phone and computer, but she'd come up to the castle to look at the spaces they were going to use for the party, and do things like measure the Great Hall so that she knew where to put the decorations.

'Oh, hi, Anna.' Deb looked up from her laptop and took off her reading glasses. 'Just ordering glassware, and organising the band. I'm ticking through my to-do list.'

She was used to throwing herself into her work to avoid thinking about her personal life. It had used to be Dan that had bothered her – thinking about whether they were really meant to be together. About whether she was truly happy in their relationship.

Newsflash – you weren't, she thought to herself as she reviewed a spreadsheet of party costs. And, now, she was avoiding thinking about what had happened with Kyle the night before.

Ugh. It certainly hadn't gone the way she'd thought it would. Not that she'd had any firm expectations – but the way she'd pushed him away had made everything feel so awkward – that was not good.

Should she have done anything she didn't feel ready to do? Of course not. But she was also frustrated at herself. Because when she was around Kyle, her body felt ready.

It was her mind that wasn't.

Anna set a pot of coffee and some delicious, sticky cinnamon rolls, still warm from the oven on the side of the capacious desk.

'*Finnegan!* Heel! Sorry, Deb.' Anna tutted at Hal's dog. The spaniel raced over to Deb, barking excitedly. Deb stood up to head him off, catching his silky body and giving him a fond head rub.

'Not at all. He's a darling. I've always liked dogs.'

'Well, he's going to be a pest while the laird's away. He loves Zelda: she takes him for good long walks most days she's here, so I think you're really going to miss her, aren't you, boy?'

'Oh. Well, if it helps, I'm happy to take Finnegan on some walks. The castle gardens are so beautiful, but I'd be keen to see the rest of the grounds, and it would give me a good excuse.'

'Really? That'd be great.' Anna nodded. 'You'd be helping me out massively. My schedule is unbelievable, especially with the party coming up.'

'No problem at all.' Deb picked up her phone as the screen flashed. It was Kyle.

Can we talk about last night? I want to check you're okay.

She frowned and put the phone down.

'All right?' Anna caught her expression.

'Oh, it's nothing. Just a personal thing.' Deb looked out of the window, distractedly.

'I'm here if you need an ear,' Anna said, kindly. 'You look a bit upset, if you don't mind me saying.'

'Hmm. I'm okay,' Deb replied, a little shyly. 'Just had a bad date.'

'Ach. Been there,' Anna tutted. 'There's not much local choice, though. If he's single, I've probably dated him.'

'Oh, lord.' Deb laughed, without meaning to. 'Actually, you might know him. Kyle Abernethy. He's involved in building some houses up on Gyle Head.'

'Kyle Abernethy?' Anna did a double take.

'Yes. Why?' Deb frowned at Anna's expression.

'Oh. Well, it's really not my business, of course. I know that Hal's had a few run-ins with him recently,' Anna said. 'Not that that has anything to do with your love life.'

'Run-ins in what way?' Deb asked, cautiously. She was keen to know what other people's opinion of Kyle was.

'Well, the land that Kyle bought? Hal sold it on the understanding that it'd be developed to build cottages in keeping with the ones already on Queen's Point. They had a disagreement because Kyle's building what looks like executive flats up there. They'll ruin the traditional look of the village. And won't be affordable fer most.' Anna raised an eyebrow. 'And when I say a *disagreement*, I mean that there were raised voices. On both sides.'

'Oh!' Deb was taken aback. Kyle hadn't mentioned anything about this to her. As far as Deb was aware, the issue with the building site was that it was threatening local wildlife, not that Kyle was cramming pricey flats onto the land. Mina and Sheila might have been more right than they knew, when they were complaining about the development bringing more commuters to the village.

Deb frowned. She was well aware of the problem of a lack

of affordable housing all across the country, at a time when people's finances were stretched further than ever. And she didn't like the idea that Kyle was lying or in some way not being truthful about what he was doing. He'd spun her a tale about him being a caring builder, but if that wasn't true, then how could she trust him about anything else?

'Hmm. Gyle Head's stayed rural all this time because Hal was picky about who he sold it to. I don't have any strong feelings about Kyle, don't get me wrong. But I know that Hal's not happy with what he's doing up there, and the locals aren't either,' Anna sighed. 'But... I guess, all I'd say is, be careful. He's a funny one. And people aren't too fond of him around here.'

'Funny, how?'

'Got a temper, I'd say. Okay to me, but as I say, him and Hal went at it. I thought he could've been more professional.'

'Okay. Noted, I guess.' Deb wasn't sure how she felt about what Anna had said. Of course, she was entitled to her opinion. But it introduced a sliver of doubt about Kyle into Deb's mind.

But, whoever Kyle was at work didn't necessarily reflect who he was in his personal life. And, to be fair to him, he'd texted her to check she was all right after the night before.

Briefly, Deb sent a reply to Kyle: *All fine, thanks. Sorry if I overreacted.*

He replied immediately: *Glad to hear it.*

'Sorry. I didn't mean to pry.' Anna gave her an awkward smile. 'I'm sure it's nothing.'

'No, that's okay,' Deb repeated. 'Thanks for letting me know.'

It was a little awkward, but it wasn't as bad as Anna saying that she had dated Kyle. That would have been worse.

Hal and Zelda had been gone a week or so already, and though he had been in sporadic email contact, she did very much get the impression that Hal was, as Anna said, not a details person. She'd sent a number of detailed emails so far, asking for signoff on a few different decisions, and asking for the contact details of the company that had supplied the waiting staff for past parties. The only reply she'd had was FANTASTIC – THANKS, ALL LOOKS GOOD in block capitals.

Clearly, Hal was not a natural multitasker – at least, when he wasn't physically present at the castle. *Out of sight, out of mind, maybe.*

However, as she talked to Anna, a reply from Hal appeared in her inbox.

Finally, she thought, and opened it.

Dear Deb,

To answer your question about pictures of parties from the history of Loch Cameron to use as inspiration for the May Day party. You should find some interesting pictures in the archive. Ask Anna to show you. I am happy for you to photo-copy or scan images as you wish.

Thank you for your sterling work in organising everything so far, and I trust your judgement in all things. Here is the number for John, the contact for the waiting staff.

Trusting you are well,

Hal

'Does the castle have an archive room?' She looked up at Anna. 'Hal says I can go down there and look for old photos and stuff for the party. Inspiration.'

'Yes. I can take you down there. Now?'

'That would be great.' Deb got up and put her phone in her pocket. 'If you don't mind.'

'Not at all. Follow me. Let me let the dog out first.' Anna

opened one of the long double doors and ushered Finnegan into the garden. 'This part of the garden's enclosed. He'll be fine out there, and he has a kennel if it gets wet,' she explained.

Anna led Deb out into the long, wide hallway outside the drawing room. Deb's boots clicked on the tiled floor; she had admired it many times and always assumed that it was probably Victorian, judging by the floral pattern.

'This way.' Anna opened a door at the end of the hallway and pulled a hanging light cord which exposed a narrow stairway going downwards. 'Watch your step. This was built when people were smaller, I think. For small feet or something. Or, whoever built it wasn't that bothered about the safety of whoever was using it.'

'Was it for the servants, then?' Deb asked as she dutifully watched where she stepped.

'Yes. Some of the servants' quarters are down here, and the main kitchen and old larder. Various store rooms we hardly use anymore. The archive's just along here.' Anna led her down a rather dark corridor, flicking on some lights as she went. Harsh, tubular light dinged on with a low hum.

'Rather dingy.' Anna opened a door, squinted in the dim light and turned on a nearby lamp. 'There you are. Not quite as shadowy now. In you come.'

Deb stepped into a medium sized room with a long wooden table in its centre. Four chairs were tucked underneath it, as if waiting for a dinner party that would never happen. Around the walls sat a variety of glass-fronted cabinets and shelves filled with books stacked high towards the bare stone ceiling.

'I suppose castles weren't built with a modern demand for light, airy spaces,' Deb said, taking in the leather trunks in the corner and the locked wooden bureau. 'I like it, though. It's atmospheric.'

'It's something, all right. Though I think that atmosphere's mostly mildew.' Anna sniffed. 'There's so much down here. I doubt even Hal knows what all of it is,' she said with a shrug. 'Do you want me to give you a hand for a while?'

'That'd be great. Thanks. Photos of parties, ideally, or written records of some of the details. If we could recreate one of the old recipes, or a centrepiece, something like that, it would be really great. Give a sense of history to the party,' Deb explained.

'Right. On it.' Anna turned away and started to look through the shelf opposite.

Deb opened one of the cabinets and looked in, curiously.

'Have you got any idea where I should start?' She looked over at Anna.

'I'm not sure, but I know that bit is mostly journals from the Chamberlain of the Estate.' Anna glanced over at her.

'These?' Deb held up a large old fashioned loose-leaf folder for Anna to see.

'Yes, that's them. I've had a little look before, here and there – they're quite interesting, sometimes. You get a bit of local scandal.'

'Hmm. This guy is talking about how one family in the village were stealing cattle from another family, and the Laird had to get involved and sort it out.'

'What did the Chamberlain of the Estate do?' Deb started flicking through the densely handwritten pages. It was all very neat, copperplate ink writing, with dates and margin notes.

'It was a kind of role like an Estate Manager.' Anna looked up from a leather-bound book she was looking at. 'He would have cared for everything on a day-to-day level for the Laird. Which one are you reading?'

'Osbert Vaughan. Not a very Scottish name.' Deb consulted the cover of the folio. 'This is dated 1813. It's amazing that it's still here.' She put it down on the table.

'I know. It's a wonderful record of the area.' Anna nodded.

'I also wanted to see if I could find more pictures of parties from the past to use as inspiration for the décor this year. And I thought maybe if there were some good ones, we could blow them up as posters and have them around for people to look at. Or even make some fun postcards or something. Tie the tradition to the past,' Deb said, thoughtfully. 'This is great, but not entirely what I was after.'

'That's a nice idea.' Anna went to one of the glass-fronted cabinets and opened it. 'I think there are some photo albums in here. Yes, look.' She brought out a few large red leather-bound albums and laid them on the table. 'These, I've seen before. I know they're from the sixties through to the eighties, so that would be Hal's parents. Now... if you wanted to go back further than that, there are some others here, too. Ah, and maps.'

'Ah, look at the dresses. These are fantastic.' Deb opened up the photo albums and started flicking through the pages. 'Really retro. Look at this suit with the shoulder pads this lady's wearing.' She pointed to one of the photos in which a woman, probably in her thirties, wore an emerald green skirt suit with a double-breasted jacket with large gold buttons.

'Ooh. Very Wall Street.' Anna smiled. 'Here, these are albums from earlier. Turn of the century, there.' She placed a smaller, grey cardboard album on the table. 'Won't be colour pictures, of course. Sadly.'

'Mmm.' Deb flicked it open and smiled. 'Ah, this is perfect! Look, there are all sorts of grand occasions here. Dinners, people dancing.' She showed Anna a series of black and white photos of ladies in ballgowns and men in Scottish formal dress doing what appeared to be Scottish country dancing. 'This is wonderful! Do you think Hal would mind if I used these? Can I take some pictures with my phone?'

'Don't see why not, and I'm sure he wouldn't mind.' Anna went back to the cabinet as Deb snapped some pictures of some of the old party photos from the different albums. 'You know that the Laird who built the folly up on Gyle Head used to have some big parties up there. I mean, that's what that whole project was all about – entertaining his London friends. You should try and find pictures of those parties. I heard they were wild.'

'I bet. There are a few details online. I know what people did in those days to entertain their social circles. The rich, that is. It wasn't everyone that could afford that kind of thing.' Deb raised an eyebrow.

'Indeed. Ah, this is interesting. Look at this old map. You can see Gyle Head here, before the old Laird – Donald Cameron, that was – built the folly.' Anna tapped her fingernail on the map as she slid it over the table to Deb. 'Look. There were four cottages there.'

'How weird. They're not there now.' Deb looked at the date on the map: 1900.

'Huh. Wait, there are other maps in here. Look, this one is 1940. No cottages.' Anna passed it to Deb.

'What happened to them?' Deb wondered aloud. 'I mean, presumably they had people living in them? Or, maybe they were derelict?'

'I don't know.' Anna frowned. 'If Hal was here, we could ask him. Wait, let's see if there were any Chamberlain notes at the time. Where did you get that one?'

Deb pointed to one of the shelves on the right-hand side of the room. Anna went over and ran her finger gently along the gold-stamped spines of the folios and notebooks.

'What year are we looking for? When did he build it?' Anna asked, over her shoulder. 'If we can narrow it down between 1900 and 1940, that would be helpful.'

'Ummm... I remember seeing something online. Wait, let me look.' Deb went back to the original article she'd read, and found the date. '1935. The inter-war years.'

'Right. Let's see... 1930, 1932... 1935. Here.' Anna took down a black leather-bound folio. 'Mackenzie Smith was the Chamberlain to Donald Cameron. Let's see what he has to say.'

She flicked through the pages, shaking her head. 'I can't see anything. It's all local disputes, castle repairs... oh, wait. Here we are.'

She read aloud from the record:

> 'Building work on Gyle Head progresses well. Laird Cameron has employed a team of architectural experts for the construction of the folly. The four cottages that stood in the area have been successfully dismantled, and the families evicted. The stone will be repurposed in the new building.'

'Bloody hell.' Deb was shocked. 'Evicted?'

'Yeah. And he doesn't seem that bothered, does he? Old Mackenzie Smith? It seems like they were most bothered about not wasting the stone that the cottages were built of.'

'That's outrageous.'

'Awful. Listen to this,' Anna continued, her brows knitting together as she read:

> 'The tenants have been moved on successfully for the most part. The Laird notes for the record that all four families – McKinley, Dalgliesh, McCarron and Sutherland – were long-standing tenant families, and will be missed.'

'Will be missed? Is he for real?' Deb countered, angrily. 'Wait. Did you say Sutherland?'

'Yes. McKinley, Dalgliesh, McCarron and Sutherland.' Anna read the list out again.

'That's my name,' Deb said, frowning. '1935...'

'Interesting coincidence.' Anna shot her a look.

Surely not, Deb's mind began to race. It was so unlikely. And yet... she thought about Grandma Elise. What happened to her.

Deb had a sudden, strange feeling in the pit of her stomach.

'My grandmother was evicted from her home when she was eleven. It ruined her life. I never knew where that was, though.' Deb thought back to her grandma's diary. Of the entries that it had broken her heart to read.

'Does it say... the individual names of the Sutherland family?' she asked, tentatively.

She thought again about Elise. About how she had been assaulted multiple times by her foster family. About how she had survived that and losing her parents, and managed to have a daughter of her own, even though her husband hadn't stuck around, either. Janice had insisted on taking her mother's maiden name, and it had been the only name available for Deb, too. They were Sutherland women, and the world had not been kind to them.

Cursed, Janice had said, so many times that Deb had lost count.

She needed to know.

'It was a William and Eilidh Sutherland, and their bairns, Elsie and Tom.' Anna looked up from the piece of paper, searching Deb's face for a reaction.

Deb closed her eyes; she felt herself needing to lean against something.

Cursed. Janice's word rang in her memory. *Poor Elsie.* She had a sudden vision of her grandmother as a child, walking away from a white-painted cottage very much like the one she was currently living in. Crying, holding her mother's hand. *Please, can't we stay?*

Deb could see it all happening in front of her, as if she was there, like a ghost.

In her mind, she held out her arms to Elsie and Tom, and ran towards them. *I'll save you*, she called out, in the dream. *I'm here.*

Yet, try as she might, she was a ghost in the dream, and her grip was too insubstantial. She tried and failed to hold their hands, and the vision dimmed. *No!* she cried, wanting to stay, wanting to connect, feeling the terrible grief and dismay in Elsie's heart at having to leave her home. She hadn't known it was going to happen, of that Deb felt sure. There had been no warning – at least, her parents had known, but they hadn't told the children. Perhaps hoping in their feckless way that it wouldn't happen.

But, it did.

Unsteady on her feet, Deb sat down at the table as fat, heavy tears spilled over her cheeks. In that moment, she had no resistance to the grief that overpowered her.

SEVENTEEN

After some thought, Deb had emailed Hal the information, taking some pictures of the relevant entries in the Chamberlain's Journal with her phone and summarising what she and Anna had found out.

As you can imagine, Hal, she'd written, this is a big personal blow. I don't expect you to know, of course, but my grandmother – who was a child when she evicted from her home on Gyle Head – ended up going into care with her brother. In effect, this ruined her life, due to a series of abusive situations. She never really recovered from those experiences.

I'm not asking anything of you, but just felt that you should know, especially because of the current developments up on Gyle Head.

She hadn't had a reply yet, but that wasn't unusual. Hal was taking forever to reply to anything she sent him.

She had also thought about contacting Kyle with the information, but she wasn't sure where she stood with him, and talking to him was just going to be awkward. So, when her phone began to buzz and she saw it was Kyle, she couldn't hide her surprise, or the warm flush that began in her belly.

'Hello,' Deb answered the call as neutrally as she could.

Playing it cool had never particularly been her strong suit when it came to men, though she was excellent at all kinds of negotiations and generally taking charge at work.

'Hi. How are you?' Kyle sounded a little guarded, and there was background noise – it sounded as though he was in the car.

'All right. You?' Deb sighed, wondering why he was calling her. She felt wrung out after the discovery this morning. She really just wanted to be alone to think.

'Fine. Listen, I'm going to be passing you in about ten minutes and I wondered if you were home. Thought it might be a good idea to chat in person, after last time.'

'Oh... Okay, sure.' It was out of the blue, but Deb felt excited at the unexpected opportunity to see Kyle in person. 'I'm home. Drop by when you're ready.'

Ten minutes later, after Deb had hurriedly brushed her hair, changed from her jogging bottoms and loose T-shirt into a casual but flattering knee-length knitted black pencil skirt and a plain white fitted T-shirt, Kyle knocked at the cottage door.

She let him in, leading him into the cute lounge with its vivid floral wallpaper, where her laptop was open on the coffee table. He took off his work boots, which were caked in mud, by the door.

'Been up at the site,' he said, by way of explanation. 'Don't want to track it into your nice pretty cottage.'

'Thanks. I was just about to make a coffee. D'you want one?' she asked, politely, trying not to think about the last time Kyle had been in her cottage, and what had happened. She worried for a moment about whether he would try to kiss her again, and then worried about the fact she was worrying about it.

'Sure.' Kyle sat down on the pink chaise longue, looking slightly incongruous on such a girly chair. 'Thanks.'

'The cottage décor is probably a bit feminine,' she called from the kitchen, replying to his earlier comment about the cottage being pretty. 'Whoever decorated it must have decided they were only going to rent it to women. Or men that like this kind of thing. I like it, though.'

'Hm. It wouldn't be my choice, but I think I can sit on a pink chair and not have my masculinity threatened,' he replied; she could hear the characteristic smile in his voice.

She made the coffee, wondering what Kyle was going to say to her about their date. And whether she should mention what she'd found out about Elise and Gyle Head.

You have to, she told herself. *It would be weird not to, especially as he's here.*

'So, I have some news,' Deb said, as she walked into the lounge, carrying two mugs of coffee. 'I found out something about Gyle Head.'

'Oh really? Not another type of bloody squirrel, is it?' Kyle sighed, taking the coffee. 'Thanks, that smells great.'

'No, no squirrels.' Deb couldn't help but smile. She thought that not everyone would appreciate Kyle's dark sense of humour, but she enjoyed it.

'Good. I can't tell you how many emails I'm getting about protected species. If it was up to me, I'd just put poisoned nuts out for them and be done with it. I'm joking, of course,' he sighed. 'I wish I could do that, though. Maybe leave out some Valium-soaked digestives for those women in the village, while I was at it.'

'No, nothing like that.' Deb rolled her eyes.

'Excellent. Listen, before you tell me whatever it is you're going to tell me – I wanted to apologise for last time. You know.' He put his coffee mug down on the little table and leaned forward, his elbows on his knees. 'I didn't like the way we left things. I feel like I'm always apologising to you about something! But I should have been more understanding. I would never want to rush you... I just thought we were having a good time, and I didn't understand why you pulled away. But I might have misread the situation altogether, and if so, I wanted to say, I'm sorry.' He frowned. 'God knows I've misread women before.'

'That's... really nice of you. Thanks,' Deb said, haltingly, thinking about how to reply. 'I had a good time on our date too. But...' she trailed off. 'Umm. I guess, since the hysterectomy, I haven't felt very confident about myself and... you know, *things*.' She blushed, feeling stupid. 'And I'm not sure what's happening with my ex. I mean, I'm here, and he's back home. Things aren't exactly great. But I don't know, we left things a bit open-ended. He's still living in my house. So, I guess, what I mean to say is, there are a lot of *I don't knows* for me at the moment.'

'I get that.' He nodded. 'I have those too. And I've never been good at knowing if women like me or not. Or, been successful at attracting the good ones.'

'Thanks?' Deb laughed, breaking the tension. She wondered what Kyle's *I don't knows* were; wondered what he meant by *not attracting the good ones*. Were there some skeletons in his closet, too?

'Present company excepted, obviously.' He gave her a wry smile. 'Anyway, it's fine, I understand if it's not a good time.'

Deb felt divided. On one hand, she didn't feel like it was the perfect time to pursue anything with anyone, but on the other, she had such a deep attraction to Kyle that just being in the same room as him and not touching him or being near to him, was torture. Since he'd arrived, she'd tried hard – and failed – not to notice his well-muscled thighs in his blue jeans, and the strength and grace with which he held himself.

But, she still felt that fear. What if she pursued things with Kyle, her body didn't work the way it was supposed to? What if she couldn't do sex anymore, or it hurt, or it was *wrong* down there, somehow? And she could never forget what Janice had always taught her: men were dispensable, not to be trusted, and certainly not with your heart.

Dan had proved it was true. But, what if Dan had only done what she'd expected him to do? What if she had set herself up for failure by choosing someone that she had never truly, deeply, loved?

If she was honest, she had been sleepwalking through her relationships for years. As a Sutherland woman, she'd been taught to be strong, and resist the vulnerability that came with love. Not that she was in love with Kyle – she hardly knew him. But the way he made her feel scared her. Perhaps that was what was stopping her kissing him, stopping her letting whatever was going to happen, happen.

'I... actually, I had something to tell you. Not about you and me, but...' She thought for a moment. 'It's kind of about you and me. Or, me, anyway. It might help this make a bit more sense.'

'All right.' He sipped his coffee. 'What is it?'

She thought about how to best deliver the news. 'The thing is, I found out that I kind of... have a personal connection to Gyle Head.'

'Really? How?' His brow furrowed.

'Umm... well, my ancestors used to live there. My grandma, when she was a kid. And my great-grandparents.'

'Wow! Really? I do seem to remember that there were some houses up there at some point. I recall seeing that in the paper-work. But it hasn't been residential for a long time. I know that, because I had to do all the applications for residential status, and organise getting water and power and sewage and every-thing else up there.'

'No, it was a good while ago. The Laird that owned the land then evicted the families and had the cottages destroyed.' Deb felt a lump in her throat, thinking again about Elise and her brother having to leave the house. How difficult that must have been.

She reflected again on how that experience would have formed Grandma Elise's outlook for the rest of her life – that lack of being able to trust that anyone would look after her, care for her, or have her best interests at heart. If she had believed that in her childhood, then life had demonstrated to her very clearly that day – and in the years afterwards – that there was nobody protecting her, and that she shouldn't trust anyone.

Deb felt that hurt in her own heart. She had been taught to hold onto the mistrust, like a shard of glass poking into her heart that she had gotten used to. She felt a rush of pain, thinking about Elise, thinking about everything she had inherited from her. Good and bad. She wanted to explain it to Kyle, but she couldn't quite get the words, or explain in a way that would make sense.

'Wow. Crazy coincidence,' Kyle replied, sounding interested, but also detached. 'How did you find out?'

'I was up at the castle looking at some old records. It's actually very upsetting.' Deb tried to say it, but she could tell by his expression that he didn't get it. And, why would he? Kyle had no idea of how she felt. He didn't know her or her family, or what it was like, having grown up learning the wrong lessons from Janice's stoic broken heart. Instinctively, anger bloomed in Deb's heart and spread up to her throat, gathering in a ball of frustrated tears. His detachment was triggering a reaction in her.

'I'm sorry. But that was a long time ago, right? It wasn't you. It was your grandma,' he replied.

'Well, yes... but that event really ruined my grandmother's life. It changed her forever,' Deb argued, feeling herself tear up, frustrated that Kyle didn't seem to understand what she was saying.

'I'm sorry. That sounds rough,' Kyle said, evenly. 'I'm just not sure what you want me to do about it. I just bought the land. I didn't evict her. You know that I'm only thirty-eight, right?'

His offhand tone annoyed her, especially when he had

seemed so concerned for her feelings earlier. She didn't understand how he could suddenly be so cold.

'Of course I know that. What I'm saying is that I have a deep emotional connection to that land. And it's come as a total shock. I guess I'd appreciate it if you sounded like you understood. Or cared,' she snapped.

'Okay. I'm still not exactly sure what you want me to say here,' Kyle replied, still sounding careful. 'What do you want me to do about this, Deb? I bought Gyle Head as a business opportunity. It's a large property development project. That's the sum total of my involvement.'

'Don't you see how this might make me feel?' Deb felt disbelief that Kyle could be so obtuse, when her feelings were so jagged: so very deep and painful.

'Umm... I guess? But, if you were going to complain to anyone, it'd be Hal, wouldn't it? As it was his predecessor that did the deed.'

'I'm not complaining. But thanks.' Deb felt increasingly irritated. 'To be clear, I'm not interested in an apology. I guess I just thought you might understand that this... I don't know. Puts our relationship in a weird position.'

'Do we have a relationship?' Kyle asked. 'I feel like you decided we didn't. It's not a good time. I'm OK with that, by the way. I just wanted some clarity, and to know that we were on decent terms with each other.'

On decent terms. The phrase annoyed her further, though, in her heart of hearts, Deb knew that her feelings weren't Kyle's fault. He couldn't be expected to understand how she felt. But she was too worked up to be grounded and calm now. The news about the eviction and Gyle Head – finally being able to put some specifics to Grandma Elise's story – had set a bomb off, it felt like, in her emotional life. She had known what had happened to her grandmother for some time now, but not the extent of it. And knowing that it had all happened so close to where she sat now – on land that she could visit and walk on – somehow brought everything to the surface, and she couldn't lock her feelings away anymore.

'Oh, for...' Deb exhaled forcefully. 'Whatever. Forget I said anything.'

Kyle looked concernedly over at her. Deb wiped tears from her eyes.

'Deb. I didn't want to upset you,' he said, slowly. 'I'm sorry... I should go.' He stood up.

'Fine.' Deb stood up and led him to the front door, her breathing shaky.

She didn't want him to go, not really. But she knew that if he stayed, she would get more and more upset, and nothing good would come of it.

He stopped to put on his boots.

'Deb...' he began, reaching out for her arm. 'Can we just talk?'

'I think it's best if you go,' she said, choking back tears. There was nothing to be gained by him staying, as much as part of her wanted to bury her head in his wide, strong chest and take comfort there.

'All right,' Kyle sighed, giving her a sad, tentative smile as he turned and left. Deb shut the door behind him and burst into tears.

Try as she might, she just couldn't make it work with Kyle Abernethy. Was it her? Was it him? Or, was it the crushing weight of her family legacy that she couldn't seem to move beyond?

Deb thought about calling Janice, but knew what her mother would say, and it wasn't helpful. Janice would tell her that Kyle couldn't be trusted, and would only bring her pain. That she could only rely on herself. But, what if that wasn't true? What if it was Deb's own family inheritance of pain – that shard of glass in her heart that all the Sutherland women shared – that was to blame?

If it was, then Deb had no clue how to pull that glass out of her own heart and move on. That glass was all she knew, and it had protected her from connecting to anyone very deeply, all her life. Because connecting to others – deeply and with love – made you vulnerable to them, and that was where the pain came from.

For the first time, Deb was starting to reflect that perhaps that story might not be true. And, if it wasn't, then she had no idea how she was supposed to live differently.

She listened to Kyle's car door slam and the engine start. She went to the window of the lounge and watched him drive away, feeling a terrible tug at her heart.

EIGHTEEN

I want to give it another go, Deb. We had something good.

Deb woke up and reached for her phone to turn off the alarm, knocking her grandmother's diary off the bedside table. It hit the rug with a soft *thunk*. She'd fallen asleep reading it again last night, and, though it made her feel sad, it also gave her a sense of connection to her grandmother.

However, when she peered owlishly at her phone, blinking at the time display and feeling like she'd only slept for an hour instead of seven, she was taken aback to find that Dan had texted her in the middle of the night.

She reached for her reading glasses and put them on to read the message again.

I want to give it another go. I'm sorry for being an idiot.

She sat up in bed. So far, she hadn't responded to any of Dan's messages.

Again, here was Dan with what *he* wanted. Did *she* want to get back with *him*? Deb let out a long sigh. She wasn't sure what she wanted right now. She had thought for a brief moment that something might happen with Kyle, but that didn't seem likely now...

Deb had replayed the last time she'd seen him in her mind multiple times. She had gone to message Kyle several times, to apologise, to try and explain, but she couldn't think of what to say. Was she wrong to want more empathy from him? Or had he really been *that* insensitive?

If I felt it was wrong, then it was wrong, she reasoned, taking her glasses off and rubbing her eyes. Better to just leave it.

And now, here was Dan.

She had been feeling quite lonely, it had to be said. The thing with Dan was, even though they had been through some hard times together, not all of what had happened had been his fault. He'd been patient with her through all of the endometriosis: it couldn't have been easy, being with a partner who was so incapacitated all the time.

If he was ready to change, would it be worth trying again? They had had some good times. And, at least Dan understood what she had gone through.

Deb had always thought that she was someone who valued personality and shared values more than looks, or "chemistry", which, frankly, she had never believed in. But that was before.

Now, she believed in chemistry. It was a real, unfortunate, cringeworthy thing and it had made her deeply uncomfortable, at this stage.

Wouldn't it be better to choose someone for whom sex wasn't really a priority?

Okay, let's talk, she replied.

The phone rang in her hand almost immediately.

'Err... hi,' she answered, clearing her throat.

'Hi. Sorry, it's early. I just thought, strike while the iron's hot and all that,' he gabbled. He sounded nervous.

'I'm actually still in bed. It's...' she squinted at the time on her phone '... seven fifty.'

'Sorry. Should I call back later?' He sounded so apologetic that Deb felt instantly guilty.

'No, it's all right.' She got out of bed and put on her robe. 'I'm just getting up.'

'Right. How are you feeling?' he asked.

'All right, thanks,' she answered, a little surprised. The last time they'd spoken, Dan hadn't seemed very interested in her recovery. In fact, it had seemed like he resented her and it.

'That's good. I was worried about you.'

'Were you?' Deb was genuinely surprised.

'Of course. And, look. First things first. I was an absolute idiot, Deb. I'm so sorry,' he sighed. 'I was an idiot about everything. I don't know why I got so... weird about everything. I should have supported you with the operation and everything... and I didn't. It was a shitty way to be.'

'It wasn't great.' Deb walked into the kitchen, filled up the kettle with water and lit the gas hob, settling it on the aged range cooker that sat at one side of the kitchen.

'I know. All I can say is that I think I got... scared... of how much you needed me. You'd never been like that before, you know? You're always so independent.'

'I'd just had major surgery, Dan. Of course I was going to lose my independence for a while,' Deb snapped. 'It would have been the decent, normal, human thing to just step up and care for me, like I would have cared for you. Or anyone.'

'I know. I don't know what to say but sorry.' Dan sounded miserable, and, despite her better instincts, Deb felt a little sorry for him.

Don't be sorry for him, she chided herself. *Don't you dare.*

'Well, I appreciate the apology,' she said, guardedly.

'Can I see you? Maybe take you out for dinner? I think there are other things we should talk about.' His voice was measured, but Deb detected a note of hope underneath. 'And, if we are broken up for good, then we at least need to discuss you coming to get your stuff, or what we do with the flat.'

She was still due to pay rent on their two-bedroom flat at the end of the month. Deb was aware of it, of course, but she'd been trying not to think about it; organising the party was keeping her busy, and the stress of the situation just made her want to turn her brain off and think about literally anything else.

'Okay. Well, I guess we do need to talk about that,' she sighed. 'A coffee and a walk would be better.'

'Okay. I'll come to you, if you like,' he volunteered. 'It'd be nice to see where you are.'

For a moment, Deb had a moment of pause. She didn't really want Dan in her new peaceful haven of Loch Cameron, but it would be much more convenient than going back to Glasgow, which she really didn't have time to do.

'Okay, then,' she said. 'I'm free next week.'

'I'll look at my calendar and see what works. I'll text you.' He sounded relieved. 'Thanks, Deb. I miss you.'

'Let's just meet for coffee,' she said, carefully. She didn't want to commit herself to anything. Dan might have wanted to get back together, but she hadn't thought about it at all, since she'd been in Loch Cameron. She couldn't say that she'd missed him. Was this really a good idea? When she had left Glasgow a few weeks ago, she would have said that she was done with Dan. But, there was a history there, and Dan had been with her through some of her darkest times.

The prospect of a relationship – or even casual sex – with a new person was intimidating. At least Dan knew her, and there were no surprises. He'd been less than understanding about the operation, but Deb also didn't feel intimidated by the thought of being naked in front of him – though the thought also didn't fill her with excitement, either.

Perhaps it would be better to aim for *comfortable* over *thrilling* – and, maybe, a second chance was what she and Dan needed. Maybe they could make it work. Maybe that was the best plan.

Maybe.

NINETEEN

'Well, you could have warned me you were coming,' Janice grumbled as she opened the door to her flat in the small block she'd lived in ever since Deb was a kid. 'I haven't cleaned up. The place is a tip.'

Nice to see you too, Mum, Deb thought, but knew better than to say it.

She hadn't been able to get Janice on the phone much over the past week or two and had been leaving constant messages. *Mum. Give me a call and let me know you're okay.* Janice had texted briefly, here and there, and there had been the evening when Deb had called her and tried to talk about the diary.

But, aside from that, Janice had been very quiet, and Deb had become worried. So, she'd decided that morning to drive over and see her mum. Plus, she still really wanted to talk to Janice about the diary.

'Well, I wanted to see you. And I didn't come to see how well you were getting on with the cleaning,' Deb replied, cheerfully. The drive over had taken hours and even though she'd got out and had a walk around a few times, her middle was aching.

'Just as well. I was wiped out yesterday,' Janice sighed. Deb frowned, looking her mother over. She didn't look well. She was pale, and her hair was scraggly. She wasn't as sprightly as she normally was. Deb could tell that because she'd surprised her mum with a visit, she hadn't had the opportunity to prepare herself for Deb and pretend she was better than she actually was. It gave Deb a terrible feeling of sadness to see her like this.

'How did it go? The appointment?' Deb took off her shoes and hung up her jacket. She'd brought a few provisions on the way and, when she opened the fridge, was glad that she had – there was almost nothing inside apart from a carton of milk and a few old-looking tomatoes. 'Mum. You need to do a shop.'

'I just haven't had the energy.' Her mum sighed, and slumped into a chair. 'I will, though. The appointment was fine. Stop worrying.'

'Good. Well, I'll do an order while I'm here.' Deb got out her phone and tapped on one of the supermarket apps she had set up. 'You know that I'll do it for you anytime.'

'I didn't want to bother you, love,' Janice said, weakly.

Until now, the arrangement had been that Janice would let Deb know if she needed groceries, but her neighbour Beatrice often went to the shops for her and Janice seemed to prefer it that way, despite the fact that Deb had her usual grocery shop on repeat order and only had to go through a couple of screens to make it happen.

'Mum. We've gone through this. You're not bothering me at all.' Deb rolled her eyes as she unpacked the bag of groceries she had with her: a loaf of bread, a couple of pints of milk, some bananas, a packet of chocolate biscuits, a few tins of baked beans. It wasn't much, but she was glad she'd brought something.

'Don't roll your eyes at me, Deborah Sutherland,' Janice reprimanded her.

'Sorry. I'm making you beans on toast, though.' Deb opened one of the tins and put some bread in the toaster. 'I read

Grandma Elise's diary, by the way. I see what you mean about it being sad. It's heartbreaking. I've been so wanting to talk to you about it.'

'I couldn't read much of it,' Janice confessed. 'Made me too depressed. I only found it a few years back, in a box with some other things of hers. Nothing much else of interest.'

'It's so sad that she lost Tom, her brother. Did you read the part about how Mrs Smith broke his ankle and his thumb, beating him? Horrifying.' Deb shook out the baked beans into a saucepan and turned the gas on underneath it, then got two plates down from a cupboard and went to a drawer for cutlery, only to find that the drawer was empty. The sink was full, and so Deb ran the hot tap and started washing up.

'Yes. Different times, but she was unlucky.' Janice leaned back in her chair, looking tired.

'That's an understatement,' Deb said, washing a stack of dirty plates and placing them on the drier. Then, she put some slices of bread in the toaster and stirred the beans. 'Her and Tom were abused, in foster care. It's shocking. And after losing their parents and their home. I mean, you can read between the lines in the diary and see that her parents were probably alcoholics.'

'Oh, very likely. Grandma never touched a drink. She had a horror of it.' Janice closed her eyes.

'Did you ever meet Tom? Your uncle, then?' Deb asked.

'No. She mentioned him a couple of times; I knew she had a brother, but that he wasn't around anymore. I never knew the story until I read the diary.'

'It's so sad that they lost each other. He could have been such a support to her in her life, and she to him. Maybe Grandma Elise wouldn't have felt so alone if she had her brother around, and...'

'Listen, love. I'll have that later. I need to lie down for a bit,' Janice interrupted her.

'You're not going to eat? It'll be ready in a minute.' Deb looked over, askance: there was so much more she wanted to talk about in the diaries. 'I wanted to ask you...'

But, Janice had suddenly slumped in her chair. 'Oh, no,' Deb muttered, and knelt in front of her mother. 'Mum? Are you all right?'

'I'm just tired, love,' Janice said in a low voice. 'Can you help me to bed?'

'Of course.' Deb turned off the heat under the beans. The toast popped, making her jump, but she left it where it was.

Fortunately, everything was on one level, so Deb didn't have far to walk with Janice, who took everything at a shuffle. Once she'd got Janice into bed, Deb went back to the kitchen, picked up a banana and made a quick cup of tea and took it into the bedroom.

'Here. Eat this, at least.' She unpeeled the banana and handed it to Janice. 'When was the last time you ate a decent meal?' she asked her mother, thinking with a sinking horror in her stomach how easy it would have been for her not to have driven over today.

'I don't know. A couple of days ago.' Janice ate the banana in careful bites, then sat up slowly to drink the tea. 'I get too tired to cook.'

Deb swore to herself.

'*Mum.* This is why ready meals exist. Or I can come over and cook for you, freeze some stuff up so you can just microwave it. Or get Beatrice to come over and make you a sandwich or something. You know she wouldn't mind.'

'I will do no such thing. Beatrice has her own life.' Janice handed Deb the banana skin. 'It's the dialysis. Let me sleep and I'll be right as rain later. Then I'll go to the shops.'

'You're not going to the shops in this state. I'll get a shop delivered,' Deb repeated, showing Janice the supermarket app on her phone. 'Look. It's ready to go.'

'Fine,' Janice sighed, drank a little more tea and handed the mug back to Deb. 'Can I sleep now?'

'Of course.' Deb took the mug and went back to the kitchen, where she ordered Janice's standard food selection. She viewed the list sadly. They were meagre choices. Janice insisted on having the supermarket value version of everything, despite the fact that Deb paid, and was more than happy to add in some better quality bits and bobs. Today, she'd added in some things she knew her mum liked: some good quality ice cream, a pack of chocolate brownies, kiwi fruit, strawberries, diet cola. They were all things that Janice viewed as occasional luxurious treats, and things that Deb knew other people didn't even think were that special.

That was Grandma Elise's influence, again, she thought, as she sat down at the small kitchen table with its ceramic tile top and ate her beans on toast alone, trying not to cry. Grandma Elise had, according to her little diary, gone hungry for much of her childhood.

Deb remembered that Janice had told her, while she'd never gone without food, as a child, there hadn't been many treats on the table. Janice had grown up on simple, cheap vegetables and the cheap cuts of meat here and there: tinned food and simple cooking. It wasn't bad – at least we ate, Janice would say – but it had given her a lifelong horror of what she thought of as *extravagance* with food.

This scarcity mindset had always made Deb so sad for Janice – and herself. Growing up, she'd been so aware of how careful Janice was with money and food, and there was something in that fervent dislike of extravagance that always made her anxious. She'd had to consciously make herself try new foods as an adult, and get out of the habit of working out how much each portion of food would cost per meal.

She finished her meal, and opened the diary again. Janice hadn't wanted to talk about her mother, again, like she never really did, despite posting Deb the diary. The resentment and anger was deep for Janice – Deb knew that. She wondered if her mother would ever get over it and see Grandma Elise for who she really was – a scared, lonely and hungry girl who had lost everything and everyone she once loved.

Deb could see that: the diary made her see it, if she had ever doubted it before. And, in a way, she wondered if that was why Janice had sent it to her in the first place: Janice knew that she couldn't forgive her mother, but perhaps also knew that Grandma Elise needed understanding. If Janice couldn't give it to her, then perhaps she knew that Deb could.

So, perhaps, on some level, that was Janice's act of love for her mother. Deb let out a long sigh, and put her head on the table.

She didn't want to leave her mum in this state, but Janice made it very hard to let anyone help her. What was Deb going to do?

TWENTY

'Lovely day for it,' Dan called out to her across the car park of the Loch Cameron Inn. It was raining and he was wearing his brown parka with the fur hood up, faded blue jeans and muddy walking boots. 'Just as well I came prepared.'

'Yes, it's a little bit damp today.' Deb laughed nervously as she approached him. 'Did you find it okay?'

'Yeah. Bit off the beaten track, isn't it? Hi.' He leaned forward shyly and planted a kiss on her cheek. 'You look great.'

'Thanks.' In fact, Deb had purposefully dressed down for the occasion, wearing a baggy jumper, jeans and walking boots as well, all of it under a bulky black puffy coat. She'd tied her mid length blonde hair up in a ponytail – thinking that she really needed to get her roots done – and applied a minimal makeup. She was going for "I'm doing fine without you, but also not making an effort for you".

When she'd checked in with Janice that morning on the phone, she had neglected to tell her that she was seeing Dan. She definitely would not approve of Deb meeting up with him. It made Deb edgy. Deep down, she had the sense that she might be making a mistake, but there was something in her that felt compelled to see Dan – if only to tie up loose ends, or make sure that she was doing the right thing, one way or the other.

'It's good to see you,' he added.

'And you,' she said, more to be polite than anything. Actually, she wasn't sure how she felt about seeing Dan. It was... strange. Dan belonged in Glasgow: in their flat, in the city, where they sometimes met for dinner or to go out with friends; he didn't belong here, in Loch Cameron. Her new haven.

'So, this is where you've been hiding out.' Dan looked around him, at the beautiful old stone inn with its small, old fashioned windows and hanging baskets. Even in the rain, they were a vivid riot of colour.

'Not really hiding. Working.' Deb zipped up her coat; the sky had been clear when she'd left the cottage. Typical.

'I know. I was just kidding. How's the job going?'

'Good, thanks. Busy.' She nodded. There was an uncomfortable silence. 'So. Walk?'

'I was thinking that we could go inside and have coffee,' he suggested, gesturing to the grey sky.

'Let's get a coffee to go and walk around the loch. I think it's going to stop in a minute,' Deb replied. She had no desire to sit in the Loch Cameron Inn so that all the locals could observe her love life falling apart. Or, whatever this was. Plus, she needed a good walk. She'd been working at her laptop all morning.

'Right you are. Just a bit of freshness in the air anyway, right?' Dan gave her a cheeky smile that she hadn't seen for a long time.

'Exactly,' she chuckled. 'Shall we?'

As Deb led the way into the Inn, she was struck by how cosy it was. Inside the front door, a coat rack and a pot of umbrellas made it seem as if they'd just walked into someone's house and not a pub. There was also a bowl of water on the floor and a shelf above it with a jar of dog biscuits; a hand-lettered sign said DOGGY FILL UP STATION.

In the main bar, there were a variety of seating areas – some wooden tables and chairs and some comfy-looking upholstered chairs in flower patterned fabrics and tartans. A log fire crackled in a large fireplace, outside which sat a number of polished copper pots, containing fire tongs and various other tools that Deb would have been hard pressed to name. The walls boasted paintings of rural scenes: cows in lush-looking pastures, stags with majestic horns, and fields of purple heather. The feel was comfortable and relaxed: a few stacks of newspapers and magazines sat here and there on tables and on the bar, not looking as though they had been artfully arranged, but more that they had just been put down after being read.

There was another room that led off the main bar, in which a couple of elderly men were sitting at the bar, watching a snooker match on an ancient looking TV that was mounted to the wall.

Deb hadn't managed to visit before, mostly because she didn't like the idea of coming into a pub on her own. Worse, she really didn't like the idea of walking into one which was likely full of locals that would stare at her, as a lone woman and a stranger.

'Hello, dear,' a smartly-dressed woman, perhaps in her early seventies, called out as they walked in. 'Welcome.' She wore a cream blouse with a lace collar and a red cardigan draped around her shoulders. Her hair was arranged in a neat, platinum blonde bob and she exuded an air of efficiency and friendliness that Deb liked immediately.

'Hi,' Deb replied, noticing the woman's smartly manicured hands, with pearlized white nails, as she approached the long wooden bar. 'Can we get some coffees to go?'

'Of course, dear. What kind? We have the machine, so, all the usuals.' The woman pointed behind her to a gleaming silver espresso machine. Deb was pleasantly surprised: she'd assumed that, in a country inn in a remote Scottish village, the only coffee options would be instant, or instant with a slug of whisky.

'Cappuccino please.' Deb looked at Dan.

'Yes, same, please. Thanks,' he said, coming to stand next to Deb at the bar. 'This is cosy, isn't it?' he said, mirroring her thoughts. 'Wouldn't mind a local like this.'

'It's nice,' she agreed. 'This is the first time I've been inside, actually.'

'Won't be a mo.' The woman was busying herself with the coffee machine. 'Havenae seen ye before, lassie.'

'Ah, no. I'm just up here helping the laird with the May Day party,' Deb explained.

'Ah! Deb, is it?' The woman turned around with a big smile on her face. 'He told me ye might be in. In which case, these're on the hoose.'

'Did he?' Deb was surprised, but then she remembered that Hal had said something to this effect in an email.

'Aye. Hal's pickin' up yer bill, whilst yer here.' The landlady nodded. 'I'm Dotty, by the way. I run this place wi' my husband Eric.' She held out her hand, and Deb shook it.

'It's lovely to meet you, Dotty.' Deb grinned. 'This is my... friend, Dan.' She didn't know how to introduce him, but Dan didn't seem offended.

'Hi.' He shook Dotty's hand in turn.

'Lovely tae meet ye both,' Dotty said, turning back to the coffee machine to finish the drinks. 'How're ye settlin' intae Loch Cameron, dear?' she said, over her shoulder.

'Fine thanks. It's really nice here,' Deb said, sincerely.

'Aye. We do alright,' she agreed. 'Yer stayin' up at the Ross cottage, is that right?'

'Yes, that's right.'

'Ah, lovely. We've had a few lassies stay up there in the past years. Funny, really – just the girls. Must be somethin' about Gretchen's auld place, eh.' Dotty chuckled.

'Well, it does have very cute décor,' Deb agreed. 'Maybe that's it.'

'Maybe.' Dotty handed them two cappuccinos in takeaway cups. 'There y'are, darlin'.'

'Thank you so much.' Deb almost felt that it would be quite nice to stay in the Inn after all now, but the rain outside had stopped and been replaced by a blue sky again. 'We're off for a walk around the loch now.'

'Ohh, enjoy! I should get oot myself.' Dotty gave them a little wave. 'Remember, Deb, anytime ye want lunch or dinner or a coffee, just pop in. On the hoose.'

'I will. That's so kind. Thanks!' Deb grinned.

'She seems friendly. Nice to have an infinite supply of free food and drink too. I'm jealous,' Dan said as they walked out of the Inn.

'It's definitely a nice perk of the job,' Deb agreed.

Outside, the loch glittered, reflecting the midday sun. Here and there, boats bobbed on the water, some moored at the edge on the pebbled beach, and, further away, a couple of small fishing boats on the wider expanse. The boats looked to be in good order, painted in smart white and blue or in jolly reds and yellows, with names like *Roamer* and *Salty Sue*.

'So.' Dan sipped his coffee as they made their way onto the cobbled high street. 'It's good to see you. I think I've said that already, actually.' He tutted at himself. 'Sorry.'

'That's all right.' She warmed her hands on the cardboard cup; even on a sunny day, it could be cold by the loch, and it was still only spring. 'Look, Dan. Things got really bad between us. I know that it was hard, having me laid up at home, recuperating from the operation. But you behaved really badly. And even though you've said sorry, you really hurt me. And, you have to admit that things weren't exactly brilliant before then.'

They turned along the muddy footpath that ran alongside the loch.

'I guess. But we always got on,' he said, catching her eye as she looked up at him. 'I valued that.'

'Did we, though?' The haunting sound of a curlew rang out across the loch; as they walked farther away from the high street, it had grown quieter, so it was easier to hear birdsong and the wind in the trees. Deb wasn't much of a wildlife expert, but she knew curlews because they were Janice's favourite bird. *I really should call mum*, she thought.

'I think we did,' he said, defensively. 'When we started going out, we had a lot of good times. Like that trip to Skye we had, in the campervan. And that first Christmas.'

'When we started going out, yes,' Deb argued. 'When you start seeing someone, you're supposed to have a good time, otherwise you wouldn't bother, right? That's the honeymoon period. A good relationship is when you still get on *after* the honeymoon period. I don't think we did.' She remembered that week on the Isle of Skye. Some people would probably have an intensely romantic time there. She and Dan had hired a camper van that had no heating and leaked, it had rained all week and he'd steadfastly refused to do anything romantic at all, like go for night time walks to look at the stars or to the Fairy Glen where she'd wanted to go. The first Christmas they'd been together had been fine, but she didn't remember feeling like it was anything special. With Dan, there was always a sense of anticlimax.

'I kinda thought we did,' he insisted. 'And, anyway, I think people have unrealistic expectations of relationships. They want them to be all sweetness and light all the time. Life's not like that.'

'Right... but you are supposed to *enjoy* being in your relationship, most of the time, still.' Deb sipped her coffee, which was surprisingly good. 'It's not unrealistic to expect to be happy. To be in love. To feel loved and respected. Have fun with, be silly.' *And have chemistry*, she thought, but didn't say.

'Of course. But I loved you. I still do.' He jammed his hands in his pockets and refused to meet her eyes. 'All right, I was rubbish at showing it. But I do. I can do better.'

'Dan... I can't respond to that,' Deb said, slowly. 'Please don't put pressure on me about this. You can't say that you love me when you treated me so disrespectfully. That wasn't love.'

'Why? Because I didn't do the washing up?' Dan swore under his breath. 'Come on, Deb. This is what I'm talking about. I'm human. I make mistakes. But I can still love you.'

'But you treated me completely awfully,' Deb said, starting to feel any remainder of friendly feeling she might have had for Dan being steadily replaced by irritation. It was like a cloud covering the sun. 'It wasn't the washing up, Dan. It was the constant complaints and implying that I was being lazy when actually it was excruciating for me even lying down. It was the gaslighting when I dared to say something about how you were acting. You made it sound like it was all in my head. Like you're doing now.'

'I'm not. You're just not listening. I...' he interrupted her.

'No, Dan. *You're* not listening.' Deb stopped walking and stood still. She took a deep breath of the cool, clear Loch Cameron air and felt it ground her. She felt the muddy path under her feet, and it was reassuring in its solidity. Loch Cameron had her back, in some kind of strange way that she couldn't explain. 'I can't continue to be in a relationship with you. Whatever feelings I had for you, you destroyed in the past months. But we were never that well suited, I don't think. We were both looking for something comfortable, unchallenging. Because we were both afraid of having something more than that, maybe. I don't know. But I don't want that anymore.'

'You've met someone else,' he replied, dully. 'That must be it.'

'Really?' Deb almost laughed. That was his go-to thought? That if Deb didn't want to go back to their substandard relationship, it must be because she was seeing someone else, and not because that was a healthy choice she had made for herself. 'That's what you think?'

'Haven't you? You look different. Glowy. Thinner. You've done your hair different, or something,' he said, a resentful tone in his voice now. Even though his words were technically a compliment, she knew that he didn't mean them that way.

'It's none of your business, but, yes, I have gone on a date.' Deb thought of Kyle, but she didn't feel compelled to say anything else. Kyle wasn't any of Dan's business. It wasn't as if they actually *were* seeing each other. *Not anymore, anyway,* she thought with a pang.

'Hm.' Dan looked away. 'Well, I did my best, Deb. I came after you. I said sorry. I don't really know what else you want me to do, but if that's not enough, then that's all I've got.' He scuffed his feet in the mud. Somehow, the gesture made him look like a sulky teenager.

'It's not enough,' Deb replied simply. It was hard to say, but she knew that she had to be honest and open. 'I appreciate you coming to see me, Dan. And I appreciate the apology. Really, I do.' She let out a deep breath. 'But, I think we can both do better than a relationship where neither of us are truly happy, just for the sake of being with someone. I want to do better than that.'

Dan gave her a long stare, then nodded.

'All right,' he sighed. 'In which case, I assume you're going to move out of the flat.'

'Yes.' Deb had been trying not to think about that, but Dan was right. If they really were breaking up and not giving it another go, then she had to find a new place to live: she couldn't stay in the cottage forever, especially as it was currently free. 'Can I finish the job off here, and then come and move my stuff out? I know it's maybe not ideal for you to have all my stuff there. But I don't really have time to look for a new place to live while I'm organising this party. And I'll keep paying my half of the rent until I move out.'

If she was still paying her half of the rent, then Deb felt that she was within her rights to keep her stuff there until she was ready to move it out.

'I guess so. I'll just move it all into the spare room.' He sounded mulish. Deb resisted the temptation to ask him whether he was going to move all of her furniture into the spare room too – considering that she'd bought most of it.

'Okay. I'll be in touch, then.' She wrapped her arms around herself; the temperature had dropped, and clouds were threatening rain again. Despite the inhospitable weather, she still felt that the village and the loch were supporting her somehow. Being here, in Loch Cameron, did make her feel connected to the land in a way that she hadn't before, and it gave her strength. Clarity, from the cleanliness of the air and the light, and strength from the dark, rich, fertile earth under her feet.

'I'm going to head off,' Dan muttered. 'Take care, Deb.'

'And you.' She wondered whether she should have kissed him on the cheek or something, but he was holding back, standing away from her, and she picked up the non-verbal cues that he didn't want to make physical contact. That was okay with her.

He turned and walked back the way they'd come, around the loch back to the high street.

Deb didn't want to have to walk with him back to the car park at the Loch Cameron Inn and watch him drive away – that was almost too sad, in some ways. Thankfully, there was another route back to the cottage from where she stood.

Goodbye, Dan, she thought, as she watched him go. She was glad that he'd come over, in fact; now, she knew for absolute sure that there was no future with him. What she had felt had just been loneliness, but that was no reason to jump back into a relationship that hadn't worked for a long time. During their conversation, she'd had the opportunity to reflect, and compare the way she had felt in her relationship with Dan with the way that Kyle Abernethy made her feel. It was a case of apples and oranges. With Dan, she'd never known anything like the excitement she got from a touch of Kyle's hand.

It started to rain again and Deb pulled up her hood. As she walked along the muddy track, the rain got heavier, but she was enjoying being cosy inside her coat: it was quite waterproof, and she was warm from marching along.

Despite the difficulty of her meeting with Dan, Deb felt surprisingly upbeat. The rain smelt good – of heather and grass and spring – and it felt as though it was cleansing her. She felt fresh and alive.

I'm grateful for this moment, she thought, as she walked along, listening to the curlew's song that she had heard earlier. *I'm grateful that I'm not Dan's girlfriend anymore. And I'm even grateful that I have to find a new place to live. Because then I can really start my new life.*

Being able to start again struck Deb as a blessing rather than a curse as she walked back to the cottage. She was aware that she wouldn't always have seen things this way, but so much had changed over the past few months.

She'd been so focused on what had changed in her body – and, now, in her work and personal life – that she hadn't necessarily realised that something had shifted in her heart, too. But it had. And the thing that had changed was that, now, she felt full of hope.

TWENTY-ONE

The Post Office sat at the far end of Loch Cameron's cobbled high street, and it was possibly the smallest that Deb had ever been in.

She was there to collect some packages that hadn't been able to be delivered to the castle: there had been some issue with a delivery truck that had broken down, and so Deb had arranged for four large boxes of floral wrist corsages to be delivered to the Post Office. She'd brought the car down, and was hoping that the boxes weren't too bulky, otherwise she'd need a hand carrying them out.

It was just a week until the party, and Deb was feeling the burn of what she liked to call the "Event Horizon". It was the same for every event she'd ever worked on: invariably, as the event got closer, she found that, no matter how organised she'd been, and how many eventualities she had anticipated, there would be last-minute crises that had to be sorted out. Mostly, she thrived on the pressure of getting everything done in time, but, this time around, she was feeling more exhausted than usual.

Hal had replied to her email about her grandmother's diary

and her discovery that Elise was one of the children who had been evicted from Gyle Head, all those years ago. But it had been a short, somewhat terse email.

> Deb – thank you for this. I will read in more detail soon and respond. In the meantime, please accept my thoughts and best wishes. Hal.

The brevity of Hal's email annoyed Deb deeply, and made her even more emotional about the diary than she had been before. The entries had been playing on her mind. She kept thinking about her poor grandmother, wishing she could talk to her. Wishing she could hug her.

Plus, she was worried about Janice. Beatrice had been popping in casually to check in on her most days, which Deb was deeply grateful for, but it sounded as though Janice was struggling. She had certainly been struggling when Deb had visited, the week before. Deb had ended up staying overnight, sleeping on the sofa, and made Janice eat a good breakfast when she'd woken up, bleary and weak, the morning after. But Deb couldn't be there all the time to make sure her mum ate and looked after herself.

Beatrice had reported that on more than one day in the past week, she'd gone in to find Janice exhausted, in bed, not having eaten or drunk anything since her last visit. Deb had called her mum's doctor, but she hadn't been a huge help. She'd asked if a carer could go around to look after Janice, and the doctor had said she would look into it, but Deb worried that while that was *being looked into*, Janice might starve or have an accident or be too weak to get out of bed, and she wouldn't know until it was too late.

She was glad that the party was almost here, because that meant she could go home soon. Being closer to Janice would set her mind at ease.

'Oh. Excuse me,' Deb said, automatically, as she squeezed past the man in the small walkway in front of the counter, between two revolving greetings card displays and the wall, which was adorned with a local noticeboard. *Dog walker, reasonable rates. Spick and Span Local Cleaner, call for availability.*

There was more than one advert for holiday homes, lettered in careful block capitals: Deb wondered who would enquire about a holiday home nowadays without seeing any pictures – but, then, she supposed that she'd ended up at the cottage she was staying in, sight unseen. All taken care of by the Laird.

'No problem.' The voice was familiar: Deb looked up to find herself staring into Kyle Abernethy's dark, soft lashed eyes.

'Oh!' she didn't have anything more sophisticated to say. 'Hi.'

They were still standing almost nose to nose, because the queue space for the counter was so narrow. Deb stepped to one side, so that her body wasn't aligned as intimately with Kyle's.

'Hi.' He looked guarded.

'Fancy seeing you here.' She attempted flirtation and was immediately mortified. *Ugh, Deb*, she thought. *Come on.*

It was uncomfortable seeing him out of the blue. *I guess that was always going to happen in Loch Cameron eventually*, she thought. It wasn't an anonymous city where you could never see the same person twice.

Deb knew that things were difficult between her and Kyle, but she didn't want them to be. She wanted to be friends again, at the very least. All right, if she was honest – more than friends. But she also couldn't reconcile the Kyle that gave her The Feelings with the Kyle who didn't appear to care about her grandmother being made homeless on the very land that he now owned. Was it his fault? Of course not. Could he have seemed more sympathetic and interested? Yes. A lot.

'Indeed. Anyway, better be off.' He nodded curtly and strode towards the Post Office door.

What? Was that it? Kyle was acting as if they were strangers. The very least he could do was to be civil and have a polite conversation.

How are you? Fine, thanks, and you? You're looking well. Ah, thank you! The weather's been fine for the time of year. It has, hasn't it? Anyway, must dash! It wasn't hard. Everyone knew the drill. You'd have that level of polite conversation with the bin men, never mind someone you'd kissed. And when that kiss had been as good as it was with Kyle, then...

The lady behind the counter called Deb forward, so she had to return her attention to her packages for a moment.

'I'm picking up four boxes, I think? Deborah Sutherland,' she said, getting her phone out. 'I have a code to scan here. I think delivery was attempted a couple of days ago.'

'Right you are, dear.' The woman behind the counter was middle aged with two auburn plaits arranged in buns at each side of her head. She wore a sweatshirt that bore the picture of a famous actor's face poking out between the broken boards of a door, and the words HERE'S JOHNNY! in black capitals underneath it. It was a famous horror movie; Deb supposed she was a little surprised that the postmistress in Loch Cameron was also, apparently, a horror movie buff.

'Over in the corner. I put them to one side,' the woman explained. 'Bit big, you see. Everyone was trippin' up on them.'

Deb looked over at the corner where four huge boxes were, indeed, piled up. They were much bigger than she'd been expecting, and she had a moment of sudden panic, wondering how on earth she was going to pick up even one of them, never mind all four. AND get them to the car outside.

Gingerly, she went over to the boxes and pried up one corner of the top one. It wasn't too heavy, but it was bulky and almost as long as she was, and Deb could see that getting it out of the Post Office was going to be a performance. She sighed, and picked up the top box as best she could, angling her body in such a way that she could hold it sideways and shuffle it along the narrow corridor.

'I'd give you a hand, but I've put ma back oot,' the post-mistress called after her.

'No worries,' Deb replied, with gritted teeth. She dragged the first box to the entrance and laid it on the floor so that she could open the door. Carefully, she edged it outside and onto the pavement, until she felt her fingers suddenly lose their grip on the box. She grappled with it for a moment, but it was no use.

The box fell flat onto the pavement outside with a flat smack.

Deb let out a loud exclamation and jumped backwards. It was an over-reaction, because the box was nowhere near her feet, and it also wasn't heavy enough to hurt her if it had landed on her boots.

Outside, Kyle stood next to the red pillar box, frowning at his phone. He looked up in surprise.

'A little help?' Deb said, knowing that her tone was sardonic, but she really couldn't help it. *Don't worry about me, I'm just struggling over here.*

'You seem to have it under control.' He narrowed his eyes slightly and put his hands in his pockets.

'Wow. Thanks.' Deb bent over and picked up the corner of the box, dragging it to her car which was parked on the kerb. She blipped her car key to open the boot, and started manoeuvring the box into it.

'Oh, for the love of... let me do that.' Kyle came up behind her and took the box, expertly slotting it into the limited boot space. 'There.' He nodded.

'There's three more, actually.' She looked up at him, combatively, although she was also aware of everyone in the

Post Office seeing her with Kyle, the least popular man in Loch
Cameron.

'Are you asking for my help with them?' He returned her
gaze, not smiling. 'Not what a rude person would do, probably.
Help a lady in distress.'

'I'm not in distress. I just have four large boxes I need to get
in the car. Help or don't help, it's up to you.'

'Well, obviously I will help,' he muttered.

'Fine. Come on, then.' She went back inside the Post Office
and pointed to the pile of boxes in the corner. 'You get one side,
I'll get the other.'

Kyle nodded, and picked up two of the boxes. 'You get the door,'
he said. Deb, not knowing what to say, turned around and opened it
as instructed. Kyle carried both boxes out to her car and added them
to the boot. 'The last one's not going to fit in there. You'll have to put
it on the back seat,' he said. Deb realised that he was dressed in a
sharp black business suit with an immaculate white shirt underneath: Kyle looked like he was on his way somewhere, and, now, she
realised, he had gotten box dust all over his jacket.

He went back into the Post Office and returned with the
final box. Deb opened the back door of the car and Kyle slid the
box in without any apparent difficulty.

'Thanks.' She smoothed her hair and wished she was
wearing something nicer than a pair of jeans and a T-shirt
under her parka. Not that she was interested in impressing Kyle
anymore, but she had standards, after all. You never wanted to
see anyone you had been on a date with, with your hair in a
tangle and no makeup on.

'No trouble.' Kyle brushed the dust off his suit.

'Going somewhere?' she asked.

'Just a meeting.' He looked away.

'So. How have you been?' Deb asked. It was just the polite
thing to say.

'All right. You?' He was very brief, and Deb could feel that there was something he wasn't saying.

'I'm okay.'

'Right.' There was a silence.

Dear lord, Deb thought. There was awkward, and then there was teenager-in-a-sulk monosyllabic. This was definitely the latter.

'Listen. I know we ended on a bad note, but I wouldn't have pegged you for this rude.' Deb felt a little exasperated.

'Oh, you wouldn't? Rude. Hmm.' He nodded. 'I just helped you with those boxes.'

'You know what I mean,' she replied. 'You're being weird with me. The least we can do is be pleasant to each other in public. Okay, we went on a date, and it didn't work out. There's no reason to be like this.'

'Well, I guess I was confused about why it didn't work out, and then I realised. Would have been nice of you to tell me,' he shot back.

'Tell you what?'

'I heard that you were back with your ex,' he said, crossing his arms over his chest. Deb did her best not to notice the way that his large biceps strained against his suit jacket.

'You heard... what?'

'It's fine. I just would have appreciated hearing it from you,' he continued.

'Hearing what from me?' Deb wanted to add, *if I'm back with Dan, it's the first I've heard about it.*

'That you were seeing him again. I don't want to get caught in the middle of... whatever that is. You using me to make him jealous, maybe. Whatever.' He shrugged.

'Umm... that's what you think I was doing, dating you?' Deb felt the anger rise in her. Kyle had a way of putting her back up like no one else she'd ever known. True, he also made her feel other things she'd never felt with anyone else, but that was by the by.

'Weren't you? It happens. I was a convenient distraction, if not.'

'I can't say that you were very convenient at all,' she retorted.

'Right. Gotcha. Well, I'd appreciate the honesty, next time. Not that there will be a next time,' he added. 'Good luck with the party.'

'But...' Deb protested, but Kyle was walking away.

'See you around, Deborah.' He crossed the street, got into his car and drove off.

What just happened? Deb stood next to her car, feeling as though her stomach had dropped into her shoes. She hadn't done anything wrong, and she definitely wasn't back with Dan. Yet, Kyle had made her feel as though she had done something utterly awful.

It was also clear that, as nice as Dotty at the Loch Cameron Inn was, she was also clearly quite chatty when it came to telling people all about what had happened on her premises. Deb shook her head, aghast at the degree to which her personal life was clearly the subject of local gossip. What exactly had Dotty said, and how had Kyle even heard that she and Dan had had a coffee? Was everyone talking about it? The crochet coven too? Or had Kyle just happened to bump into Dotty – and then just happened to end up talking about Deb? She had no idea.

Well, that's a small community for you, she thought. *But, I don't have to explain myself to anyone, let alone Kyle Abernethy.*

Part of Deb wanted to call Kyle and explain to him everything that had happened with Dan. How she had realised that Dan and her were a hundred per cent not going to happen again. But the obstinate part of her hated that idea, and resisted it.

If Kyle didn't have the patience or interest to talk to her

properly, then he could stay in the dark. If he wanted to jump to conclusions, then he was welcome to.

The fact that Deb was being just as stubborn as Kyle was being resistant occurred to her, but she ignored it.

It's his loss, she thought. It was what Janice would have said.

Part of her felt sad at the thought, but Deb was too busy to consider his feelings – or, even her own – right now. She had a week to finish getting ready for the party, and there was so much that needed to be done.

It was Kyle's loss but, maybe, it was hers too. Yet, she couldn't consider being with Kyle – even if that was an option, and he seemed to have very firmly indicated that it wasn't – knowing that he'd brushed off such a seismic event in her family history with a kind of *oh-well-it's-in-the-past* shrug. Family trauma was never just in the past. Deb could feel that loss resounding down the years from the 1930s to her life now, like an echo. That loss had affected Janice's life, and in turn, hers.

Okay, Kyle didn't know everything about her life. He didn't know what Janice was like. He didn't remember Grandma Elise. But he could have shown more compassion – especially if he cared about her, like he said he did.

She sighed and got into the driver's seat. Maybe after the party was over, she'd let herself think about that.

Maybe.

TWENTY-TWO

'Mum?' Deb had answered the phone when Janice had called, but instead of her usual cheery hello, there was the sound of panicked breathing at the other end of the line. 'Mum?' she repeated, frowning.

She was standing in the middle of Loch Cameron's bi-weekly food market, which was bustling with people wandering in all directions. At Anna's suggestion, she'd been checking out some of the local food producers with an eye to enlisting some of their products for the May Day party: so far, she'd talked to a lovely couple who ran a bakery stall, which was practically heaving with delicious cinnamon buns, hot cross buns, lemon Danish, chocolate pastry twists and all manner of other mouth-watering sweet treats. Deb had also sampled olive bread, crusty sourdough loaves and classic farmhouse granaries, as well as a moist and utterly delicious cherry madeira cake, a carrot cake which was frankly to die for, and a wonderfully moist pistachio and lavender sponge which she thought would be perfect for the party.

Janice was of the generation that found tech a little counter-intuitive, to say the least, so Deb waited for a second, assuming that her mother had done something like dropped her phone. She walked to the side of the street, by the iron railings that ran alongside a pathway alongside the loch edge, where it was a little less busy.

'Mum?' she repeated.

'Darling, I'm not too well.' Janice's voice was weak at the end of the line, and Deb felt a blooming panic tug at her middle. 'Can you come over? I wouldn't normally ask... it's just that I've... had a fall.'

Deb knew her mother well enough to know that if there had been any other option open to her instead of calling her daughter, then she would have done it.

'Where are you, Mum?' Deb turned away from the market stalls, and put her fingers in the ear that didn't have a phone next to it.

'I'm at home, darling.' Janice's voice wavered; Deb was shocked to hear that Janice was trying not to cry. Janice never cried. 'I... I can't get up. I think I might have broken my ankle.'

Oh, no.

'Mum!' Deb cried out, her heart pounding. 'You're... on the floor?'

'Yes.' Janice's voice was reedy. 'Can you come? I know it's a way. But I'm in a lot of pain.'

'Oh, god. Okay. I mean, it'll take me a few hours.' Deb looked at the time on her phone: it was midday, and to get to Glasgow, where Janice's flat was, would take at least three hours.

Three hours was too long to leave her mum lying in agony on the floor.

'All right. What I'm going to do is call an ambulance and then Beatrice, next door. I'll drive over, but you need help before I can get there.' Deb's crisis management skills kicked in, and she was grateful for them. 'Okay? I'm going to call Beatrice now.'

Beatrice had a spare key for emergencies.

'Uh, no. Don't bother her.' Janice was breathing heavily. Deb could only imagine how much pain she must be in. 'Please, I just want you. I don't want anyone to see me like this.'

'Mum. I literally can't get there for hours. You cannot lie on the floor with a broken ankle. No one could, not least a woman with ongoing kidney failure. Oh! You're supposed to go to dialysis today too.'

'Yes,' Janice said, weakly. 'I was just getting ready to go and I fell in the hallway.'

Deb swore under her breath.

'All right, Mum. I have to get off the phone so I can call an ambulance. If you're not there by the time I get home, then I'll follow you to the hospital. Okay?'

'Deborah. Please don't make a fuss,' Janice said.

'Mum. That is completely unreasonable,' Deb sighed. 'You've broken your ankle. You need your dialysis. An ambulance is not something you can refuse. Just keep your phone near to you.'

She ended the call, choking back tears. Deb had hardly ever witnessed Janice being vulnerable at all, even though she had been ill for a long time. Janice was impermeable, like a rock. That meant that if she was asking Deb for help now, then things were very bad. Deb tried not to think about her poor mum, lying with her ankle twisted under her, or the bone shattered and sticking through the skin, or in a pool of blood... there were so many possible scenarios.

Deb called the emergency services and gave them her mum's address, explaining what had happened and saying that she hoped a neighbour would be there to let them in. Next, she called Beatrice.

The phone rang several times before Beatrice's voice appeared at the other end of the line. Deb felt relief wash over her: for a moment, she had wondered what the ambulance would do if they hadn't been able to get in. Break the door down? Deb supposed that might be something they did, from time to time.

'Beatrice? It's Deb Sutherland. Janice's daughter,' she said, slightly out of breath as she was walking as fast as she could up the single track road that led from the end of Loch Cameron high street up to Queen's Point. She was lugging several bags of shopping.

'Oh, hello, dear.' Beatrice sounded as cheery as usual. 'How are you?'

'I'm all right, but Mum's had a fall. She says she's broken her ankle.' Deb huffed as she climbed the track, feeling the burn in her legs. She hadn't returned to her usual level of fitness yet after the operation, and as well as this making her out of breath, she could feel the soreness in her abdomen. She wanted to stop, but she was in a rush, and panic was driving her.

'Oh, lord! Why didn't she call me herself?' Beatrice cried. 'I'll go round now, dear. Are you coming?'

'I'm going to drive over, but it's going to take hours. I've called an ambulance. Can you be there and help her, say I'm on my way?' Deb felt her voice begin to crack. She suddenly felt powerless, being so far away and not being able to help.

'Of course! Poor Janice!'

'I know. I think she was too proud to call you,' Deb sighed, out of breath as she reached Queens Point. 'I'm coming now. I'm literally going to jump in the car now.'

'All right, dear. You take care, and I'll call you back on your mobile and let you know what's happening. Okay?' Deb knew that Beatrice was probably just as worried as she was, but she appreciated someone caring about her feelings enough to try and reassure her too. Tears choked Deb's throat at the kindness, but she swallowed them. She didn't have time for emotions right now.

'All right. Thanks, Beatrice. Thank you so much.'

Deb reached the cottage, dumped the bags of groceries in the kitchen, not even bothering to put anything away, grabbed a bottle of water and a banana for the drive and ran out to her car, pulling the cottage door shut behind her. Her heart was hammering.

Oh, god, please be all right, Mum, Deb prayed as she started the car and drove down the lane, onto the high street and out of Loch Cameron. *Please.*

TWENTY-THREE

The hospital smelt like all hospitals: antiseptic, vomit and despair. At least, that was how it smelt to Deb, who had always hated them. *Who liked hospitals?* she wondered, as she walked down one long corridor after another, looking for the ward that Beatrice had texted her the details of an hour earlier. Probably, if you worked in one, you got used to them, at least.

In fact, it had taken her five hours to reach the hospital in Glasgow – two hours longer than she'd expected, due to part of the motorway around Glasgow being closed. It had meant an excruciating detour, and at least an hour of bumper-to-bumper traffic. Deb had sobbed in frustration, desperate to get to Janice, but feeling that everything that could go wrong *was* going wrong. While driving and when stuck in traffic, she'd been checking her phone constantly for updates from Beatrice, and then, repeatedly calling the hospital, trying in vain to find out where her mum was. Her phone was dying, and she'd been in such a rush leaving the cottage that she hadn't picked up a charger for the car.

When she had finally pulled up to the hospital, she saw that her phone was on ten per cent battery, which just about summed up how she felt, too. She saw that she had a text and opened it, thinking that it was from Beatrice, hopefully telling her where to go when she got inside, but it was from Hal.

Deb – hope you're well. Sorry for my brief email about your family discovery the other day. I have now responded properly via email but you haven't responded, and I wanted to make sure you were all right. Do drop me a line or give me a call if you'd like to. Hal.

Deb stared at her phone for a moment. Of all times, *this* was when Hal chose to respond? She didn't have time to look at her emails right now, and her phone was about to die, anyway. She swore under her breath, then put her phone in her bag. She'd have to read Hal's email later.

'Mum!' After asking at the hospital reception and jogging up and down various long corridors and stairwells, Deb finally burst into the small room, finding a whey-faced Janice in bed with her leg in plaster and hooked up to a dialysis machine. Beatrice sat in a chair next to the bed, drinking a cup of tea.

'Oh, darling. You shouldn't have come,' Janice said as Deb buried her face in her mother's neck. 'I'm all right.'

'You're not all right!' Deb started crying again. All the tension of the drive over, being desperate to be with her mother and not being able to, worrying about her, imagining the worst, imagining how much pain Janice was in and how scared she must be – it all spilled out of her now, as she hugged her mother. 'I was so worried!' Her throat was so constricted with worry and tension that she could hardly get the words out.

'You shouldn't worry about me.' Janice gave her daughter a brief hug, and then pushed her away. 'Beatrice looked after me.'

'You've broken your ankle, and you're on dialysis. And you called me and *asked me to come*,' Deb said, angrily. She knew she shouldn't be angry with Janice, but after her horrendous journey and all the worry, her mother's typical push back – *I'm all right, I don't need help, I'm independent* – hurt.

Deb had no doubt that Janice was only ever acting out of love. She knew that her mother really believed that the best thing she could do for her daughter was *not to be a burden*, as she saw it. But she had never understood that every time she refused Deb's help, it felt like a slap in the face. It felt as though she was refusing her daughter's love.

That was how it felt now. Deb felt as though – on top of the worry and the panic – she had been punched in the chest by Janice's refusal of her love and her concern.

'Oh, I was in a bit of a state. I shouldn't have called you, but I wasn't thinking straight,' Janice sighed. 'I'm sorry you've had a wasted journey, sweetheart.'

'Well, it's not wasted, is it? You're lying in a hospital bed looking like death warmed up,' Deb argued. 'What kind of daughter would I be if I refused to come when you needed me?'

'Well, the ambulance people were very good. Got to me very quickly. Beatrice let herself in and she even made us all a cup of tea. I must say I felt better after that, and after they gave me some pain relief. So, you see. All fine.'

'Beatrice? Could you give us a minute?' Deb turned to her mother's elderly neighbour, who had been tactfully staying out of the conversation. 'I'd like to have a private word with Mum.'

'Of course, my pet.' Beatrice got up from the chair and took off her reading glasses, letting them hang on a chain around her neck. 'I'll pop down to the café and get us some tea.'

'Thank you. And thanks for everything today. I'm so grateful for your help,' Deb said, hoping that Janice had had the presence of mind and the politeness to thank Beatrice also; however, she doubted that she had. She wanted to turn to her mother and say, *this is how we thank people when they help us*, like she was talking to a child. But, she didn't, knowing that

Janice wouldn't take kindly to being talked to like that by her daughter.

'Look, Mum. I'm really happy that you say that you're okay.' Deb sat down heavily in the chair that Beatrice had vacated. She was really tired. 'But you had a fall, and you are vulnerable, because of the kidney failure. I know that you don't want to be vulnerable. I know that you don't want to be a burden on me or anyone else. And you aren't a burden. You never have been, because I love you, and part of being a family is taking care of each other when we need it.' She took Janice's hand.

'Deborah, please don't lecture me,' Janice said, an edge in her voice. 'It's my job to look after you, not vice versa. You are the child. Not me.'

'I'm not saying that you are a child. And I'm not lecturing you, Mum.' Deb made an effort to keep her voice level. 'But I am saying that you are, unfortunately, at the stage of life where you have to accept some help from someone. And that should be me, because I am your family. We're all the family we have. So don't push me away, please. It's hurtful.'

Janice looked at her daughter for a long moment, not saying anything.

'I would never want to hurt you, darling. That's the opposite of what I want,' she said, quietly. 'I never wanted to get in the way of you living your life. I only ever wanted the best for you, and I'm so very proud that you have achieved so much. I don't want you to have a sick old woman to look after. I'd rather die, and not be a burden.'

'Mum. I don't want you to die!' Deb felt the tears spilling down her cheeks once more.

'Oh, darling. Don't cry.' Janice's voice softened, and she reached up to wipe away the tear from her daughter's cheek. 'I'm sorry. I didn't want to upset you. That's the last thing I wanted to do.'

'I know.' Deb tried to wrestle her emotions back under

control. 'But you have to understand how it makes me feel when you say those things.'

'I see that it upsets you.' Janice took both of Deb's hands in hers. 'Listen, sweetheart. You have to understand how I grew up with Grandma. She was... strict. And cold. She'd had a hard life, and I suppose it made her look at the world in a certain way. She taught me that life was hard, and that you shouldn't complain. Just get on with it. With you, I never wanted to give you that message, about life being crappy. Because I think, if you think that, then you make it happen. You create your reality according to your expectations. But I also never wanted to get in your way. I love you so much, Deb. I know I'm ill. But I want you to go out there and shine your light in the world because I know how bright it is. How bright you are.'

'Oh, Mum.' Deb couldn't hold back the tears now: she felt them gushing from her like someone had turned on a rusty tap.

'It's all right. Let it out.' Janice held her, and rubbed Deb's back in slow circles as Deb sobbed. 'I promise to be better at letting you help me. Okay? I can't promise to change overnight, but now that I know how you feel, I'll do what I can.'

'Thank you.' Deb got the words out, laying her head lightly on her mother's shoulder. 'It doesn't mean I think you're weak. It's just because I love you, Mum.'

'I love you too, sweetheart.' Janice smoothed her hair. 'I'll love you forever.'

TWENTY-FOUR

It wasn't until the next day when Deb had driven back to Loch Cameron that she finally checked her emails. She'd ended up staying at her mum's flat overnight rather than face the long drive back to Loch Cameron, and by the time she and Beatrice had got home from the hospital, Deb was exhausted. She'd fallen into bed fully clothed, and woken up not knowing where she was.

After tidying up her mum's flat and saying a quick goodbye and thank you to Beatrice, Deb had gone back to visit her mum in hospital. Janice was looking a lot brighter, but she was being kept in until a care plan could be put in place to make sure that she could access her dialysis and get around all right with the broken ankle, which was going to take a while to heal.

Get on with you, I'm all right. Janice had given Deb a big hug. *I'm okay.*

I'll come back and see you soon, Deb had promised, feeling the tears well up in her eyes. She had to get back to Loch Cameron – there were too many things she had to be there for. There were deliveries up at the castle that she had to sort out with Anna, and decorations that needed putting up, inside the castle and outside in the grounds. Anna was great, but Deb knew that she had to be there to oversee things.

It was hard leaving Janice, but she had to go. She'd be back soon, she promised herself.

When she got back to the cottage, she dropped her bag in the hallway and let out a long sigh, bringing in some packages that the postman had left on the porch while she was away. There was often post for Gretchen, which she now knew was likely books, and she had ordered some things for the party. Deb didn't have the energy to open the packages right away, so she stacked them inside the doorway.

Then, she put her phone on charge, made herself some tea and a cheese and ham sandwich, and ran a bath.

While she was waiting for the bath to fill – it was one of those huge antique cast iron baths with feet, which Deb absolutely adored; she suspected it had been Zelda's addition to the cottage when she'd renovated it, rather than an original feature – she sat on the floor of the lounge next to her phone and flicked to her emails while she ate her sandwich and drank her tea.

Dear Deb,

I'm so sorry this has taken me a while to respond to. Please let me assure you that my delay in responding has no reflection on you, or the gravity of the situation. Things here have just been frantically busy, and I've been with Zelda most of the time. And, if I'm honest, I was horrified when I read your email. It's been hard for me to take in – the fact that someone related to me could have done something so heinous. And, yet, as time goes on and I learn more about the history of Loch Cameron and of my family – things that I was never told, growing up – the more I understand, and sometimes, the sadder I am that we did not do better as landowners, protectors and community leaders.

First, let me say how sorry I am to learn of your grandmother's story, and her sad connection to Gyle Head. I had no idea about what happened – I knew that my ancestor Donald Cameron built the folly in the 1930s, of course, in the same way that I knew about the stone circle that was erected in the castle gardens in the past, too. My ancestors were fond of parties, and it was quite the fashion at one time to build interesting attractions on your land to entertain visiting guests – and, no doubt, to help entice reluctant southern friends and allies up to the freezing north.

Of course, I am in no way excusing what Donald did. To turn people out of their homes, just to build something with no actual community function, is unforgivable. As lairds, we have a responsibility to care for our tenants and our community. I have always worked hard to look after the people of Loch Cameron, as I believe my father did before me. But, there have been failings, and I take responsibility for the Clan Cameron because I am the Clan Chief, and responsibility can lie nowhere else. I wear the Clan tartan, I live in the castle and the swords and the claymores of the battles that the Clan fought for our land and our sovereignty hang on my walls. I, alone, am responsible. For all of my ancestors. I wear their successes and failings like a cloak.

I believe that it's fate that has brought you here to Loch Cameron, Deb. Somehow, this land has a way of pulling back its own. And, in this case, Loch Cameron is demanding that I right the wrong that was done to your family, and help you reclaim your heritage here as a daughter of our sacred, special land. You belong here, your heart belongs here and your grandmother belonged here, and it was wrong and terrible that she was ever ripped away from her home. In losing those four families, Loch Cameron lost some of its rightful community and for that I will be sorry, always.

Let's talk about this when we can. I have some ideas – things I'd like to do, perhaps, but I would value your input too. For now, please know that whatever you decide and wherever you end up, you will always be a treasured daughter of Loch Cameron, and to that end, I have asked Anna to send something over to you.

With my deepest regards,

Hal x

Deb started to cry. Hal's email was so kind, and Deb's emotional battery was pretty low right at that moment. She put her phone back on the carpet and wrapped her arms around her knees, feeling her body shake with sobs. Sometimes, it was the times when people were the kindest to you that made you the saddest.

When the tears had ebbed away, she went to check on her bath and turned off the taps. She finished the sandwich, grateful for having some food in her stomach: food always made her feel better, more grounded. After undressing and balancing the cup of tea in her hand, she eased into the water and closed her eyes, letting the warmth calm her.

I have asked Anna to send something over to you.

After she'd luxuriated in the deep bath for a good while and the water was starting to go cold – she considered letting some of it out so that she could top it up with more hot water, then decided that would be frivolous – Deb opened her eyes, remembering Hal's final line in the email and the fact that she had brought a number of packages in from the porch when she'd got in. Was one of them from Hal?

She got out of the bath and pulled out the plug, standing on the mat and visualising all her stress from the past couple of days spiralling down the plug hole. Then, she wrapped herself in a fluffy robe and padded to the hallway to look at the packages.

Some were definitely books, addressed to Gretchen. But there was one large box which was addressed to her, without any postage. Someone had hand-delivered it: *it must be from Anna at the castle*, she thought.

She carried it to the kitchen table and slit the tape open carefully with a knife. Inside, there was a handwritten note on a thick piece of cream paper with the Cameron clan crest embossed at the top.

Dear Deb

Hal asked me to send you this. If you're not sure what it is, it's a shawl in the Cameron tartan that belonged to his mother (just in case you thought it was a small blanket or something). There's also a brooch here that also belonged to the late Lady Cameron which I put in a black box. The shawl has been dry-cleaned a while back and kept in a cedar blanket box, so it should be fine. As you probably know, the brooch is to fasten the shawl – you'll have your own way of wearing it.

He asked me to tell you that the brooch is gold with a Citrine stone, and that it now belongs to you, as a daughter of Loch Cameron. Lady Cameron used to wear it a lot, so I know that it's a very sincere gift on his part.

All the best,

Anna

'What?' Deb breathed, as she put the note to one side and

reached into the box, pushing aside the white tissue paper that lay under the note and drawing out a large, square woollen shawl. The tartan was red with a thin yellow line and a black woven check design, and, as Anna's note had indicated, smelt pleasantly of cedar. She held the shawl against her, not quite believing that Hal had sent her this.

Deb reached into the box again and drew out a small black jewellery box, just as Anna's note had promised. Opening it, she gasped as she discovered a beautiful, circular gold brooch featuring celtic knotwork and with a large golden-yellow stone in the centre. It was a stunning piece of jewellery and Deb turned it over in her hands, holding it up to the light. Was it really gold? Surely Hal wouldn't give her a family heirloom that was so valuable? But Anna's note said that it was, and she had no reason to lie.

It now belongs to you, as a daughter of Loch Cameron. Deb blinked, unable to contain her surprise. Hal's email had said that he wanted to talk, and to be able to make amends for what had happened to Grandma Elise. This wasn't quite what she had expected, but it was a lovely gesture.

Deb hadn't expected anything, really. It was more about an acknowledgement of what Grandma Elise had been through. She wanted her grandmother to matter. To be remembered, and for her story to be heard. It seemed as though Hal was taking this seriously, and Deb was grateful for that.

She wrapped the shawl around her shoulders, and fastened it with the brooch. It was warm and voluminous, and Deb could imagine how nice it would be to wear on a cold evening, walking in the castle grounds. She wondered what the late Lady Cameron had been like, and where she had worn the shawl.

It was a thoughtful and lovely gift, and Deb was touched by its significance. In response to her tale of her family's loss, Hal Cameron had given her something that was dear to him, and

that belonged to his family. Deb thought of his words again: a
daughter of Loch Cameron.

*You belong here, your heart belongs here and your grand-
mother belonged here, and it was wrong and terrible that she was
ever ripped away from her home.*

She re-read the email, and closed her eyes. *Grandma Elise,
this is for you,* she thought.

TWENTY-FIVE

'Lookin' fer anythin' in particular?' The young woman made her way over to Deb as she stood in the middle of the shop, looking around her. 'I dinnae think we've met. I'm Fiona.' She held out her hand, and Deb shook it.

'Hi. Deb Sutherland.'

'I've seen ye around recently. Holiday?' Fiona enquired.

'No. Work.' Deb explained about the party, briefly. 'I'm staying at the Ross cottage,' she added, having learnt by now that this was what the locals called her little place on Queen's Point. She'd already started thinking about it as *her* cottage: she'd miss it when she had to leave. Somehow, the thought of leaving Loch Cameron made her feel sad, even though she'd always known that she was only here for a few weeks.

'Ah, it's lovely up there.' Fiona nodded. 'Ah miss Gretchen, though. She's a character. Ah actually have tae visit her up at the home, because she wants a new outfit fer the party an' I said I'd take up some suggestions.'

'Oh, I'm sure she'd love that,' Deb agreed. 'I love Gretchen. She's had quite the life, too, from the sounds of things.'

'Och, aye,' Fiona laughed. 'She's got tales tae tell. So, what can I help ye with today? Havin' a sale on thermal undies. Ye can never have too many layers, even in the spring.'

'Ha. No, I think I'm all right for those. I'm after a dress for the party, as well, actually.'

Deb felt like she could think about fripperies like dresses, now that she knew her mum was on the mend. She'd be back and forth to check on Janice and Deb was hugely relieved that she'd agreed to having a carer who would pop in twice a day to keep an eye on her once she got home.

That seemed like a massive win to Deb, who had never got Janice to agree to anything before. It felt like a weight had been lifted that Deb hadn't really noticed she was carrying.

'Oh! Lovely. I've been supplyin' evenin' dresses for the May Day party a few years now.' Fiona led Deb to an area at the back of the shop. 'Come this way, hen. The main shop's mostly waterproofs, boots an' the like. But you'll find what ye want out here.'

The back of the shop was sectioned off with a large mirrored screen. 'I like tae keep it separate. An' make it a bit special back here, for the ladies,' Fiona added as they walked through the gap.

'Oh, my!' Deb exclaimed.

Behind the screen, Fiona had transformed the little alcove into a magical wonderland of diamante, fairy lights and jewel tones. Two velvet armchairs – one plum, one navy blue – sat to one side, facing a rack of long dresses. Deb could see silks, lace and satins in various colours; she went over to the rack immediately and reached out to touch the garments. There was a full-length free-standing gold rimmed mirror by the back wall, and shelves holding evening bags and a selection of heels next to it.

'I've got costume jewellery as well, aye. If ye wanted a statement piece tae set off a dress.' Fiona smoothed the pile on one of the chairs. 'I love it back here. Sometimes I just come an' sit back here an' have a coffee, do the accounts.'

'It's gorgeous, Fiona!' Deb felt like she used to as a child when Janice had taken her into the local toyshop, once a year, before Christmas. Just once a year, she had been allowed to roam her favourite aisle – the one full of dolls in their pink boxes, all with beautiful, sparkly ball dresses and cute little outfits – and choose one. Choosing just *one* had been so difficult. She'd wanted them all, but of course, Janice couldn't afford more than one.

'Ah, thanks, hen.' Fiona looked pleased. 'Nice tae be able tae help local ladies feel special for the night, aye. Ah rent or buy the dresses, up tae you.'

'The thing is, I brought a dress up with me. I wear it to all of my events. But I tried it on yesterday and it's too big.' Deb began flicking through the rail of treasures. 'I used to be a size fourteen, but it's hanging off me. I haven't been trying to lose weight, but I guess I've been really busy with organising the party.'

'These things happen. Ye should try a twelve. Maybe even a ten, lookin' at ye.' Fiona sized Deb up with a swift look.

'Maybe. And, also, Hal Cameron gave me this amazing shawl, and I want to wear it to the party. Around my shoulders. So, a dress would have to go with this.' Deb pulled the shawl out of her bag and unfolded it for Fiona to see.

'Ach, it's gorgeous. Cameron tartan. He gave that tae ye?' Fiona raised an eyebrow, then turned away and started flicking through a long rail of dresses.

'Yes. Out of the blue. It's a long story, but I found out that my family were from here, originally. I grew up in Glasgow. But my grandmother lived here, but she and her family were evicted, back in the 1930s. I got a very nice email back from Hal about it and he sent this over as a gift, with a brooch. It belonged to his mum, apparently.'

'Oooh. What's the brooch like?' Fiona turned back to her, curiously. 'I bet it's bonny if it belonged to Lady Cameron. I remember her, aye, when I was a kid. She was always well turned oot. No' a hair ootae place, always coiffed, you know? An' she always wore fantastic outfits. Chanel twinsets, that kindae thing,' Fiona sighed. 'I always had a passion for fashion, so I used tae take notice of what Lady Cameron wore, aye. She was like the Lady Di of Loch Cameron.'

'Here. It's gold. I feel a bit awkward about taking it, to be completely honest.' Deb took the brooch out of the black box that she'd brought with her, and showed it to Fiona. 'It must be worth quite a lot of money.'

'Wow. I'd say so.' Fiona's eyes widened. 'That's stonkin'. What a beauty. Hal's a generous guy. He obviously thought ye deserved it. Ye dinnae need tae feel awkward, hen.' She patted Deb's hand. 'Okay. Let's find a couple o' dresses that'll set off the shawl, then.' She returned to the rail.

'Hmmm. Red, or black, or even gold or yellow, tae go with the stripe,' Fiona mused. 'This one'd suit ye, I'd say.' Fiona pulled out a floor-length bias-cut satin dress in a pillar box red and held it up to Deb. 'Wi' yer colourin'. Or this one.' She flicked through a few more and pulled out a knee-length bodycon dress in black.

'Gosh. I'm not sure I could pull off either of those. They're a bit... bold.' Deb looked at both dresses doubtfully. 'I mean, I love them... on someone else.'

'Aye.' Fiona handed her both dresses. 'But it's your party. You should stand out. Ye've a crackin' little figure on ye,' she added.

'I don't know. I'd feel so... exposed.' Deb took the dresses from Fiona cautiously.

'Well, give them a try. No pressure,' Fiona said, warmly. 'I'll look for jewellery while you're tryin' them on. Somethin' in gold, I'd say, tae go wi' the brooch. No' that I stock actual gold, just costume jewellery.' She hummed under her breath. 'Get on wi' ye. Changin' room's just in the shop.'

'All right.' Deb thought it was best to do as she was told, going into the little changing room in the main shop and pulling the curtain across. She stripped off her jeans and sweatshirt, and slipped on the red satin dress first. It felt both luxurious and sensuous against her skin, and also completely flimsy and insubstantial. Deb wasn't used to wearing anything as... lingerie-like... as this, in public.

She slipped the tiny straps over her shoulders and shimmied the diaphanous fabric over her hips, sliding her hands over her hips. The dress felt lovely, but she wasn't at all sure about how it looked. There was a mirror in the small changing room, and Deb stared at herself in consternation.

The dress looked good. Surprisingly good. But she almost felt as if she was looking at a stranger in the mirror. There was the fact that she had lost a lot of weight after the operation, and the bloated tummy she'd got so used to from the endometriosis had completely disappeared. Deb didn't think she could remember the last time she had a flat stomach: in her teens, perhaps. There was also the consideration that she didn't ever usually wear dresses like this, and she felt very self-conscious in it. She'd never felt she had the figure for something so revealing before, or the confidence.

'How is it?' Fiona called out. Deb walked back out into the shop and found Deb in the little dress cove. 'Awww, look at ye! Ye look like a princess!' Fiona cooed.

'It's a bit... revealing, isn't it?' Deb pulled at the silky fabric, self-consciously. 'Look at these tiny straps! A brisk wind could blow them off!'

'Well, yer no' supposed tae pull at them.' Fiona tutted. 'An' it's an evenin' dress. It's supposed tae look glamorous. Dinnae be scared o' a bit o' attention. Anyway, wi' a shawl on the top, you'd be a bit covered up, an' ye'd want tae take the shawl off later, I expect.'

'Yeah, I expect so. It's been a while since I wore anything

this nice, I guess.' Deb twirled in front of the full-length mirror. 'Oooh. It moves when I spin!'

'Aye.' Fiona giggled. 'Nice fer dancin'. I assume there's goin' tae be a good band up at the castle, for the party? An' a ceilidh?'

'Yes. We've got a band that can do traditional Scottish music for the ceilidh, and modern songs for later. Well, not particularly modern, but you know what I mean. Things people like to dance to.'

'That sounds great. The ceilidh's always ma favourite part.' Fiona gave Deb an appraising glance. 'This one looks killer on ye. But ye should try on the other one too.'

'All right.' Obediently, Deb went back to the changing room and slipped out of the red dress. The black dress was one of the bandage-style bodycon dresses she'd seen models wearing in shop windows. She'd never envisaged herself wearing one, though: it felt so daring. But, the fact that Fiona had said how nice she'd looked in the red dress had bolstered her confidence. She reached back and did the thick silver zip as far as she could, and then went back to Fiona.

'Can you do the zip for me? Couldn't quite get it to go all the way up,' she explained, smoothing her hands over her hips and stomach. 'I can't believe it fits, to be quite honest. I don't think I've been this thin since I was eighteen. I hardly recognise myself.'

'You've lost quite a bit, then?' Fiona did the zip up deftly and stood back to look at Deb. 'Ye know what? I like this one more. The colour's even nicer wi' yer hair, an' the dress shape is very flatterin'. I like that pencil skirt length. To the knee. Very elegant an' sexy.'

'Thank you. It's surprisingly comfy.' Deb walked around the little fairy-light bedecked area. 'I guess because it's stretchy. I feel like I could run around in this one. You know, because as the event organiser, I'll be working all night. I can't be wearing something I can't move in.'

'Fair enough. I can understand that.' Fiona handed her a stylish gold costume jewellery necklace. There was a chain at the back, and the front featured six large gold coins that, when Deb held it up against herself, sat nicely on her collarbone.

'Oh. That's nice.' Deb admired herself in the mirror for a moment. 'Do you really think I can get away with this dress?' She turned and looked at herself from the side, not quite believing how flat her tummy was. 'Thing is, I had endometriosis for a long time. I was always really bloated – some days, I looked six months pregnant. I had an operation a few months back, but I'm still getting used to... my new body, I guess.'

'Of course. Ye look fab.' Fiona nodded. 'An' as I say, ye'll have the shawl on as well here an' there. An' you'd be surprised how many ladies come in who've had similar things. Or still do. Bein' a woman is hard, hen,' she sighed. 'I envy ye – hysterec- tomy, was it?'

Deb nodded.

'Aye. I'd love not tae have a uterus anymore. Nothin' but trouble.' Fiona shook her head. 'An' when it comes tae hormones, sometimes I think, how much of how I am is ma actual personality, an' how much is the hormones, ye know?'

'Oh, I know.' Deb blew out her cheeks. 'I'm grateful to have it done and dusted. I do sometimes think about what it would have been like to have a child, though. But that's never going to happen now.'

People had even asked Deb, sometimes, when the baby was due. Once, on a train, someone had stood up and let her have their seat, obviously believing that she was with child.

Now, she never would be. The thought gave her a pang of loss, even though there had never been a baby to lose. It was more that one potential future life had disappeared, or, more accurately, had had to be sacrificed.

The condition had also made it almost impossible to lose

weight. She hadn't ever been one for dieting, but she had tried various exercise regimes, because she wanted to feel fit and healthy. Before the endometriosis, Deb had been a keen jogger and enjoyed dancing. Yet, when it got really bad, she hardly had the energy to walk to the shops, some days. The prospect of running a few miles wasn't all that appealing when you had to wear a maximum strength tampon and a brick of a sanitary towel just to leave the house. Plus, the various hormone-based medicines the doctor had tried with her had made her feel depressed and lethargic – and, she was convinced that they stopped her losing weight, too.

So, it was really weird to Deb that now, without paying any attention to it at all, she'd dropped probably two dress sizes. All as a result of having healed from the hysterectomy, not needing to be on any hormone medication anymore, and the endo itself having been shown the door. Finally, her body was able to regulate itself normally. And, with a busy lifestyle, and eating well, this was apparently the result.

'I'm sorry, hen.' Fiona frowned. 'I know we've just met, but I'm here if ye want tae talk aboot it. Anytime.'

'Thanks, Fiona. That's kind of you.' Deb felt a little uncomfortable, but only because she wasn't used to opening up to strangers. Yet, she was also grateful to Fiona for being so nice, and she liked her. 'It's nice to make a new friend, as well. Especially one with such good fashion sense,' she said with a grin.

'Back atcha, darlin'. Now. Have ye got shoes? Nice ones, but I guess heels that ye can still run around in, if ye need tae?' Fiona put her hands on her hips, all business again.

'Yeah. I've got some comfy heels. Black.' Deb nodded. 'That should be all right. Okay. I've decided. I'll take the black dress.' She gave another little twirl in front of the mirror. 'You're right. It does look good.'

'Aye, be brave, hen.' Fiona gave Deb's shoulder a little squeeze. 'You're gonna rock that party, ah promise ye. There willnae be a man there who can keep their eyes off ye. An' some of the lassies, too,' she laughed.

Unbidden, Kyle Abernethy's face popped into Deb's mind. Had she been actively trying not to think about Kyle since their run in at the Post Office? Yes. Had it worked? Not in the slightest.

He wouldn't be at the party, so it didn't matter. Kyle wouldn't see her in her new, beautiful dress. Anyway, she wasn't there to be pretty. She was there to do her job, which she was being paid handsomely for. And that should be enough.

TWENTY-SIX

The castle looked magical.

It had rained all day the day before, causing Deb to almost tear her hair out with worry – she didn't want people to be tracking mud from the fields into the castle, and she also didn't want it to be raining when the fireworks were planned – or the bonfire, which was such a key part of the May Day celebrations. But, the forecast had promised a dry, fine day for the day of the party, and by the time the evening arrived, the castle grounds felt reasonably dry underfoot, and Angus, who was managing the fireworks, had been happily setting them up in the topiary garden a couple of hours earlier.

She had had the dream about the skipping girl again. It wasn't an anxious dream, or a memory. Deb knew that she wasn't dreaming about herself. It was as if she was watching a sepia reel from something in the past.

It played on her mind, but she couldn't think about it now. The party had to be her main focus.

As far as Deb could see, everything was set, and *mostly* everything was perfect.

Not everything, of course. As with any event, there were

always a few things that didn't go to plan. The fireworks and the bonfire were under control, the band had arrived and had started playing, the bar was running under Dotty and Eric's expert supervision and the caterers had arrived and had settled into the castle kitchen.

However, the glassware that Deb had hired for the evening had arrived with half of the wine glasses broken, and the napkins had come in the wrong colour: she'd ordered forest green, and she'd gotten a very un-Scottish mint colour which didn't match any of the decorations. Still, if that was all that was going to go wrong, then she'd take it. She'd managed to get Anna to make up the shortfall in the wine glasses from the castle's own supply of crystal – which she did feel a little cautious about using but, frankly, she had no choice – and they'd use the paper napkins that the caterers had brought as standard, instead of the fabric ones that Deb had planned.

Deb had stationed herself in the vestibule at the castle entrance, where tourists usually bought tickets. She sat at the wooden table that was always there, with the boxes of wrist corsages and the buttonholes she'd had to manhandle out of the Post Office in front of her. Her idea had been to provide traditional Clan Cameron flower tokens to all of the guests as a thoughtful gift – each corsage or buttonhole featured a purple thistle, representing Scotland, some oak leaves, which were featured in the Clan Cameron crest, and lilac, which was abundant everywhere in the village at that time of year. After all, part of the reason for the party was to celebrate the togetherness of the community, and Deb had thought that the flowers would be a good way to symbolise that.

She was slightly self-conscious in her black bodycon dress and heels, though she had to admit her outfit was surprisingly comfy. She'd draped the tartan shawl around her shoulders and fastened it with the brooch, and was grateful for the warmth on a chilly evening.

'Look at you! Glamourpuss.' Zelda Hicks sashayed through the door from the Great Hall to the vestibule where Deb was sitting. 'Deb! It's so good to see you!'

Deb stood up, and Zelda wrapped her up in a warm hug.

'Hi, Zelda. When did you get back?' Deb had known that Zelda and the Laird were coming back for the party, but they had been a little vague about details.

'Last night. I'm jetlagged like you wouldn't believe.' Deb always noticed Zelda's New York accent, and it stood out even more in a Scottish castle than it had done when Deb had first met Zelda in London. 'Hal's here somewhere. You look fantastic, I'm not even joking. You've lost a lot of weight. Not that that's important, but... you have.'

'Yeah. It's a combination of being busy and the post-operation recovery, I think.' Deb shrugged.

'Well, you look fab. And I love the dress.'

'I got it at Fiona's, in the village.' Deb fiddled with one of the wide shoulder straps. 'It is actually weirdly comfy.'

'Ah, I love Fiona! That's a great little shop. You know, I helped her out a little, setting up her Instagram account and stuff for it. Have you seen her feed? She's got like, thousands of followers now. She's probably going to post a lot from the party. You should definitely make sure she takes a picture of you in that dress.' Zelda winked. 'Belle of the ball.'

'Oh, hardly.' Deb blushed a little. 'Look at you! You look absolutely stunning.'

'That's what I told her.' Hal Cameron walked into the vestibule, and pulled Zelda in towards him, planting an affectionate kiss on her cheek. 'I've never known you look anythin' other than perfect.' Zelda was dressed in a long Cameron tartan ball dress that looked to be made especially for her. It had short sleeves, a sweetheart neck and nipped her in at the waist before billowing out into a wide, floor-length skirt. She looked every bit the Lady of the Manor.

'Oh, this old thing?' Zelda held out the skirt to one side, exposing a long slit up one leg. 'Ha. I'm joking. I had it specially made in Edinburgh to match Hal. Gotta be sharp and look good next to the Clan Chief.' She looked up into his eyes, and planted a little kiss on Hal's clean-shaven cheek.

Hal was wearing full Scots evening dress, which comprised a Cameron tartan kilt, a black evening jacket with tails, crisp white shirt, black socks with a matching tartan tab, and a black bow tie. Over his kilt, he wore a traditional fur and leather sporran, and an ornamental knife – the *sgian dubh* – tucked into one sock.

They were one of those couples that you could see straight away absolutely adored each other – it warmed Deb's heart to see them so in love. And, just for a moment, she felt alone, even though she was surrounded by people.

'Deb, you look amazing too. The shawl looks beautiful.' Hal planted a kiss on Deb's cheek. 'This was my mother's,' he said, to them both. 'As was the brooch.' He nodded, looking pleased. 'It looks great on you, Deb. Zelda actually suggested I give this tae ye. After we read yer email, we were both in bits.' He shook his head. 'I'm so sorry for what happened tae yer granny, Deb. I really am.' Hal looked grave. 'I've actually been thinkin' a lot aboot what I can do tae remedy the situation, an' I think I've come up with somethin'. We'll talk, okay?' He reached for Deb's hand and squeezed it.

'Okay. Thank you, Hal.' Deb was touched. 'I really didn't expect ... all this.' She touched the brooch, which sat on the shawl at her shoulder. 'But it was a really kind gesture.'

'No' a bit of it.' He nodded. 'We wanted tae show ye that yer part o' Loch Cameron. It's only right.'

'Lady Cameron had some really cool stuff,' Zelda added. 'Hal's still got loads of her couture, up in one of the rooms here. You should come and see it sometime. I need to persuade one of my old fashion buddies to come and do a feature on it or something because there are some hella good dresses up there.' She grinned at Deb. 'We should invite Fiona, and try it all on. Make a day of it.'

'That sounds really fun.' Deb smiled, grateful for Zelda's warmth.

'And you've done such a great job with everything! The castle looks fantastic!' Hal turned to her. 'Thank ye, Deb. I really appreciate the fact that we've been able to be away and just leave it in your capable hands.'

'You're most welcome.' Deb felt a glow of pride in her chest eclipse her temporary loneliness. She was really proud of how the party had come together.

'Now, listen.' Hal looked serious. 'I'm goin' tae make a bit o' a speech, later. An' I want tae mention yer granny. Is that okay?' He looked concernedly at Deb. 'Reason bein', I've got tae address the issues aboot the housin' project up on Gyle Head, an' connected wi' that, I want tae be completely honest with the community aboot the past. I think it's important.'

'Oh. Right. I guess so,' Deb said, feeling suddenly on the back foot. There was a part of her that felt protective of Grandma Elise, but then, on the other hand, she thought that people *should* know. It was important to tell her grandmother's story. 'Yes. Yes, okay.'

'You're sure?' Hal asked, his eyes crinkling kindly at the edges. 'I just think, honesty is important, aye. I want tae say an official apology to you. In front of everyone.'

'You don't have to do that, Hal,' she said, feeling emotional.

'I know. But I want tae,' he said, softly.

'Thank you,' Deb replied. A thought struck her. 'Hal? I have a question, actually. My grandmother had a brother, Tom, who lived in the cottage with her and her parents until they were evicted. I don't know if you remember from what I sent you, but according to my grandmother's diary, they went into care, and were separated. I think she spent the whole rest of her life without him.'

'Oh, no! That's terrible!' Zelda put her hand to her mouth. 'I can't imagine how horrible that would be!'

'I know.' Deb nodded. 'I can't, either. I mean, I doubt that he would even be alive now. But, Hal... would you have any way of tracing him, do you think? Would there be something in the archives at the castle? It's a long shot, I know, but...'

'Deb! Oh, thank goodness I found ye.' Dotty burst into the vestibule, wringing her hands. 'Ah, sorry if I'm interruptin'. Hello, Zelda dear. Ye look bonny. An so do you, Hal. Handsome as ever.'

'Hi, Dotty.' Hal stepped forward and gave Dotty a kiss on the cheek. 'Looking bonny as always yoursel'. You have tae save me a dance later.'

'Oh, get away wi' ye.' Dotty flapped her hands at him, impatiently.

Hal turned back to Deb. 'Umm, Deb – aye, let me have a think aboot that. There might be somethin' I can do. Leave it wi' me.'

'All right. Thanks, Hal.' Deb turned to Dotty. 'Hi, Dotty – do you need me?'

'Umm, aye. Deb, dear, can I steal ye for a wee minute?' Dotty had an air of panic about her, which Deb – as a seasoned event planner – knew all too well.

'We'll take over here, if you like,' Zelda offered. 'I can give out the favours, and Hal can welcome people. I've got the schedule on my phone, so we know when everything is due to happen.'

'All right. Great, thanks.' Deb looked at her phone for a minute, discombobulated by Dotty's sudden arrival, and what Hal had said before that. 'Ummm. Right. I'll need you both for the welcome and toasts, and starting the dancing. Then we've got the bonfire lighting at nine, if Hal wants to do his customary poem reading.' Deb had researched the poem, Tam O' Shanter by Robert Burns, and she had to admit that she was intrigued to see Hal Cameron perform it.

'Right you are.' Hal nodded.

However, she felt odd when she thought about her grandmother's story being shared with the whole village: a rubbing of the edges of her family history and the lairds of Loch Cameron.

It had been Donald Cameron, the laird at that time, who had changed Elise's – and therefore Janice's, and her own – life, so suddenly and without warning. His decision had had an impact on the generations of Sutherland women. Now, Hal Cameron was about to apologise for that decision in front of the whole village. Generations later, had Deb in some way balanced karma between the two families? She didn't know, but it felt... fitting, at least.

She couldn't think about all of that now, though.

'Dotty. I'm all yours.' Deb adjusted the wireless headphone in her ear, which was there so that she could receive calls easily. You never knew what was going to happen at an event, and since Deb had had to call an ambulance at a previous event because someone had fallen over on some steep steps and fractured their ankle, she was prepared for anything.

'There's a problem wi' the drinks,' Dotty whispered. 'It's the chamomile liqueur for the Clan Cameron cocktail. I thought Eric put it in the car, an' he thought I did. It must still be at the Inn, behind the bar.' She rolled her eyes.

'Oh, right.' Deb frowned. 'Can we do without it? I mean, can we substitute something for it?'

'No' really, lassie.' Dotty shook her head. 'It's the signature cocktail fer the evenin'. I prepared the chamomile liqueur and the herb syrup weeks ago. It won't be the same without it.'

'No, I don't suppose it will.' Deb sighed. 'Okay. People are arriving now, so I need you and Eric on the bar. If you give me the keys to the Inn, I'll take the car down and get the chamomile thing, and the herb syrup and bring them back. Just give people wine and beer for now, and soft drinks.'

'Right ye are, lassie.' Dotty reached into her pocket and brought out a set of keys. 'This is the main lock fer the front door, an' this is the deadlock. Thank ye.'

'No problem.' Deb took the keys and picked up her handbag from under the table of buttonholes and corsages, where Zelda had taken a seat and was now handing favours out to a line of villagers who were starting to stream into the castle. 'Zelda, can you hold the fort? I've got to pop down to the village for something.'

'Will do.' Zelda gave Deb a wink.

'Thank you! Won't be long!'

She dashed out onto the gravel drive at the front of the castle, where groups of villagers were gathered, talking and laughing, and got into her car.

Driving carefully down the long gravel driveway that led away from the castle, Deb wound down her window, despite the cold of the air outside. The air was cold, but she felt she needed it.

Was she stressed out by the event, and the last minute dash to the Inn? No, that wasn't it. She was a seasoned enough event organiser not to let something like that get on top of her.

The party was starting, and everyone was enjoying themselves. So, why did she feel so low, all of a sudden? It was good that Hal was going to talk about Elise. She felt glad about that, but it was tinged with sadness. It was sad that her grandmother couldn't be there to hear the apology. It should have been her.

At the same time, Deb realised that she'd had the party to focus on, all this time, and now, it was almost over. Tomorrow, she would have to think about her life again, and it was that, too, that was making her anxious. She would have to organise moving out of her flat with Dan, find somewhere new to live, and be single for the first time in years.

I was supposed to be happily married by now, she thought, as she drove over the narrow, blue painted bridge that linked the castle grounds to the village, crossing the loch at its narrowest point. *Or, something. I was supposed to be settled, to know what I was doing. But I don't. Not like Zelda and Hal, or Dotty and Eric.* They had each other, and they had lives. They knew what they were doing.

She drove to the Inn, parked in the car park and stared into the darkness. She knew she should be in a hurry – to pick up the chamomile infusion and the herb syrup and take them back to the castle – but she just sat and looked up at the moon, which glowed in a black sky, garlanded by grey clouds.

What am I doing? she asked herself. *What will I do, now that this job is over? I've found roots here. Do I want to stay? Or go back to Glasgow?*

You're making a new start, the answer came, as if the moon had heard and replied.

Yes, she'd lost Dan, and her flat – that was never hers, anyway – they'd just shared the rent. She had lost her uterus, and her chance at having a baby in the usual way, but she'd also lost the pain and the bleeding, the bloating and the general terrible impact on her life that endometriosis had had. That could only be a good thing. And she knew that Dan wasn't right for her.

Deb thought, as she got out of her car and walked towards the front door of the Inn. Yes, some people seemed to be living their life in a romance novel, like Zelda and Hal, but they were the privileged exception. For some reason, something had blessed them both with love and luxury, and an international, jet-setting life anyone would be envious of. But that didn't mean that Deb couldn't have love. Just because Hal and Zelda were a power couple, deeply in love, didn't mean that it couldn't exist for her, too. Deb knew in her heart that there was no lack of love in the world, even if she'd been brought up to believe in the scarcity of love by Janice. That was an old story, and it wasn't Deb's story anymore. Especially not now, when Elise's story, though it could never be forgotten, was at least being acknowledged and brought into the open by Hal.

That's not my story. Not anymore, she thought, as she went into the bar, switched the light on and went behind the bar, looking for the bottles. Dotty had texted her with a description of where they were.

Happy Every After can be for me too. I don't know when or how, but I believe that it can, she thought. And that gave her a good feeling. Hope.

TWENTY-SEVEN

Deb slowed her car, seeing that a car had stopped ahead of her. It was parked at an angle, half blocking the entrance to the blue painted bridge that linked the castle to the village, with its hazard lights on. She swore under her breath and pulled up behind it.

Unbelievable.

She'd already had to dip out of the party to pick up the liqueurs that Dotty and Eric had forgotten, and now the universe was apparently conspiring against her even further by putting a literal obstacle in her way as she rushed back to the party.

Deb got out of her car, taking her bag with her. If the driver had broken down, then she might need to call a rescue service – not that anyone was coming out to Loch Cameron in the middle of the night, she guessed.

'Hey. Are you okay?' she called out, walking around to the driver's side of the car. 'Oh, for goodness' sake. *Really?*' she exhaled with a mixture of irritation and disbelief when she saw Kyle Abernethy behind the wheel.

'And a good evening to you too, Deborah.' Kyle opened his partially-open window fully.

'What's happened?' she asked, aware that she sounded terse. 'I need to get over the bridge to the party.'

'Well, I thought I'd just stop here and admire the view, sitting in my freezing cold car,' he replied, a definite sarcastic tone in his voice. 'Beautiful at night, don't you think? I definitely wouldn't rather be at home, warming myself by a log fire.'

'Ha ha. Seriously. You broke down?' She had got out of the car without putting her coat on, and now she was seriously regretting it. Kyle was right: it was absolutely freezing.

'Yeah. It's been a bit temperamental recently, and then it just cut out when I was driving up to the bridge,' he sighed.

'Right. Have you called a rescue service?' Deb had clicked into practical mode. 'I need to get up to the castle. It's urgent.'

'Okay, well, I was heading up that way, too. Also, fairly important I'm there,' he said, levelly. 'I have called someone, but they said it's going to be hours. I was just going to push the car to one side a bit so I don't block the road, then walk up, actually.'

Deb resisted the urge to ask why Kyle, the most hated man in Loch Cameron, was going to the May Day party. She thought that the evil eye he'd get from the crochet coven as soon as they saw him would probably dissolve him like a slug under a salt shaker, but she didn't say it.

'Oh. Well, I'll give you a lift, then.' She looked behind her, glad that there wasn't likely to be a line of traffic forming behind her: everyone was at the castle. 'And I'll help you push the car to the side of the road. We don't want to block the cars when people leave the party.'

'All right, then. You're not exactly dressed to push a Land Rover in the mud, though.' Kyle gave her a quick look up and down as he got out of the car and handed her the keys. 'It'll start, but it doesn't seem to want to do much else. Put it in neutral and steer. I'll push, and then you can put the handbrake on when we've moved it.'

'Okay.' Deb climbed up into the cab of the black pickup, surreptitiously pulling down the hem of her skirt so that she didn't accidentally give Kyle an eyeful of thigh and knickers. Not that there was an exciting knicker situation going on – in fact, Fiona had sold her some shapewear to wear underneath the bandage dress, so Deb was well and truly trussed up and covered in spandex.

'Ready!' Kyle shouted from the back of the truck.

She adjusted the driver's seat so that she could reach the pedals – another reminder of just how large a man Kyle really was – turned on the engine and set the truck in neutral and let off the handbrake. Slowly, the car moved forward, and she steered it to the left of the bridge, where there was a narrow passing place.

'That's good,' Kyle called out, and she put the brake on, grateful that she didn't have to drive the big pickup properly. 'Thanks.' He reappeared at the driver's side window, and she closed it and then got out of the cab gingerly, lowering herself down to the muddy side of the road.

'It's okay,' she said, handing him his keys. 'Right. Well then, you'd better come with me, before I die of the cold.' She hugged herself, shivering.

'I'm sorry.' He followed her to her car and got in. 'Did you spoil your nice shoes, or your dress?'

'No, I think they're all right.' Deb cast a quick eye over her comfy heels, which seemed to be bearing the brunt of her sudden jaunt down to the Inn and back, including an impromptu car rescue, quite well. She started the engine, and resumed her drive up to the castle.

'Sorry... You're going to the party, too?' she asked, curiously. 'I didn't think you were invited.'

'I wasn't. But the laird called me a couple of days ago and

invited me.' Kyle raised an eyebrow. 'We had a bit of a chat. Cleared the air about some stuff, I think.'

'You'd had a disagreement, I heard.' Deb was still freezing, so she turned up the heating in the car to maximum. 'Sorry. I need to defrost my toes.'

'That's okay. I was turning into a ice lolly in the car myself.' Kyle shivered. 'Well, it's a lot to explain. We'd been at logger-heads over the use of the land, and of course, you know that there's been local opposition to the project. Anyway, we were finally able to hammer out a plan that I think will make everyone happy on a call last week. Part of the issue's been that I couldn't ever get a hold of him while he was off in New York this past month or so.' Kyle sighed. 'It's good, I think. He says he's going to make a big announcement about it, so I'll leave it to him to tell you at the same time as everyone else. But he's a good guy. I think what we've got planned will work.'

'Well, now I'm intrigued.' Deb returned her gaze to the road and shifted gears as she rounded the end of the long gravel drive leading back to the castle.

'Yeah. Listen, Deb...' It was unusual for Kyle to sound as unsure of himself as he did in that moment, and Deb shot him a curious look. He looked nervous.

'I also wanted to say that I'm sorry,' he continued, his voice halting. 'When you told me about your grandmother and the cottages up on Gyle Head, I wasn't as kind as I could have been. Hal told me that you'd told him about it, and I have to admit that when I started talking to him about it, I realised that I'd been really insensitive to you. Now, I don't want that to sound like I listened to Hal because he's a man and not to you when you said exactly the same thing.'

He held up his hand as if to ward off a comment from Deb. 'I know how that sounds. It was just, when he told me the details of what you'd told him, I started thinking about how it must feel for you. I'm sorry I didn't think of that before. It just felt like you were accusing me, like it was my fault, and I got my back up. I can be an idiot sometimes. And I guess I've got really defensive about the project, too, because of the local resistance.' He sighed and put his head in his hands. 'Basically, I messed up, and I'm sorry.'

'Well, thank you. I appreciate the apology,' Deb said, as they drove towards the castle. She felt awkward with Kyle's sudden openness, but it also gave her a glow of happiness in her belly. She had wanted to reconnect with Kyle, and she hadn't known how to broach the subject. Unexpectedly, he'd done it for her.

The gardening team had done brilliantly in winding what was probably miles of fairy lights around the trunks of the tall fir trees, and over and through the thick rhododendron bushes. Now that it was fully dark, the drive looked magical. Deb gasped a little at the enchanted effect as she drove along.

'This your doing?' Kyle asked, looking out of the window. 'It's gorgeous.'

'Oh. Thank you.' She was surprised at the compliment. They drove on in silence, and Deb parked in front of the castle. 'Here we are, then,' she said, awkwardly. Her initial irritation had worn off, and had been replaced by the simmering attraction that she always felt in his presence.

However, Deb was still unsure of where things stood between her and Kyle. He'd been lovely, and apologised for the thing that had been bothering her, all this time. But she still wasn't sure what he wanted with her, if anything.

She wanted to say something, but before she had a chance, he'd hopped out of the car and slammed the door.

'Thanks for the lift,' he said, as she got out of the car, adjusting her dress self-consciously.

'No problem.' Deb started walking in, and then realised that Kyle had made her totally forget the whole reason she'd left the party in the first place. She gave herself a light smack on the hand and turned back to the car. 'I've got to get something. I'll see you in there.' She waved him away.

'Okay,' she heard him reply.

So. Back to party organising, she thought to herself. *You are actually here to work, unless you'd forgotten.*

No, I hadn't forgotten. Perhaps just got temporarily distracted.

She opened the back seat of the car and reached into the footwell, where she'd put the box of bottles from the Inn. It was heavier than she remembered, and she felt her ankle wobble threateningly with the unexpected weight.

'Let me get those. You'll twist an ankle on these flagstones in those shoes.' Kyle appeared at her side. Deb jumped, not expecting him to be near; she'd thought he'd gone into the castle.

'Oh. Thanks.' She handed him the box, and locked the car. 'Dotty forgot these ingredients for the signature cocktail for the evening. It's called a Clan Cameron.'

'Not the only yummy thing around here,' he murmured, and gave her a brief, unusually shy grin.

Deb didn't know how to reply to that, so she said nothing. But her heart pounded. What did Kyle mean? Was he flirting with her?

With a lump in her throat, she followed him into the castle, where the party was in full swing.

TWENTY-EIGHT

'SAVE OUR SQUIRRELS AND CAPERCAILLIE!' the shout rang out across the Great Hall, and Deb's heart sank.

Oh, no.

She thought that she had persuaded Mina and the crochet coven not to make a scene at the party, but, apparently, she had been far too subtle in her efforts.

Mina, Sheila, Sue and some other women were carrying the finished protest quilt into the Great Hall between them, like a large flag. Deb could see the slogan in capitals, which had been sewn in green and black on a white quilted background.

'WOMEN SEWING AGAINST ECOSYSTEM COLLAPSE!' the group chanted as they made their way into the room.

'Oh, for ...' Deb swore under her breath as she caught Hal Cameron's eye. 'Sheila!' she hissed as the women passed her. 'Is this really the time?'

'It's always the time for activism, Deb,' Mina said primly as she walked past, holding up one side of the quilt.

There was a hubbub of noise. Mina, giving her corner of the

quilt to Sheila, went up to the band at the front of the hall and tapped the microphone.

'Sorry to interrupt the party,' she began. 'But as this IS a community gathering, we wanted to make our voices heard. Say no to new houses on Gyle Head!' she shouted. The microphone squealed, and Deb recoiled from the volume.

It was typical. She'd worked so hard on the party and tried so hard to get everything right. In fact, Deb was really proud of everything she'd done. And now, Mina and Sheila and the rest of them were ruining everything. She was mortified.

Hal must think I'm the worst party planner in the world, she thought, running to the stage. She didn't have a plan in mind per se, but it was a panic reaction. If she could get there and reason with Mina... if she could persuade her to let it go, then they could let the party continue.

Deb looked back at Kyle, standing at the back of the room. A look passed between them. *I'm sorry*, she wanted to say. *You don't deserve this.*

Yet, before she could get there, Hal Cameron was smiling kindly at Mina and taking the microphone out of her hands. He gestured for quiet.

'Thank ye, Mina,' he said, kindly. 'That quilt is absolutely stonkin'. I know that you all must've worked really hard on that, aye. An' you're right. This is a community celebration, an' you've got a right tae be heard.'

'Thank you, Hal,' Mina replied, smugly. 'I think we can all agree that something needs to be done about the development on Gyle Head. I'm sorry that we had to bring it up in this way, but we didn't feel like there had been any action. It's been frustrating, seeing all the work starting, and not being listened to.'

There was a general murmur of agreement in the crowd, and Hal nodded seriously.

'I understand. An' I'd like tae respond, if I may,' he said.

'Of course, Hal.' Mina nodded.

'Aye, well then. We know aboot the housin' development up on Gyle Head,' Hal began, as the crowd began to quiet. 'I know a lot o' you have opposed it. An' I'd never want to restrict your right tae be heard.'

'Good thing, too,' Dotty muttered, crossing her arms over her chest. 'Those new houses are a menace!' She shot a dirty look at Kyle, who was standing at the other side of the room and looking self-conscious.

Deb smiled politely, not keen to incur Dotty's wrath by disagreeing, but feeling awkward at standing next to someone who was throwing daggers at the man she had just brought up here in the car.

'Well, that's no' strictly true,' Hal continued, frowning. 'It's true that Kyle and I – that's Kyle Abernethy, the developer – had a differing vision fer the development at first. The problem seems to have come up because he changed the plan fer the houses he was plannin' up on Gyle Head. I thought that meant that he wasnae goin' tae be buildin' affordable housin', but in fact that's no' the case. Sixty per cent o' those houses're goin tae be fer some o' the poorest families, because I'm goin' tae be subsidisin' them.'

There was a whoop of surprise from the audience. Mina looked completely taken aback.

'Well... that's not what I heard,' she argued, shooting a glance over at Kyle at the back of the room.

'That is what Kyle and I have agreed,' Hal said, firmly. 'We've been meeting about it over the past few weeks, an' he's also been workin' really hard tae protect those bird an' squirrel environments yer all so worried aboot. Rightly o' course. I think Kyle's plannin' tae tell ye all aboot everythin' in a community meetin' very soon. Okay?'

'All right.' Deb could see that Mina didn't know what to say. 'Thank you.'

'Aye. I'm goin' tae leave that tae Kyle, when he's ready.

Now, unfortunately, I do have somethin' else tae say which isnae so happy.' Hal frowned, and paused a little before he continued. 'Deb knows about this already. She was the one that brought it tae my attention.'

Hal caught Deb's eye, as if to check with her that it was all right for him to go ahead: she nodded, with a feeling of nervousness. She understood that this would be part of Hal's *making it right*, but she was still a little nervous that everyone here was going to hear about Grandma Elise. She reminded herself that this was good. Clearing karma. Righting wrongs.

'What ye might no' ken is that there was an unfortunate bit o' history up on Gyle Head, an' I'm afraid that one of ma ancestors was responsible,' he said. 'It seems that when the former Laird was Clan Chief, he decided that he wanted tae turn Gyle Head intae a kind o' pleasure garden for himself. You'll know that there's a stone circle he built on the castle grounds, down by the loch. Well, that was the same Laird as built the auld Folly up on Gyle Head. It's in ruins now, but I've got pictures of when it was new. Very bonny, with ornamental gardens, an' a lake.

'Unfortunately, so that he could build all o' that, so that he could entertain his friends on the weekends when they came up from the city, an' in the summers, the Laird decided tae knock down some cottages tae make room for his amusements. An' he evicted the families that lived there. I had no idea about this awful abuse of a landlord's power until Deb Sutherland unearthed some auld maps of the area, an' brought them tae me. I did some research an' found the truth.'

A murmur went around the crowd, and several heads swivelled in Deb's direction.

'Now. It seems that there were four families affected. The McKinleys, the Dalgliesh family, the McCarrons, and the Sutherlands.' The Laird consulted a piece of paper he'd been holding in his hand. 'In fact, the Sutherlands were Deb's own ancestors. This was an abuse of power that never should've happened, and I wanted tae be open about it. And I'll be makin' reparations. I'm no' sure exactly what, yet, but I'll try tae make it right as best I can. I pledge that to you, Deb, and to the descendants of the other families too.'

Deb nodded gratefully at Hal, but there was a strange feeling of heat coming up from her middle, and she felt suddenly as though she very much needed to sit down.

The room spun around her and she reached out for Dotty, who was standing next to her.

'Ach, she's gone pale!' Deb heard Dotty call out. Her legs felt suddenly wobbly, as if she couldn't hold herself up anymore. She closed her eyes, and felt herself falling.

TWENTY-NINE

'Deb. Talk to me. Come on.'

She came to when the cold night air tightened her skin and made her shiver. Deb opened her eyes.

They sat on a bench at the side of the castle, on a sheltered patio that overlooked the castle gardens. The sounds of the party thumped behind them, but out here it was tranquil. A light breeze stirred the leaves of the nearby trees, and Deb blinked at the castle's topiary garden, which was lit up with fairy lights in the same way as the drive on the way in. Kyle sat next to her.

'What... what happened?' She swallowed; her mouth was dry. 'How did I get out here?'

'I carried you,' Kyle replied, looking concerned. 'You passed out. Thought you could do with some air.'

'I passed out?' She sat up, realising that she had been leaning on him. 'You didn't have to... I mean... thank you.'

'That's okay.' Kyle handed her a glass which she recognised as containing a half-drunk Clan Cameron cocktail. 'Here. Have a few sips. You could probably use the scotch, and the sugar.'

'Thanks.' She took it and sipped the drink. 'Hm. That's delicious, actually,' she commented, not yet feeling that she had totally returned to the real world.

'Yeah, it is.' He watched her. 'So, what was that all about?'

'I have no idea. I've never fainted.' Deb took in a deep breath. 'But I have been feeling really tired. I think with the past week, all the party organising... usually I'd manage it fine, but I guess with the recovery from the op...' she trailed off.

'That's understandable.' Kyle watched her face, seriously.

'It's cold out here,' she added. Her shawl had come off, and she was just in her dress.

'Here.' He took off the suit jacket he was wearing and draped it around her shoulders.

'Oh, no! You'll get cold!' Deb protested, to which he tutted.

'Don't be daft. I'm not the one that just passed out.'

'Well, all right, then, I suppose.' Deb pulled the jacket around herself gratefully. 'Thanks.'

'Welcome.'

For a moment, neither of them said anything. Kyle stared out at the garden, but Deb could see that he had something on his mind.

'You dead fainted against Dotty. I ran over because she couldn't hold you up, and people were just standing there, watching,' he explained.

'Thank you. Again,' she added.

'It's no bother. Would have done it for anyone,' he said, shortly.

'Right,' she replied. There was another silence.

We are good at awkward silences, she thought.

'Well, maybe I wouldn't have run to help just anyone,' he said, after a pause. 'I've actually been wanting to talk to you for a while, Deb. I guess now is as good a time as any.'

'That sounds ominous.' She looked up into his light blue eyes. They could be icy, but now they were filled with an intensity she hadn't seen before.

'I hope it isn't,' he said, looking away for a moment. 'Deb... I need to say something to you.'

'Okay...'

'This isn't easy for me. I'm not a romantic guy, as a rule.' He exhaled. *Romantic?* Deb's heart started beating faster: she couldn't control it. 'But I have to say this. When we met, I was going through some difficult stuff. And I know that you thought I was kind of an idiot. I *was* an idiot. I was rude to you.'

'You were,' Deb agreed. 'But we got past that. Or so I thought.'

'So did I. I feel like we really connected. But then... I felt like you pushed me away. And then I found out that you were back with your ex.'

'I wasn't. I'm not. If you'd bothered to ask me directly, and not listen to gossip, you would have known that,' Deb sighed. 'We met for a coffee. He wanted us to get back together, and I guess I thought about it for a while. I was lonely. I felt like I couldn't do any better. Then I realised that wasn't really a good way to look at life.' Deb pulled Kyle's jacket around her shoulders.

'It isn't. But I've been there too.' Kyle nodded. 'I was engaged, until about a year and a half ago. She was actually pregnant, with my baby.' Deb could see that the words were difficult for him to say, and she wasn't surprised at all.

'What happened? You're not still together?' For a moment, Deb wondered if this was what Kyle was trying to tell her: that he was married, or partnered, and a father. That was why he'd been so distant.

'No. The relationship broke up. She lost the baby at four months,' he said, pain crossing his face. 'I was broken. I poured all of myself into my work. This development project became everything to me.' He let out a long breath. 'That was why I was so intense about it, I guess. When people started protesting, it just made me really angry. I wasn't doing anything wrong, and I guess I wasn't in the best place to take criticism.'

'Oh, Kyle. I'm so sorry!' Deb reached for his hand. 'That's awful. The relationship broke up because of losing the baby?'

'Yeah. It was just too much for us to take. Maybe if it hadn't happened, we'd be married now, maybe with more than one kid. I mean, we didn't plan the pregnancy. But I still wanted it. All of it.' His eyes had teared up, and when they met Deb's, her heart broke for him at the sadness behind them. 'I still do. Not her, I mean, we had problems before that, and in retrospect, she wasn't the right one for me. But I still want... someone special, you know?'

'I understand that feeling,' she said, carefully. She wanted to protect herself. 'And... children? Is that still something you want?' she added, thinking, *because if you are saying what I think you're saying, then that's not something I can do now. Or ever.*

He paused for a moment. 'When Catriona got pregnant, I was happy. I adjusted my view of the future to include a baby, because I loved her. I thought I loved her. I thought that was what I wanted. It might be still, I don't know. But I've changed a lot since then. I think I was just trying to please her. Fit in with what was happening. I'm not ready to go there again – the emotional upheaval was intense. Losing a baby...' he trailed off, and looked away. Deb could see his eyes had filled with tears.

'Why are you telling me all this?' Deb asked, still cautious. Her heart was so bruised from Dan that she felt almost afraid of how much Kyle was opening up to her. Yet, she also wanted nothing more than to be sitting here with him. To be close to him and listening to his beautiful voice.

'God, Deb. Isn't it obvious?' Kyle ran a hand over his face. 'I like you. More than like you. I'm... I've fallen for you. And I can't go another day without saying it.'

'You... you have feelings for me?'

'Yes.' He looked deep into her eyes, and Deb felt an over-whelming rush of electricity through her whole body. She swallowed hard. 'When I thought you were back with your ex... it killed me. I couldn't stop thinking about it. About you. We have this... powerful connection. I've never felt it with anyone else.'

'I know,' she whispered. 'I feel it too. From the first moment we met.'

'Do you... do you think you could have feelings for me too?' he asked, almost shyly, and Deb was taken aback by the realisation that Kyle didn't know – had no idea – of how she felt about him. How much she had thought about him. How intensely she had reacted to just being near him; the chemistry that she felt with him, like they were opposing poles of a battery.

But, the spectre of her infertility nagged at Deb. She remembered that stupid magazine article.

WHAT WOULD YOU DO FOR A BABY? Six women told us how they achieved a woman's greatest goal – becoming a mum.

If Kyle had wanted a child once, he might want one again. And she couldn't give him that. She felt perfectly fulfilled not having children – it was her choice, and she was happy with who she was and what she had chosen. But she needed to make sure that he understood that.

'You know I can't have children. The hysterectomy, and everything,' she said, her voice firm. 'And I don't want a family. I've never been the maternal type. I love my job. Sure, it might change at some point, and there are options if so. But, honestly, I can't see that happening. I come from a line of fiercely independent women, and I've come to appreciate that about myself.'

'I know.' He nodded. 'That's the thing that first attracted me to you. You're tough. You stood up to me. Didn't take any crap. I need someone like you. I can be insensitive, sometimes, though I don't mean to be. I love that you love your work. I love what I do, too. I couldn't be with someone who didn't have their own stuff going on.'

Deb's heart bloomed. She didn't think she had ever been liked – loved, even, possibly – for her independence and the steel spine she had inherited as a Sutherland woman.

'Thank you. That means a lot. Are you sure?' she asked, then corrected herself. 'I mean... thank you.' She was a Sutherland woman, after all, and she didn't need to second guess anyone.

'I told you, it's not a priority. Anyway, if at some point in the future we both wanted to, then there are other ways. The important thing is that I want you. Totally and utterly. I don't need anyone or anything else.' Kyle took her hand. 'Do you... do you think you could have feelings for me too? Maybe in time?' he repeated.

'I don't need time,' she murmured. '*Kyle*. From the moment I met you, I knew that this was something special. Even when you were being completely unbearable.' She tilted her head up towards him, and he reached down for her chin with his fingers. 'I want you. I have feelings for you. Big feelings.'

'Deborah. Like a queen,' he breathed, and his lips brushed hers. 'I've longed to hear those words.'

Kyle had kissed her before, but this time it felt like they were connecting on another level entirely. Deb felt her heart open like a rose as his lips gently met hers. First, they brushed hers softly, and she felt the tip of his tongue flicker on her lips. A rush of sensual pleasure ignited in her abdomen, and she surrendered to the kiss.

Slowly, it deepened, and Kyle's hands found her waist, and then her hair. He stroked her hair gently as he kissed her, and this act of tenderness opened Deb's heart even more. He murmured her name as he kissed her, and then held her close, against his broad chest. Deb stared out at the castle gardens, full of the simple warmth and delight of knowing that Kyle had feelings for her, and that hers were allowed to flourish in his arms.

Finally, she knew what all the love songs were about. Tears sprang to her eyes suddenly, as she realised what she'd been missing, for all this time. For all the time that she'd compromised with Dan; for all the time she'd thought that love wasn't for her. That it was something just for the privileged few, like Hal and Zelda. The beautiful ones.

Janice had always brought her up to believe what Elise had taught her: that life was full of hard knocks, and that you couldn't depend on love. Love was fleeting, and life was hard. That was how it was as a Sutherland woman, and Deb had taken that on board, unconsciously, as a young girl. She had never seen this for herself. And, yet, here it was. Here Kyle was.

Granted, she had no guarantee how long this would last. But she did have something that she had never had before, which was the pure and one hundred per cent sureness that she had fallen for someone: hook, line and sinker. And, more than that, that he had the same feelings.

It was a terrifying feeling, but it was also the most wonderful thing in the world. And Deb resolved, in that moment, that she would no longer believe that she was cursed. Because – if it was a curse, and Deb didn't for a second believe that it was – that curse had brought her here to Loch Cameron. She had come home.

EPILOGUE

It was a windy day up on Gyle Head, and Deb tucked a shawl around Janice's shoulders.

'You're sure you're warm enough?' she asked her mother, who was sitting in a wheelchair next to her, but Janice gave her that familiar frown that Deb knew meant *don't fuss*.

'I'm fine, for goodness' sake, Deborah. It's June,' Janice hissed.

Some things never change, Deb thought, as she stood up.

Kyle stood at the centre of the gathering, looking uncharacteristically nervous. Hal Cameron stood next to Deb and Janice, who had been persuaded to be pushed up to Gyle Head in a wheelchair. Zelda, looking characteristically glamorous with her sleek black ponytail – even in jeans and mud-covered wellies – held his hand.

Next to Hal, the crochet coven was in attendance, along with Fiona, Dotty and Eric from the Inn, and a variety of other locals.

'Thanks, everyone, for coming today.' Kyle raised his voice over the wind. 'I thought it was important to explain exactly what's been going on up at the development, and answer some of your concerns. I'm sorry that I haven't done so until now.' He took a breath, and Deb caught his eye and smiled.

'I know that many of you – rightly – had concerns about the building work, and how it was going to impact on the wildlife up here. I did consult with the environment agency before I began work, about the capercaillie and the red squirrel habitats on Gyle Head. We've been working hard to rehome the resident populations in the nearby forest, and you'll see from the handouts I've given you that we've been very successful. That's the environment agency report, saying that they're happy we've provided alternative arrangements and put a variety of structures and techniques in place to protect the local wildlife, going forward.'

Deb looked over at Mina, who was leafing through the handout she'd been given, an unreadable expression on her face. The crochet coven had got what they wanted. Deb wondered if a little bit of Mina was sad to have lost an adversary, but she was glad that the antagonism could be over now.

'And, I'd like to add, on a personal note.' Kyle cleared his throat. 'I know that I haven't been the easiest person to deal with over the past few months, and I apologise for that. Someone here made me see that diplomacy and communication wins the day, and not always brute force and obstinacy.' He smiled ruefully, meeting Deb's gaze. 'Thank you, Deb. You improve me, and I'm so grateful to have you in my life.'

Deb blushed as everyone turned to look at her. She was mortified at the attention, but her heart felt full.

It had been just a few weeks since the May Day party when Kyle had shared his feelings for her, and since then, she'd made some big decisions. That job was over, but Deb had known for a while that she wasn't going back to live with Dan. She was a free agent, and working freelance meant that she could live anywhere.

For the moment, she'd agreed with Hal that she'd stay at the cottage and rent it for six months, and then see where she was. She and Kyle were taking things slowly, but she was feeling happier than she had for a long time.

She had almost gone back to Glasgow. It was very tempting to want to go back and look after Janice, but her mother had persuaded her out of it. They'd come to a compromise: Janice's carer came in twice a day and could take her to hospital appointments. Deb would go back and visit often, and if she wanted to, she could stay with Janice in the flat for a few days if she thought her mum needed it. But Janice was doing much better now that she had someone looking after her every day, and Deb felt more at peace about the situation. It might change – it would, at some stage – but for now, it was okay. It was doable.

'As you know, there's also a history on Gyle Head that some families were unfairly evicted from their homes here, many years ago,' Kyle continued. 'I'd like to invite Hal Cameron to talk for a moment about that. Hal?'

'Right, yes.' Hal moved forward so that he was in the centre of the space with Kyle. 'So, as some of ye might remember from the party, we did discover that there was a terrible scandal here, years ago, where four families were evicted from their cottages because the previous laird – my ancestor, Duncan Cameron – wanted tae build the auld folly up here an' have the land for his parties an' what have ye. Now, as it turns out, one o' those families were the Sutherlands, which Deborah is actually a direct descendant of. An' her mother, Janice, who's here today. I believe that it was Janice's mother, Elsie? Who was evicted from here as a child.'

'Elise,' Janice corrected Hal, making Deb smile. 'Her name was Elise. Her, and her brother Tom, and their parents, my grandparents. My mother lost her home and then her parents and her brother when she was young. It changed her life. Not in a good way, I'm afraid.'

'I'm so sorry. And on behalf o' the Cameron clan, though it can never make up for your loss, I propose that I'll fund a community hub on Gyle Head as reparation. I've included some plans in your handouts here, and Kyle's company website has the details online. But you'll see that we're planning a state-of-the-art playground, a café, toilets an' baby change facilities, an' a swimming pool. With yer permission, Janice, it'll be called the Elise Sutherland Centre.'

Janice looked up at Deb, and then at Kyle and Hal.

'Are you serious?' she asked, her voice wavering. Tears were in her eyes. Deb squeezed her mother's hand, feeling the same rush of grief as Janice was. Standing there on Gyle Head, on the land that her family had once lived on, Deb felt the terrible sadness of being ripped from it with no warning. Now, she understood – viscerally, in her heart and soul and in the fibre of her being – why she had felt so connected to this place.

'Totally.' Hal stepped forward, knelt down and took Janice's hand. 'I'm so sorry that your mother lost her home, and her family, as a result. Deborah, I'm sorry that my family hurt yours in such a deep and essential way as takin' away their home. As a chieftain of these lands, I take ma responsibility to all of ma tenants incredibly seriously. I would never, ever do such a thing.' Hal took Deb's hand in his.

'Thank you,' Deb whispered as she dashed away tears with the back of her other hand. 'This means so much, Hal. Thank you from both of us.'

'It can never change what happened. But in some small way, I can make reparations. It's something I have tae do more than you'd think. Bein' a landowner, in a family that's owned land fer generations – it has repercussions,' Hal continued as he stood up. 'Land is never truly owned by anyone. It can't be. By God, maybe.' He smiled wryly. 'The king granted the Camerons this land hundreds of years ago. Was it his to give? Arguably, not. Do I have more right tae make decisions about this land than any of you, that also live here and care for it? I don't think I do. Which is why I try tae work in partnership with the community as much as I can.'

'So, as well as the community hub, Hal has also agreed to subsidise the sale of over half of the houses I'm building up here. Homes that are environmentally sustainable, with solar power and sedge roofs, by the way. Those houses will be available at well below the market rate and will be sold only to families that need them. I'm not going to let middle class commuters, or holiday letting companies, swoop in and buy them.' Kyle took over for a moment.

Deb felt a rush of pride in him. She knew how hard he'd worked on this project, and what a difference it would make to local families who would have no chance of having such a nice home otherwise. She was learning that this was how Kyle showed love: in acts of service. And he had managed to make his work – a huge house building project – into an act of service for the whole community, as well as actively persuade Hal Cameron to help heal the wound in Deb's past.

That was the biggest loving gift that Deb had ever received, and it continued to blow her away every time she thought about it.

'So, that's pretty much it. Any questions, we're here – and I believe that Sheila's organised teas and coffees, and a celebratory cake.' Hal pointed to a trestle table that had been set up nearby. The crowd started to disperse, chattering animatedly.

Deb looked down at Janice, who was wiping her eyes with the cuff of her sweatshirt.

'Are you all right, Mum?' she asked.

'I just can't believe it.' Janice blinked and cleared her throat. 'Yes, I'm okay, love. It's just very emotional, to be here, where Mum was. You know? We might be standing in her footsteps right here. Sitting, in my case.'

'I know. It's so strange. But also lovely.' Deb crouched down next to Janice and looked out onto the horizon. 'Kyle said that the old houses were just over there. At the edge of where the folly got built. Do you want to see?'

'Yes. Wheel me over.' Janice nodded.

Deb pushed her mother's wheelchair carefully over the grass, which, mercifully, had been mowed recently.

'Kyle is intending to integrate a bit of the folly wall into the new community development,' she said, as they approached the site of her grandmother's house. 'So, I guess it's nice that there will be children playing on the site where Elise used to live. Families having good times here. It's good to know that.'

'Yes, it is.' Janice let out a long sigh. 'It's strange, though, being here. Thinking about Mum. Thinking about her being here, playing in these trees, sleeping here, eating, maybe exactly where we're standing. From what she said, she was so happy here, before it was taken away. It's also strange that she never told me where she'd lived, but I understand why. It was too painful, I suppose. There are so many things she never told me. Things we'll never know, now.'

'I wish she'd been here to see this.' Deb nodded.

'I know,' Janice said, and they fell silent.

'Sorry tae interrupt.' Hal had walked over to Deb and Janice and nodded politely to them both. He reached into the pocket of his khaki oilcloth coat, took out an envelope and handed it to Janice. 'This is also fer ye, Ms Sutherland,' he said, formally.

'What's all this?' Janice asked, taking it and opening the flap of the envelope. 'Surely, you've done enough, Hal.'

'Ah, no' at all. Deb asked me tae look intae the local records fer any indication o' yer brother Tom. I didnae forget,' he said to Deb, who felt a stab of excitement mixed with apprehension in her stomach. 'I did find somethin'.'

'Tom?' Janice opened the envelope, and unfolded the paper. 'Oh, my.' She looked at it for a long moment, then handed it to Deb.

It was a death certificate. Deb felt her stomach clench in disappointment: she'd known it was a long shot to find any trace of Tom at all, never mind finding him alive. He had been a little younger than Grandma Elise, yes, but he still would have been in his nineties by now. Still, she'd hoped.

Thomas Sutherland. Date of death, January 10th, 2010. Loch Awe it read. Deb looked up in surprise.

'Loch Awe? That's not far from here, is it?' she asked Hal.

'It isnae. It looks like Tom came back tae the area at some point in his life. When he was an adult, I guess. The second piece o' paper should be of interest,' Hal said, his eyes crinkling kindly. 'Somethin', at least.'

Deb turned over the second piece of paper and exclaimed out loud, passing it to her mum.

'What is it?' Janice asked, taking the paper. 'Oh!' she looked up at Deb. 'We can go, can't we?'

'Yes. We can,' Deb said, looking at the photo that Hal had printed out for them. It was a picture of a grave stone with Tom's name on it, and underneath, Hal had handwritten

Loch Cameron Chapel, left corner.

'He's been here the whole time,' Deb breathed. 'I can't believe it.'

'Aye. Ye both came back home, in the end.' Hal put his arm around Deb's shoulders. 'We can do some more investigation. See if we can find the family. Someone paid for him tae be buried up at the chapel, and sorted the stone, aye? It wasnae that long ago. He might've had a family.'

'Goodness. I might have cousins.' Janice looked up at them both. 'That's such a strange thought! Thank you, Hal.' Her voice was a little choked up. 'You've done so much for our little family. I really can't thank you enough.'

'It's no more than what's right,' Hal replied. 'I'll leave ye tae it for a min. Have some time tae digest, an' we can catch up when yer ready.' He gave them both a formal nod, and walked back over to Zelda, who was handing out cups of tea.

'Well. I didn't expect that as well, today.' Janice let out a long breath. 'I'm going to be ready for a lie down when we get back to the cottage.'

'Me neither. I did ask Hal to look into Tom, but I didn't think...' Deb trailed off. 'He was here! All that time. Well, his body was. His bones, anyway.'

'It's something, isn't it?' Janice shook her head in wonder. 'I wouldn't have expected him to be alive, but to think that he came back to Loch Cameron in the end. It's so strange you got drawn here for that job. Seems like fate, doesn't it?' She reached for Deb's hand.

'It does. In more ways than one,' Deb replied, looking back over Gyle Head at Kyle, who was talking to Sheila and Mina, a cup of tea in his hand. They were laughing and smiling.

'I'm glad you came here,' Janice said. 'I feel like... it's healed something in our family. I could never have predicted that.'

'I know. Me either.'

Deb closed her eyes and thought of Grandma Elise. Of the days on the allotment, learning how to grow tomatoes and courgettes by the phases of the moon. Elsie – Elise – had, perhaps, spared Deb the stoic upbringing that she had given Janice, and for that, Deb was grateful. She was grateful for the peaceful times they had had together.

A vision formed in Deb's mind, as she stood on Gyle Head, breathing in the clean air and the smell of pine. She saw Elise, as a girl, her long, light brown hair in two plaits tied with white ribbons. She wore a brown smock dress with a white apron over the top, and she was skipping with a rope, just where Deb and Janice stood.

For a brief moment, Deb could almost feel the breeze of the air from the rope whipping past her face.

Granny's in the kitchen, doing a bit of stitchin'
Down comes a bogeyman and knocks her out
Ah! said Granny. That's not fair!
Ah! said the bogeyman. I don't care.

She opened her eyes, feeling as if she had slipped into a dream. Just for that moment, it had felt as though she had seen Elise, right there, where she was standing. As if she could have reached out and touched her.

That had been her dream, all along. She had been dreaming of her grandmother. Of a happy time, before she had lost everything.

And now, Deb felt as if Elise was happy again. That there was a part of her that would always be on Gyle Head.

'I think Grandma would be happy about all this,' Deb said. Janice was right. Something had shifted and healed. Between her and Janice, and in the memory of the Sutherlands on Gyle Head. There was a peace here, now; a break that had been mended.

'I think she would, too,' Janice agreed, quietly, and reached for her daughter's hand.

A LETTER FROM KENNEDY

Dear reader,

I want to say a huge thank you for choosing to read *An Invitation to the Cottage by the Loch*. If you did enjoy it, and want to keep up to date with all my latest releases, just sign up at the following link. Your email address will never be shared and you can unsubscribe at any time.

www.bookouture.com/kennedy-kerr

I hope you loved *An Invitation to the Cottage by the Loch* and if you did I would be very grateful if you could write a review. I'd love to hear what you think, and it makes such a difference helping new readers to discover one of my books for the first time.

I love hearing from my readers – you can get in touch through social media or my website.

Thanks,

Kennedy

facebook.com/kennedykerrauthor

x.com/kennedykerr5

instagram.com/kennedykerrauthor

AUTHOR'S NOTE

Keen history fans and readers of my previous Loch Cameron titles will know that I based Loch Cameron Castle on Inveraray Castle. Inverarary – a stunning castle in its own right, which has also been used in various film and TV productions – is owned by the Campbell family whose titular head is the Duke of Argyll. In this story, I borrowed some details of the history of the Dukes of Argyll to use as part of Hal's heritage. All of my inventions are purely mine, and for fictional purposes.

The skipping rhyme in Deb's dream is one I found when searching online for traditional skipping rhymes that Elise might have known. This was recalled by a couple of respondents in an online forum.

> *Granny's in the kitchen, doing a bit of stitchin'*
> *Down comes a bogeyman and knocks her out*
> *Ah! said Granny. That's not fair!*
> *Ah! said the bogeyman. I don't care.*

I am indebted to the work of Dr Louise Newson (@menopause_doctor), a GP and menopause specialist who continues to do great work in the field of menopause treatment and awareness, particularly about the benefits of hormone replacement therapy.

Dr Newson battles outdated and incorrect misconceptions about HRT, promoting its benefits in halting post-menopausal conditions such as osteoporosis, vaginal dryness and atrophy, depression, loss of sex drive, weight gain, foggy brain, memory loss and all kind of other conditions that women are expected to deal with on a daily basis. Even in 2023, I myself have observed an appalling lack of awareness of menopausal symptoms in women my age and younger/older, which is only the fault of a lack of public information, research and support from the medical community.

Menopausal women are still typically either dismissed by doctors and told that their serious symptoms – which can easily and safely be cured by HRT – are "just women's problems" or that they are "making too much" of symptoms that they are expected to live with. Recently, the UK government has recommended that menopausal women are prescribed with CBT (cognitive behaviour therapy) as an alternative to hormone replacement therapy, which strikes me as utterly ridiculous. Depression as a symptom of menopause is hormonal, not mental. No amount of positive thinking is going to address what is being caused by a very straightforward hormone imbalance.

Deb hasn't started to need HRT yet because in her hysterectomy procedure, her doctor was able to avoid taking her ovaries, but I mentioned it in the book as, if you have a hysterectomy where your ovaries are removed, you will go into menopause with immediate effect and will need to take hormones as a result. I have seen that many women – including those who have had a full hysterectomy – are not aware of this fact, and suffer needlessly as a result, because their doctors (in some cases) haven't explained what will happen to them when their ovaries are removed.

I myself had a hysterectomy because of endometriosis in 2020, and it gave me my life back. But I had to fight very hard to get it, and if I had listened to the ill-informed doctors that had told me it was just heavy periods, or prescribed me horrible, archaic and ineffective treatments, then I would still be suffering, with no life, depressed, bleeding constantly, and in pain.

Fortunately, I am a stubborn so-and-so, and I also could find the money to pay to have my operation done privately. I found an amazing gynaecologist who finally did understand what was going on with my body, and could explain it clearly to me, and could help. I was lucky.

There is still a dire lack of research about many gynaecological conditions, including endometriosis, which Deb has suffered from in this book. There is no cure for endometriosis, though patients can be offered often invasive and painful treatments such as ablation and uterine coils. Hysterectomy is an effective but extreme final resort, and patients can still suffer complications afterwards, including the increased risk of prolapse. I care passionately about this subject, and about anyone with a uterus who is suffering as a result of having one.

Deb and Dan's relationship issues were also inspired by (sadly) many, many accounts of women I saw in a Facebook hysterectomy support group of which I am still a member, whose male partners were thoroughly appalling and unsupportive to them during and after their operation. Men who complained that their partners were recovering in bed and "being lazy". Men who complained that the housework wasn't done, children not looked after, or the dinners made (they could have done it!). Men who, perhaps most disturbingly of all, pressured their partners for sex way before they were ready.

This kind of behaviour should never be tolerated. It's also true that when we are recovering from major surgery, we might not be feeling strong enough to challenge that bad behaviour, and so, let's remember to look in on our friends and family often, and be there to support them if they are experiencing this kind (or any kind) of domestic abuse.

Clearly, of course, there were and are many women who have surgery and illness of all kinds, and whose partners are nothing but loving and supportive – which is the normal response. To them, thank you.

Elsie/Elise experiences the UK care system as it was many years ago. According to the National Archives website, from 1930 county borough councils took responsibility for the administration of children's homes and fostering, although the voluntary sector continued to provide residential homes. Institutional care remained widespread but fostering became increasingly popular, particularly after the Curtis Committee on the Care of Children recommended the use of fostering in preference to institutional care in 1946. It is therefore conceivable that Elsie could have been fostered in private homes in the mid-1930s – and also, sadly, conceivable that there might have been less rigorous monitoring and care of foster homes then, especially if we look to the hugely varying levels of the care of children e.g. in evacuation during World War II.

Nowadays, charities like the Care Leavers Association are doing excellent work in supporting people of all ages leaving care arrangements. However, leaving care is still a time fraught with difficulty, and we are honour bound as a society to care better for these vulnerable young people.

Last, I am indebted to *Town and Country* magazine for inspiring the Clan Cameron whisky cocktail Dotty and Eric make at the May Day party, and include the recipe here, so that you too can enjoy a taste of Loch Cameron. If you don't want to include whisky, it will be just as nice without, and you could substitute elderflower cordial for the vodka-based chamomile liqueur.

Clan Cameron

Ingredients

- 1.5 oz whisky
- 75 oz chamomile liqueur
- 5 oz lemon juice

- 25 oz herb syrup with thyme

Instructions

Add all ingredients to a cocktail shaker with ice. Shake. Strain cocktail into chilled glass half-filled with ice. Rub the outer edge of glass with lemon peel and serve.

*How to make chamomile liqueur: Place 5 oz chamomile flowers, one strip of lemon zest, and a pint of vodka in a jar. Cover tightly and shake to combine. Store in a cool, dark place for 2 days, shaking occasionally. After 2 days, strain through a fine mesh strainer lined with cheesecloth, pressing all of the liquid out of the solids. Return infused vodka to a clean jar and add sugar. Cover and gently shake to combine.

*How to make the herb syrup: Heat ¾ of a cup of sugar and 5 oz water in a small pan over medium heat, whisking frequently until sugar has dissolved. Stir in 12 thyme sprigs and cool completely. Strain through a fine mesh strainer into an airtight container and discard the solids.

Inspired by *How to Cocktail: Recipes and Techniques for Building the Best Drinks* by America's Test Kitchen, featured in *Town and Country* magazine.

PUBLISHING TEAM

Turning a manuscript into a book requires the efforts of many people. The publishing team at Bookouture would like to acknowledge everyone who contributed to this publication.

Commercial
Lauren Morrissette
Hannah Richmond
Imogen Allport

Cover design
Eileen Carey

Data and analysis
Mark Alder
Mohamed Bussuri

Editorial
Kelsie Marsden
Sinead O'Connor

Copyeditor
Claire Rushbrook

Proofreader
Tom Feltham

Printed in Great Britain
by Amazon